Praise for *The Darkness Knows*

"*The Darkness Knows* is slowly and deliberately plotted. . . . Indridason is a consummate storyteller, one of the cream of the Nordic-noir crop, and if methodical police procedurals are your thing, you have come to the right place." —*BookPage*

"Indridason, a well-seasoned writer, has created an intricate plot with a diverse cast of players, acutely probing the relationships within Iceland's tightly knit communities." —*The Seattle Times*

"*The Darkness Knows* is a tragic tale. . . . The intrepid Indridason reveals that the only escape from the past is death." —*The Times* (London)

"In this rewarding gumshoe investigation focused on complex deceptions and unlikely coincidences, introspective Konrád faces his failures, both in marriage and policing here, and finds resolution, if not peace." —*Booklist*

"One characteristic of Scandinavian noir is the way that inhospitable weather plays a role in the story, and this has never been truer than in Arnaldur Indridason's *The Darkness Knows*. In the Icelandic crime-writing standard-bearer's invigoratingly atmospheric thriller, the frozen body of a man who's been missing since 1985 is found on the Langjökull glacier. . . . A multifaceted thriller." —*Shelf Awareness*

"Indridason methodically builds a portrait of Iceland with a large cast of nuanced characters unsettled by past events. . . . The intricate plot poignantly depicts community crosscurrents, past and present."

—Kirkus Reviews

"As fascinating as this caper is, it is Konrád's persona that holds the reader. A recent widower with a checkered past, Konrád is greatly flawed."

—David Rothenberg, WBAI Radio

Praise for The Shadow Killer

"Indridason fills the void that remains after you've read Stieg Larsson's novels."

—USA Today

"A haunting and elegant novel . . . a writer of astonishing gravitas and talent."

—John Lescroart

"What's Icelandic for 'We have ourselves a winner'?" —Newsday

"Indridason's austere, clear-cut prose coldly reveals 'all the disruption the military occupation had brought to this sparsely populated island and its simple society.'" —The New York Times

"Indridason does a fine job evoking the place and time."

—Publishers Weekly

"Indridason builds suspense through a steady progression of extensive interviews, with his sleuths doggedly prodding witnesses with dark, probing questions. The result is a haunting and foreboding mood that will attract fans of Nordic noir."

—Library Journal

"Indridason's voice, straightforward and tinged with sadness, works particularly well here, as he coaxes out tragic secrets and captures the occupation's impact with intriguing period detail, particularly the social impact of Reykjavík's emerging nightlife and the Icelandic Nationalist Party's Nazi legacy." —*Booklist*

"Mesmerizing." —*The Wall Street Journal*

Praise for Arnaldur Indridason

"There's always a solid sense of history in Arnaldur Indridason's moody Icelandic mysteries. With his usual delicate touch, Indridason weaves in just enough folklore to remind us that a nation can never live down its legends."
—*The New York Times Book Review* on *The Shadow District*

"Indridason is an international literary phenom."
—Harlan Coben

"One of the most brilliant crime writers of his generation."
—*The Sunday Times* (London)

"The undisputed king of the Icelandic thriller."
—*The Guardian* (London)

Also by Arnaldur Indridason

Arnaldur Indridason

THE DARKNESS KNOWS

*Translated from the Icelandic
by Victoria Cribb*

MINOTAUR BOOKS
NEW YORK

Published in the United States by Minotaur Books, an imprint of St. Martin's Publishing Group

THE DARKNESS KNOWS. Copyright © 2017 by Arnaldur Indridason. English translation copyright © 2021 by Victoria Cribb. All rights reserved. Printed in the United States of America. For information, address St. Martin's Publishing Group, 120 Broadway, New York, NY 10271.

www.minotaurbooks.com

The Library of Congress has cataloged the hardcover edition as follows:

Names: Arnaldur Indriðason, 1961– author. | Cribb, Victoria, translator.
Title: The darkness knows / Arnaldur Indridason ; [translated by Victoria Cribb].
Other titles: Myrkrið veit. English
Description: First U.S. edition. | New York : Minotaur Books, 2021. |
Series: Detective Konrad | "First published in Iceland under the title Myrkrið veit by Vaka-Helgafell"
Identifiers: LCCN 2021015678 | ISBN 9781250765468 (hardcover) | ISBN 9781250765475 (ebook)
Subjects: GSAFD: Mystery fiction.
Classification: LCC PT7511.A67 M9813 2021 | DDC 839/.6934—dc23
LC record available at https://lccn.loc.gov/2021015678

ISBN 978-1-250-76548-2 (trade paperback)

Our books may be purchased in bulk for promotional, educational, or business use. Please contact your local bookseller or the Macmillan Corporate and Premium Sales Department at 1-800-221-7945, extension 5442, or by email at MacmillanSpecialMarkets@macmillan.com.

First published in Iceland under the title *Myrkrið veit* by Vaka-Helgafell

Previously published in Great Britain by Harvill Secker, a Penguin Random House company

First Minotaur Books Trade Paperback Edition: 2022

10   9   8   7   6   5   4   3   2   1

There are secrets that only the darkness knows,
— my mind is sore oppressed.
Often I saw the black desert sand
scorching the grassy meadow land.
In the glacier, cracks are rumbling deep as death.

Jóhann Sigurjónsson

THE DARKNESS KNOWS

1

You couldn't have asked for better weather. She was sitting with her tour group, admiring the view of the glacier and rummaging in her daypack for a sandwich, when her gaze happened to fall on a bump in the snow crust. It looked like a human face.

It took her a moment to register what she was seeing. Then she was on her feet, screaming her head off, shattering the silence of the ice cap.

The German tourists sitting in a huddle around her almost jumped out of their skins. They couldn't understand what had triggered such a violent reaction in their Icelandic guide, an older woman who up to now had seemed so calm and unflappable.

They were coming to the end of their glacier tour. Yesterday they had gone for a hike on the famously unpronounceable Eyja-fjallajökull. It had become a popular tourist destination following the notorious 2010 eruption, when European air traffic had been brought to a standstill by the ash cloud produced by the volcano under the ice. For a long time afterwards the surrounding landscape had been buried under a thick layer of ash, but now it had mostly blown away or been washed into the soil, and the mountainsides had reverted to a vivid moss-green.

The tour was scheduled to last ten days and take in four ice caps. They had left Reykjavík just over a week ago in specially modified vehicles. Their nights were spent at the best hotels in the south-west so that the Germans, a group of wealthy friends from the car manufacturing town of Wolfsburg, wouldn't have to go without any of their creature comforts. Gourmet lunches on the ice caps were followed by good dinners back at their hotels in the evenings. During the day, they undertook hikes of a moderate length, with rest stops for refreshments. They had been unusually lucky with the weather: every day that September the sun had shone from a cloudless sky, and the Germans kept asking about global warming and the impact of the greenhouse effect on Iceland. The guide was fluent in German – she had studied literature at the University of Heidelberg – and the tour was conducted entirely in that language, apart from those two words in English: *global warming.*

She told them how the Icelandic climate had changed in recent years. The summers had become warmer with more hours of sunlight and – obligatory joke – no one was complaining. Gone were the old, unsettled summers; now you could almost rely on the good weather to last for days, even weeks at a time. The winters had become milder too, with lighter snowfall – though, on the minus side, this did nothing to diminish the gloom of the long dark nights. But the most striking change was to be seen in the glaciers, which were receding at an alarming rate. Snæfellsjökull was a good example: the ice-capped volcano, famous as the starting point for Jules Verne's *Journey to the Centre of the Earth*, was a shadow of its former self.

Now they were on the last glacier of their tour, Langjökull, which had also seen better days. In 1997 to '98, she told them, it had lost a whole three metres in height, and recently its area had shrunk by 3.5 per cent. At guide school they'd taught her to trot out figures like these, including the usual spiel about ice caps making up 11 per cent of Iceland's surface area and containing a volume of water equivalent to twenty-five years' precipitation.

They had spent the previous night at Húsafell and set off for the glacier at eleven this morning. It was a very easy group; they were almost all fit and equipped with top-of-the-range walking boots and protective gear. There had been no awkward incidents, no one had fallen ill or complained or made a scene, and everyone seemed set on getting the most out of their trip. Earlier they had hiked along the edge of the glacier before picking their way onto the ice itself. The compacted snow crunched at every step and the surface was covered in trickling streams. She led the way, feeling the cold air rising against her face. There was quite a bit of traffic up here. Seeing all the jeeps and snowmobiles roaring over the ice, the Germans had asked her if glacier driving was a popular sport among Icelanders and she had answered non-committally. Although she was well prepared, they often caught her out with unexpected questions, like the one at breakfast: how many cheeses do you make in Iceland?

She had enrolled at guide school after tourism really began to take off. By then she had been unemployed for eight months. On top of that she had lost her flat, as she hadn't been able to pay off her mortgage in the wake of the financial crash, and the man she was seeing had moved to Norway. He was a builder by trade and, finding more than enough work there, had declared that he was never coming back to this shitty little island now that a bunch of idiots had managed to bankrupt it. Then someone had mentioned that tourism was the next big thing. With the bottom falling out of the króna, Iceland had suddenly become an affordable destination. At guide school, they taught her that foreign visitors loved Iceland for the landscape, the pure air and the peace and quiet.

They'd said nothing about frozen corpses on glaciers.

The Germans gathered round, following her gaze to what appeared to be a human head, emerging from the ice.

'What is it?' a woman asked, moving closer.

'Is it a man?' asked another.

Though the face was almost covered by a thin layer of snow, they could see the nose, the eye sockets and most of the forehead. The rest of the head and body were buried in the ice.

'What can have happened to him?' a third member of the group wondered aloud. The guide recalled that he was a retired doctor.

'Has he been there long?' someone else asked.

'It looks like it,' said the doctor, kneeling beside the face. 'He didn't freeze to death yesterday.'

Carefully, using his bare hands, he brushed the snow away until the whole face was revealed.

'Don't touch anything,' his wife warned.

'It's all right, I'm not doing any more than that.'

When the doctor straightened up and stepped back, they could all see the man's face, looking as if it had been moulded from porcelain, so paper-thin that it would break at the slightest touch. There was no way of telling how long he had been there, as the ice had treated him kindly, preventing decomposition. He appeared to have been around thirty when he died. His face was broad

4

across the cheeks, with a large mouth, strong teeth, and deep-set eyes above a handsome nose. His hair was thick and blond.

'Shouldn't you notify the police, dear?' asked the doctor's wife, turning to the guide.

'Yes, of course,' she said distractedly, unable to tear her eyes away from the face. 'Of course. I'll do that right now.'

She took out her phone, confident that there would be a signal. She was always careful to stick to areas with phone or radio reception, in case of accidents.

'We're not far from Geitlandsjökull,' she explained to the emergency services, after describing what they had found. As she was speaking, her gaze fell on the flat-topped volcano from which the south-western flank of the glacier took its name. She had read when preparing for this trip that if the ice cap continued to shrink at the same rate, by the end of the century it would have almost entirely disappeared.

2

By the time he finally emerged from the sports bar into the driving snow, he was seriously drunk. He hadn't seen his friend for at least an hour, so he must have gone home. As usual, they'd met up early to watch the football. It had been a good match and afterwards he'd got talking to some lads he didn't know, while Ingi had lapsed into a gloomy silence. Ingi often got like that when he drank: just sat there, not saying a word.

He lowered his head, clutching his jacket tightly around his skinny frame, and set off into the blizzard. The snow immediately started settling on his clothes, and in no time at all he was freezing and cursing the fact he hadn't put on his work overalls, which were thickly lined enough to protect him from anything the elements could throw at him. On winter mornings it could be hard to leave the warm hut for the exposed construction site, but two mugs of coffee, a cigarette and the blue overalls all helped. It wasn't complicated. Simple pleasures – you just had to know how to appreciate them. Football and a cold beer. Coffee and a ciggie. And thick overalls in winter.

He moved quickly but unsteadily along the pavement, his thoughts as erratic as his footprints in the snow.

He'd thought the guy looked vaguely familiar as they sat chatting at the bar, but it had taken a while for the penny to drop. The lights were low and the guy had been wearing a baseball cap and kept his head down. They'd exchanged a few remarks about the game and discovered that they both supported the same team. In the end, unable to restrain himself, he'd started talking about Öskjuhlíd and asked the man straight out if it had been him he ran into there. Asked if he remembered that evening too.

'No,' the man said. But the glance he shot him from under his cap removed all doubt that it was him.

'It *was* you, wasn't it?' he exclaimed, pleased and incredulous. 'It *was* you! Don't you remember me? I can't believe it! Did the cops ever talk to you?'

Instead of answering, the man ducked his head even lower.

But he wouldn't let go of the subject. He told the man how he'd gone to the police about it several years ago but they hadn't taken any notice of him. The cops had received a million tip-offs and he'd only been a boy when it happened, so maybe it was –

'Leave me alone,' the man muttered.

'What?'

'I don't know what you're on about,' the man said angrily. 'Just leave me alone!' Then he got up and stamped out of the bar.

He'd been left sitting there, hardly able to get over the coincidence that it was the same guy. He was still marvelling at the fact when he staggered outside himself a few minutes later and headed for home. By the time he reached Lindargata, the snow was so impenetrable that he could barely make out the next street light as he hurried across the road, thinking that he would have to inform the police as soon as possible. Just as he was about to reach the other side, his befuddled senses registered that he was in danger. His surroundings were lit up by a sudden dazzling glare, and over the noise of the wind he heard the roar of an engine approaching at speed. The next moment he was flying through the air, an agonising pain in his side, then he crashed down head first onto the pavement that had been swept clear of snow by the storm.

The booming of the engine receded and everything grew quiet again, apart from the screaming of the wind. But the blizzard went on raging all around him, the stinging flakes pelting his exposed flesh and penetrating his jacket. He couldn't move, his whole body was a mass of pain, his head worst of all.

He parted his lips to call for help but couldn't emit a sound.

Time passed but he was no longer aware of it. He couldn't feel the pain any more, or the cold. The alcohol had dulled his senses. His thoughts drifted back to the man in the sports bar, then even further back in time to the hot-water tanks on Öskjuhlíd hill, where he'd loved to play, and the incident he'd witnessed there as a boy.

He was absolutely sure. They'd met once before.

It had been the same man.

There was no doubt in his mind.

3

Konrád opened his eyes at the sound of his mobile phone ringing. He hadn't been able to get to sleep, but that was nothing new. Pills, red wine, rather aimless meditation – nothing made any impression on his insomnia.

He couldn't remember where he'd put his phone. Sometimes it was on the bedside table, sometimes in a trouser pocket. Once he'd lost it for several days, only to find it at last in the boot of his car.

He got out of bed, went into the sitting room, then followed the sound to the kitchen, where the phone was lying vibrating on the table. Outside, the autumn night was pitch-black.

'Sorry, Konrád, I know I've woken you,' whispered a female voice at the other end.

'No, you haven't.'

'I think you should come over to the mortuary.'

'Why are you whispering?'

'Am I?' The woman cleared her throat. Her name was Svanhildur and she was a pathologist at the National Hospital. 'Haven't you heard the news?' she asked.

'No,' Konrád said, wide awake now. He had been going through some of his father's old papers and this time his insomnia could partly be blamed on that.

'They brought him in at around eight o'clock,' Svanhildur said. 'They've found him.'

'Found him? Who? Sorry, who are you talking about?'

'Some German tourists. On Langjökull. He was in the ice.'

'On Langjökull?'

'It's Sigurvin, Konrád! Sigurvin's turned up. They've found his body.'

'Sigurvin?'

'Yes.'

'Sigurvin! No, it . . . what are you talking about?'

'After all these years, Konrád. It's quite incredible. I thought you might want to see him.'

'Is this some kind of joke?'

'I know it's hard to believe but it's him. Beyond a doubt.'

Konrád was floored. Svanhildur's words seemed to be coming from a long way off, as though from deep in some bizarre dream that had faded from his consciousness. They were words he'd never expected to hear. Not now. Not after so much time had passed. But, on another level, it felt as if he had always been expecting this phone call. Waiting for this news out of the distant past that continued to haunt him like a shadow. Yet now that the news had finally come, he was utterly thrown.

'Konrád?'

'I can't believe it,' he said. '*Sigurvin? They've found Sigurvin?*' He sank into a chair at the kitchen table.

'Yes. It's definitely him.'

'German tourists, you say?'

'On Langjökull. There were some experts on earlier, saying the glacier's shrunk substantially since Sigurvin vanished. Don't you ever listen to the news? It's the greenhouse effect. I thought you might want to see him before everything kicks off tomorrow morning. The ice has preserved him uncannily well.'

Konrád was dazed.

'Konrád?'

'I'm still here.'

'You won't believe how good he looks.'

Konrád pulled on his clothes in a stupor. He threw a glance at the clock on his way out to the car: it was nearly three in the morning. He threaded his way through the empty streets, heading west towards the centre from his home in the suburb of Árbær, on the eastern edge of the city. Svanhildur had been at the National Hospital for more than thirty years. They'd known each other a long while, having worked on various cases together during his time as a detective in CID, and he was grateful to her now for the heads-up. As he drove, he thought about the glacier and Sigurvin and all the long years that had passed since his disappearance. They had dragged harbours, combed beaches, searched ditches, buildings, cars and volcanic fissures, but it had never crossed anyone's mind to scour the country's ice caps. Konrád thought back to all the people the police had interviewed over the course of the inquiry but couldn't remember a single connection to glacier tours.

He turned onto Miklabraut, the city's main artery, without meeting another car. Although he and Erna had moved into the small terraced house in Árbær in the early 1970s, he had never really felt at home there. He was a city boy who had grown up in the centre, in the old neighbourhood evocatively known as the Shadow District. Erna had been contented with the move, though, and so had their son, who had gone to a decent school in the new suburb and made friends with whom he invented imaginary worlds in the green area between the ski slope on Ártúnsbrekka and the Ellidaár Valley. Konrád, on the other hand, found the place too suburban, complaining that it was so cut off from everywhere else, it felt like being marooned on an island in Greater Reykjavík. He didn't like the convenience-store culture that he used to grumble was the only culture of any kind in the area. Nowhere in the country, he reckoned, did people eat more Lion bars, judging by the wrappers that littered the streets. When Erna got fed up with his moaning, he grudgingly admitted that the natural beauty of the wooded valley between the Ellidaár rivers went a long way towards compensating for the ugly dual carriageway that sliced across the hillside at Ártúnsbrekka, with its infernal fumes and noise.

He parked in front of the mortuary, which was based in an unassuming house in the hospital complex, and locked the car. Svanhildur was waiting for him by the entrance. She opened the door for him and led him inside in silence, her face solemn. She was wearing her lab coat, a white apron, and some sort of head covering made of netting and cardboard that reminded him of a sales assistant in a bakery.

'They carved out a big block of ice around him and transported the whole lot here,' Svanhildur explained, going over to one of the tables.

The block of ice stretching the length of the table was melting fast. Protruding from it was a body so well preserved that the man could have died that day, were it not for the oddly hard, glazed texture of his white skin. His arms lay by his sides and his chin had sunk down onto his chest. Meltwater had pooled on the floor, where it was trickling into the drain under the table.

'Will you be doing the post-mortem?' Konrád asked.

'Yes,' Svanhildur replied. 'I've been asked to examine him once the surrounding ice has melted and the body's thawed out. I won't be able to open him up until then. I expect his internal organs will be as well preserved as he is on the outside.' She paused. 'It must be a strange feeling for you to see him like this.'

'Did they fetch him down by helicopter?'

'No, they brought him in by road. They've been searching the area where he was found and I gather that'll continue for the next few days. Has no one from the police been in touch with you?'

'Not yet. I'm sure they will be tomorrow, though. Thanks for giving me a bell.'

'He's your man,' Svanhildur said. 'Beyond any doubt.'

'Yes, it's Sigurvin. It's weird seeing him like this after all these years, as if time had stood still.'

'While we've got older,' Svanhildur remarked, 'it's like he's got younger by the day.'

'It's a hell of a thing,' Konrád said quietly, as if to himself. 'Have you any idea how he died?'

'From what I could see as they were bringing him in, it looks like a possible blow to the head,' Svanhildur said, pointing. The man's head was largely free of the ice now and if one bent down, it was just possible to see what appeared to be wounds on the back of his skull.

'Was he killed on the glacier?'

'Hopefully that's one of the things we'll be able to work out.'

'Was he lying on his back like that when he was found?'

'Yes.'

'Isn't that a bit odd?'

'Every aspect of this case is odd,' Svanhildur said. 'As you should know better than anyone.'

'He doesn't seem to be dressed for a glacier trip.'

'No. What are you intending to do?'

'How do you mean?'

'Are you going to make yourself available to the investigation team or are you going to stay out of it?'

'They can take care of it,' Konrád said. 'I've retired. You should too.'

'I'd get bored,' Svanhildur said. She was divorced and said she sometimes dreaded the prospect of having to give up work. 'How are you, by the way?'

'Oh, you know. All right. If only I could sleep.'

They stood there in silence, watching the ice dripping from the body.

'Have you ever heard of the Franklin expedition?' Svanhildur asked suddenly, apropos of nothing.

'Franklin . . . ?'

'In the nineteenth century, the British sent out a lot of unsuccessful expeditions to look for the Northwest Passage through the sea ice north of Canada. The most famous of them was the Franklin expedition. Have you really never heard of it?'

'No.'

Svanhildur seemed pleased at this chance to relate the story. 'Franklin was a captain in the British navy,' she said. 'He undertook the expedition with two ships but they became trapped in the ice and vanished along with everyone onboard. But, earlier in the voyage, three crew members had died and the expedition had stopped at an island to bury them in the permafrost before continuing on its way. About thirty years ago the graves of the three men were exhumed, and their bodies turned out to be so well preserved that they were able to provide rare evidence of conditions at sea in the nineteenth century. Analysis of the three men's remains confirmed one of the theories about the main problem affecting long voyages like the Franklin expedition, which often lasted at least two or three years. It was known that sailors on these voyages would often become weak and confused, then lie down and die for no apparent reason. There are countless painstakingly recorded instances of this phenomenon but scholars have disagreed about the reasons for the men's strange lethargy. One of the many theories is that it might have been caused by lead poisoning, and the bodies found in the permafrost supported this. When they were examined, they revealed elevated levels of lead, consistent with the method of preserving food that was pioneered during the nineteenth century: in other words, tinned food.'

Having finished her account, Svanhildur glanced down at the body again.

'It's just one of those fascinating anecdotes from the world of pathology,' she said. 'The ships carried extensive supplies of tinned food that were contaminated by the lead that leached into the contents from the seams round the lids.'

'Why are you telling me all this?' Konrád asked.

'Oh, just because I immediately thought of the Franklin expedition when they brought Sigurvin down from the glacier. He reminded me of the sailors found in the permafrost. It's like he died yesterday.'

Konrád stepped closer to the body and stared down at it for a long while, marvelling at the preservative powers of the ice.

'Maybe we should start burying people in glaciers,' Svanhildur said. 'Move our cemeteries there if we can't face the idea of worm-eaten corpses.'

'I thought the glaciers were disappearing?'

'Yes, sadly,' Svanhildur said. As if to illustrate her words, a large chunk of ice broke off and fell to the floor, smashing into a thousand pieces.

Konrád drove home through the unrelieved darkness and got back into bed, exhausted, but sleep still refused to have mercy on him. As he lay there, the memory of the inquiry descended on him like a heavy weight. The thought of Sigurvin in the ice was almost more than he could bear. He couldn't shake off the image of the man's frozen face.

He shuddered.

He could have sworn that there had been a strange grin playing on Sigurvin's mouth as he lay there on the mortuary slab. His lips were peeled back like cracked leather to reveal his teeth, as though he were laughing in Konrád's face as a reminder of Konrád's miserable failure to solve the mystery of his disappearance all those years ago.

4

Two days later, the phone rang late in the evening. Normally Konrád would have been startled, as he'd largely stopped receiving phone calls at night and early in the morning since retiring. It was the biggest change he'd noticed, apart from the silence. But now the phone wouldn't stop ringing. This time it was a friend who used to work with him in the police. Konrád had been hoping to hear from her.

'He wants to talk to you,' the woman said. Her name was Marta and she was chief inspector at Reykjavík CID.

'He's not going to confess, is he?' Konrád had read online that a man had been arrested following the discovery of the body on the glacier. It didn't surprise him that it should have been Hjaltalín. The whole circus was starting up again. This time, though, Konrád was determined to stay out of it. Reporters had been pestering him for a quote about the discovery but he'd told them he had nothing to say on the subject. He'd left the police: others had taken over the case.

'He insists it's you he wants to see,' Marta said. 'He won't talk to us.'

'You told him I've retired?'

'Hjaltalín knows that. He wants to talk to you anyway.'

'What's he saying?'

'Nothing new: he's innocent.'

'He used to own a big four-by-four.'

'Exactly.'

'Which would have been capable of driving onto the ice cap.'

'Yep.'

'Are you allowing him visitors? Isn't he in custody?'

'We'd make an exception in your case,' Marta said. 'You'd be working for us in a temporary capacity – as a consultant.'

'I have absolutely no interest in getting mixed up in this again, Marta. Not now. Could we talk about it later?'

'We don't have much time.'

'No, I realise that.'

'I'd never have believed Sigurvin would turn up.'

'Thirty years is a long time.'

'Don't you want to see the body?'

'Already have,' Konrád said. 'He looks like he died yesterday.'

'Ah, of course – Svanhildur's been in touch with you. So, are you going to see the prisoner?'

'I'm retired.'

'All right, no need to go on about it.'

'I'll talk to you later.' Konrád rang off.

The truth was he couldn't stop thinking about Sigurvin and the visit to Svanhildur at the mortuary, but he was reluctant to reveal his interest to the former colleagues who'd been in touch over the last couple of days. He'd retired, he told them, and had no intention of going back, under any circumstances. Over thirty years had passed since they'd begun searching for Sigurvin. Since then Konrád had lost count of the people they'd interviewed, but no one had ever been charged. The investigation had quickly become focused on a man called Hjaltalín, but they'd never managed to prove anything against him. Hjaltalín had consistently denied ever having laid a finger on Sigurvin, and in the end they'd been forced to release him due to lack of evidence. The body had never been found: Sigurvin had simply vanished off the face of the earth.

And now he was lying in the mortuary, looking almost as if he'd only been gone a few days. Svanhildur hadn't been exaggerating when she'd said his body was uncannily well preserved. Although they hadn't embarked on the full post-mortem yet, a few facts had been established. Sigurvin was wearing the same clothes as he had been when he met his fate: trainers, jeans, shirt and jacket. The cause of death appeared to have been a heavy blow to the head with a blunt instrument. The skin had been broken and blood had been found on the back of his skull and on his clothes.

Konrád thought about all the years that had passed since the man died. He had sometimes imagined what the moment would be like; how he'd feel if Sigurvin ever turned up. Although he had long ago stopped searching, he'd never managed to put the case entirely behind him, and the suspicion that one day the phone would ring with the news that the missing man had been found had always been there, lurking just below the surface. Yet, ironically, when the news finally came, he'd found it almost impossible to process. Sigurvin's fate had been a mystery for decades. They hadn't even been sure he was dead, let alone had any idea how he'd died. Now they knew both the cause and the fact he had died at the time he went missing. They had never known exactly what he had been wearing when he vanished but now they could see for themselves. His body would provide those in charge of the inquiry with a variety of important new details, including a rough idea of the murder weapon. Those vital missing pieces were finally falling into place.

Konrád sat down at the kitchen table with a glass of red wine and lit a cigarillo. He sometimes smoked them when he felt a craving for nicotine, but apart from that he wasn't a big smoker. The phone rang again. This time it was his sister, Elísabet. She asked how he was doing.

'Fine,' he said, sucking down smoke. 'The phone hasn't stopped ringing.'

'I hear that bloody case is blowing up again,' said Elísabet, who was known to all as Beta. Like everyone else, she had been gripped by the news reports about the body.

'Apparently Hjaltalín's trying to drag me into it,' Konrád said. 'They've taken him into custody and he wants to see me. They've told him I'm retired but he won't take no for an answer.'

'Does anyone ever retire from a case like that?'

'That's a question I've been asking myself.'

'Aren't you curious to hear what he's got to say?'

'I know exactly what he'll say, Beta. He'll say he's innocent. The fact the body's turned up won't change a thing. We had nothing on him thirty years ago and we won't find anything now, "because he's innocent". That's what he'll say. I've no idea why he wants to repeat it for my benefit.'

Beta was silent. They hadn't been close when they were young, having been brought up in separate households following their parents' divorce, but they'd been trying to make up for it ever since, each in their own way, though it wasn't always easy.

'You weren't entirely convinced he'd done it at the time,' she said after a moment.

'No, unlike the rest of them. But he was always our most likely candidate.'

It was common knowledge that Hjaltalín had been the only serious suspect for Sigurvin's murder in 1985 and that, despite a spell in custody, he'd never confessed. The police had failed to prove beyond all doubt that he'd been involved in Sigurvin's disappearance. Yet he was the last person to have been seen with him, and the two men had reportedly quarrelled bitterly just before Sigurvin vanished. Hjaltalín was also known to have threatened him.

'Have they asked for your help with the investigation?' Beta asked.

'No.'

'But they want you to see Hjaltalín?'

'They think he might tell me something he won't tell them. He's refusing to talk to them.'

'Thirty years is a long time.'

'He did a good job of hiding Sigurvin. The reason he got away with it was because we never found the body. The question is whether he'll get away with it so easily this time round.'

'But you had nothing on him.'

'We had various things on him, just not enough. In the end, the prosecutor didn't feel he had a good enough case to take before a judge.'

'Don't let yourself get drawn in again. You've left the police.'

'Yes, I've left.'

'Talk to you later.'

'OK, bye.'

The discovery was all over the media but Konrád had got the inside story from Svanhildur. Ever since the body was recovered from the ice, four members of Forensics had been stationed on the glacier, conducting a search of the area. Police officers from the little west coast town of Borgarnes had been first on the scene after the German tour group had rung the emergency number. The local volunteer search and rescue team had also been called out, and this had alerted the press to the fact that something was up. The police officers from Borgarnes had made their way onto the ice, despite being inadequately equipped, and had confirmed that the body was that of a man, aged around thirty, who had evidently been there a long time. They had been ordered by their superior not to touch anything, and to keep the tourists well away. At this point, Forensics in Reykjavík had been notified. By then, the Borgarnes rescue team had reached the edge of the glacier in their specially equipped vehicles. They conveyed the Germans down to the hotel at Húsafell, along with their guide, a woman in her early sixties called Adalheidur, who had found the body. That evening, the group had travelled back to Reykjavík. Detectives from CID had questioned the woman closely and spoken to the Germans with her help. An older man, who informed them that he was a doctor, explained that he'd brushed some snow from the man's face but that otherwise they'd been careful not to touch anything.

In order to minimise disturbance of the evidence, a block of ice weighing almost two hundred kilos had been carved out around the body, then freed and hoisted onto the rescue team's ice truck. A forensic technician had accompanied the chunk of glacier to Reykjavík, keeping a close eye on anything it produced as it melted. Later that evening, most of the police and rescue team members had gone down to Húsafell where they had spent the night, leaving four officers behind on the glacier to prevent any unauthorised individuals from approaching the site.

One of the country's top glaciologists, interviewed on the radio in connection with the discovery, was quick to point out that since 1985, when Sigurvin's body had been hidden on the glacier, the ice cap had shrunk by more than seven cubic kilometres. It was now around six hundred metres thick, but experts calculated that during the next quarter of a century the glacier would shrink by almost 20 per cent as a result of global warming.

'And some people are still sceptical about manmade climate change!' Konráð had heard the glaciologist saying in a tone of exasperation on the radio that morning.

'Would the body have been laid on top of the ice or buried somehow?' the radio host had asked.

'Hard to say. It's possible he was dropped into a crevasse. He went missing in February, when freezing temperatures would have made it extremely difficult to dig into the ice. But he would have been covered with snow quickly enough. Another possibility is that a crevasse subsequently opened and swallowed him up, and he remained there until his recent reappearance.'

'Did the ice just melt to reveal him, then?'

'Of course, that will require further analysis, but it sounds plausible. It would be the simplest explanation for why he's turned up now.'

Yet again Konráð's mobile phone shattered the silence of his house in Árbær. This time it was Svanhildur, wanting to know what he was planning to do. She'd heard that Hjaltalín was asking to see him.

'I don't know,' Konrád said. 'Maybe it wouldn't hurt to talk to him – to hear what he's got to say.'

'Oh, come on! You must be dying of curiosity. This is Sigurvin we're talking about! Surely that must spark your interest?'

'Hjaltalín wasn't even thirty when we arrested him,' Konrád remarked.

'I remember it well.'

'He must be pushing sixty now. I haven't seen him for donkey's years.'

'Do you think he'll have changed much?'

'I think he'll be the same idiot.'

'You two weren't exactly best mates.'

'No,' said Konrád. 'Though he seemed to think we were. I don't know what he wants to talk to me about. The fact is, I wouldn't trust Hjaltalín as far as I could throw him. He wouldn't be in custody now if they hadn't thought he was trying to make a run for it. He was on the point of leaving the country when they arrested him. That was the day after Sigurvin was identified. He claimed it was a complete coincidence.'

'Are you sleeping any better these days?'

'Not much.'

'You know you can always call me if there's something bothering you,' Svanhildur said. 'If you want to chat.'

'Yes, but I'm fine,' Konrád said brusquely.

'All right.' Svanhildur was about to ring off, then added, as if she couldn't help herself: 'You never get in touch any more.'

'No, I . . .' Konrád didn't know what to say.

'Just call if . . .'

He didn't respond and they ended the call. He took a sip of wine and lit another cigarillo. He and Erna had sometimes talked about downsizing and moving away from Árbær. Not to some block of flats for pensioners but to a cosy little place near the city centre. Though not in Thingholt or any of those old streets east of the lake, Erna had said, as there were too many party animals living there nowadays. To the west end, rather. Nothing had come of it, though. He remembered how often they had discussed the Sigurvin case at this kitchen table, and how she had always been there for him, whatever happened.

The table in the sitting room was covered with old papers of his father's that Konrád had been looking through the evening Svanhildur had rung with the news about Sigurvin. They'd been in a cardboard box in the basement and he hadn't given them so much as a glance in decades. It had been getting mixed up in an old case from the Second World War, involving fraudulent spiritualists, that had resurrected his long-buried interest in his father's fate. He had been discovered one evening in 1963, lying fatally stabbed in front of the South Iceland Abattoir on Skúlagata. Despite an extensive investigation, the murder had never been solved. Konrád had banished the incident from his mind during all the long years he had worked as a detective. His father had been a troublesome, vindictive man, who had made enemies on every side. He had done stints behind bars for smuggling, theft and fraud. And that wasn't the half of it. He had also conspired with at least one, if not more, fake mediums during the war. Konrád's mother had eventually fled their home, taking Beta with her, but her husband had refused to let her take their son, who had remained behind, growing up with his father in the Shadow District.

Konrád leafed through the yellowing papers. His interest had been piqued by a handful of newspaper cuttings on spiritualism and the paranormal that his father had kept. Among them was an article about conmen, and an interview with an Icelandic psychic in a long-defunct weekly newspaper. Another cutting was from a publication by the Society for Psychical Research, discussing the afterlife and 'the Ether World'. The articles dated from about two years before Konrád's father had been stabbed outside the abattoir. They had led Konrád to wonder if, in the final months of his life, his father could have returned to his old bad habits of swindling money out of people through fake seances.

5

Konrád had not been happy when the custody facilities were moved to the Litla-Hraun prison ten years back. He was soon fed up with having to drive sixty kilometres over the Hellisheidi mountain road and down through the Threngsli pass, crossing the River Ölfusá where it flowed into the sea, then heading east along the coast towards the villages of Eyrarbakki and Stokkseyri. Some of his colleagues, on the other hand, found it a pleasant break from the city and the constant stress at the police station. Konrád had got his car stuck in a snowdrift on Hellisheidi twice in the same winter, but there were other times when he had been able to enjoy the journey, using it as a chance to relax and take a detour through the Sudurland towns of Hveragerdi and Selfoss, even stopping to buy himself an ice cream on the way.

For many years before that, the custody facilities had been at the prison on Sídumúli in Reykjavík, conveniently close to the police station. That was where Hjaltalín had been detained during the original inquiry. But times had changed, Konrád thought, as he took the main road out of town across the seemingly endless expanse of moss-covered lava fields, passing the familiar landmarks: the green-roofed building of the Little Cafe, standing alone among the wastes, and the distinctive black-cinder slopes of Mount Vífilfell.

He had finally come round to the idea of visiting Hjaltalín in custody. Not because Hjaltalín had insisted and refused to speak to anyone else, but because Konrád had invested so much time and energy in the original investigation. He'd never really stopped looking for answers. All the hard graft that he and other members of CID had put into the inquiry had ultimately been wasted. The case had been a rarity in that it hadn't been wrapped up in a matter of days, like most major crimes in Iceland. The investigation had quickly ended up all over the place, badly lacking direction; they'd never found a body, and although Hjaltalín had been the main focus, countless other people had been interviewed as potential suspects. Now, the discovery of Sigurvin's body had cracked the case wide open again.

At some point Hjaltalín had got it into his head that Konrád was the only member of CID he could trust, and due to the way things worked out, Konrád had conducted most of his interviews. He assumed this was the main reason why Hjaltalín was demanding to talk to him now. The police had caved in to his wishes and, in the end, so had Konrád. But Konrád had no intention of doing anything else for the police. He had got too used to the comforts of retirement: the leisure time, the freedom to organise his own life, the lack of onerous duties and responsibilities. He had done his bit for society: it was someone else's turn to take over. If his meeting with Hjaltalín provided the police with a lead, fine. Apart from that, Konrád was staying well out of it.

His son had called as soon as he heard the news. He knew all about his father's biggest unsolved case and wanted to hear what Konrád was thinking now that Sigurvin had finally been found. Konrád told him he was glad that new information had come to light and that his thoughts were mainly of Sigurvin's family and the distress they'd endured as a result of having to live all these years without closure.

Konrád's recent insomnia hadn't been helped by the fact that his brain was now working overtime on the old case, preoccupied with thoughts about how he had conducted the original investigation and whether there was some obvious angle he had neglected. It wasn't the first time these questions had caused him sleepless nights.

The world had changed beyond recognition in the last thirty years. It seemed unbelievable now that beer had still been illegal in Iceland in 1985. There had been just one, state-run TV channel. And only a couple of aluminium smelters. Kárahnjúkar, the biggest hydroelectric dam in Europe, hadn't even been conceived of. Reykjavík used to have regular snowfalls in winter. There had been no internet or mobile phones, and hardly any personal computers. The privatisation of the banks and the ensuing chaos; the arrogant, reckless stupidity of government and economic leaders; the financial collapse – they were all in the future. The new millennium had seemed as remote as science fiction.

One cold February afternoon in those far-off days, as the light was failing and a bitter wind was gusting through the streets, the police station on Hverfisgata received a phone call. The woman at the other end wanted to report the disappearance of a thirty-year-old man – her brother, Sigurvin. She had last spoken to him two days earlier on the phone, when they made an arrangement to meet up. When he failed to appear at the appointed time, she had tried to get hold of him. He wasn't answering at home, so she called him at work, only to learn that he hadn't been in for the last two days. After that she had gone round to his house and knocked on the door in vain, before finally calling out a locksmith, afraid that Sigurvin might be lying ill indoors, unable to get to the phone, or that he might have unplugged it for some reason. Once inside, she had gone from room to room, calling out his name, but he wasn't there. As far as she was aware, he'd had no plans to travel abroad. He usually let her know if he was leaving the country and, anyway, she'd come across his passport in a drawer in the sitting room. He lived alone, was recently divorced and had one daughter, who lived with her mother.

The police took it for granted that the man would turn up, since he hadn't been missing long, but they noted down his description and got a headshot from his sister, which they then circulated to all the newspapers and police stations in the country. The presence of his passport showed that he couldn't have left Iceland by air, unless he had done so under an alias or somehow slipped through passport control undetected. When this possibility was put to his sister, she dismissed it as absurd: what possible reason could he have had to travel on a forged passport?

Before long, the volunteer search and rescue teams were called out and the standard missing-person response was put into action. All the beaches in the Greater Reykjavík area were combed. The press became interested in the case and carried detailed articles about the missing man. The public were urged to come forward with information if they knew anything about his movements, however insignificant it might seem, and in no time his jeep was discovered. It was parked at the foot of the hot-water tanks on Öskjuhlíd, the wooded hill close to the centre of Reykjavík. A special incident line was set up and tip-offs soon started flooding in, some more plausible than others, though the police did their best to follow them all up. One was an anonymous phone call from a woman who had delivered her message in a rush, then hung up immediately afterwards. She claimed that Sigurvin's former business partner had been overheard threatening to kill him in the car park in front of the company offices.

It had fallen to Konrád to follow up this lead. He learnt that a man called Hjaltalín had been threatening Sigurvin for some time, claiming that he had been swindled out of millions of krónur. It transpired that the two men had owned three boats and a fishing business together. Sigurvin had been responsible for the day-to-day management; Hjaltalín had only been a sleeping partner. In fact, he liked to boast about being a total landlubber. His main concern was a couple of clothing shops in Reykjavík and an import business, along with shares in one or two other companies. The two men had met as students at the Commercial College. They had both been similarly bold and driven; young men on the make. Sigurvin had persuaded Hjaltalín to go shares on a boat with him and before long there had been two boats, then three, then it had developed into a whole fishing business. Eventually, at Sigurvin's suggestion, Hjaltalín had agreed to sell his share to him and they had signed a contract to that effect. But it wasn't long before Hjaltalín began to accuse Sigurvin of ripping him off. The company had been worth far more than his friend had led him to believe, he argued. And that wasn't all: the value was likely to increase dramatically if Sigurvin played his cards right, since the recently introduced quota system would restrict access to the fishing grounds, resulting in massive share rises for existing companies. Hjaltalín had started having misgivings when he learnt more about the new arrangement and consulted experts, who presented him with a very different picture of the company's prospects from the one Sigurvin had sketched out for him. Aggrieved, Hjaltalín told his friend he had trusted him, but Sigurvin flatly denied cheating him. Business was business, he said, and Hjaltalín had signed the contract of his own free will. End of story.

According to witnesses, relations between the two men had been acrimonious ever since. Hjaltalín had turned up at Sigurvin's office on more than one occasion, yelling, banging doors and issuing threats, even lying in wait for him outside in his car.

'You'd better watch out!' Hjaltalín had shouted, on one of the last times he came round. 'You'd better watch out, you bastard! You won't get away with treating me like this!'

That had been three weeks before Sigurvin went missing. His last known movements had been in the late afternoon on the day he talked to his sister on the phone. One of his employees had seen him standing by his jeep in the company car park, talking to a man who the employee later confirmed was Hjaltalín. The witness had not come forward of his own volition, because he had a criminal record, having done time for theft and other offences, and wanted as little to do with the police as possible. But he had confided in a couple of people about what he'd overheard, one of whom had subsequently called the police with the tip-off about a former business partner threatening to kill Sigurvin. Konráð had eventually tracked the witness down.

It turned out that he hadn't caught much of what had passed between the two men, apart from the moment when Hjaltalín raised his voice, shook his fist at Sigurvin and stormed off, yelling: '. . . do you hear me . . . kill you, you bastard . . . !'

6

The blue gate opened to admit Konrád. He parked his four-wheel drive in front of the administrative block of Litla-Hraun Prison, got out and surveyed the imposing building which had been designed to resemble a traditional gable-fronted farmhouse. It was painted white, the colour of innocence.

The director was an old acquaintance, so Konrád sat down with him in his office first for a coffee. They discussed the extraordinary discovery of Sigurvin's body and speculated whether the glaciers, receding year by year, might be concealing further secrets under the ice.

'We'll find out sooner or later,' the director said. He escorted Konrád over to the small wing that housed prisoners who were being held in custody. 'It's unlikely Hjaltalín will be with us for long. The Supreme Court's currently reviewing the decision to arrest him. It looks like he'll be released.'

'To be honest, I was surprised that he was arrested at all,' Konrád said. 'They haven't found any evidence on Sigurvin's body to justify it.'

'He was about to leave the country – Hjaltalín, I mean.'

'So I hear.'

'Did you know he was ill?'

'Who?'

'Hjaltalín. He took a turn for the worse when he was brought here.'

'No, I wasn't aware of that. What's wrong with him?'

'He's just finished a course of chemo for throat cancer, so his arrest's being reviewed on humanitarian grounds as well. He's been in bed since he got here and has to be careful not to overdo it. He asked if he could talk to you in his cell to avoid having to sit up in the interview room. We've given him a dispensation. I thought Marta and co. would have told you about that.'

'No,' Konrád said. 'They didn't. Is it serious, then? Is he going to pull through?'

'That's anybody's guess.'

At the door to the custody wing, a prison officer took over and showed Konrád to Hjaltalín's cell. Two detectives were there to keep on eye on things but they remained outside in the corridor. There was no sign of Hjaltalín's lawyer. The official story was that Konrád had been brought in temporarily to work on the investigation, but news of his meeting with Hjaltalín wasn't supposed to get out.

The officer opened the door to the cell, ushered Konrád in, then closed it carefully behind him. His footsteps receded down the corridor.

Hjaltalín was lying on a narrow sleeping platform that was fixed to the floor along one wall. Apart from that, the cell contained only a chair, a small desk, a sink and a toilet. White light filtered through a barred window above the bed. There was a Bible on the desk and a faint whiff of disinfectant in the air.

'I heard about your illness,' Konrád said. 'They shouldn't have banged you up.'

Hjaltalín smiled. He didn't sit up but remained lying flat on his back with one arm behind his head, regarding Konrád with half-closed eyes, as if he wasn't particularly interested in his visit. Yet he had requested it, or rather insisted on it. They hadn't seen each other for decades, except on one occasion that Konrád would sooner forget. It took him a moment or two to assimilate the changes. Hjaltalín had aged and lost an awful lot of weight – as a result of the cancer, Konrád assumed. The treatment had caused his hair to fall out, accentuating the long, narrow face with its prominent blue eyes and colourless skin. His skull was almost snow-white. It was as if he had morphed into an ageing albino.

'They don't care,' Hjaltalín whispered hoarsely. 'You look well.'

'They thought you were trying to do a runner.'

'Are they recording this? Our conversation?'

'No,' Konrád said. 'Not as far as I'm aware.' He pulled the chair over and sat down. The Bible, which belonged to the prison, was much thumbed, with a broken spine and worn covers.

'I knew they'd come for me,' Hjaltalín whispered. 'I was going to take myself off.'

'To Thailand, I hear.'

'Wonderful place.' Hjaltalín stared up at the ceiling. 'I didn't want to end up in a cell like this again.'

'I don't think they're listening but they'll ask me afterwards what you told me. I gather you won't talk to anyone, not even your lawyer.'

'The moment I heard who they'd found – that it was Sigurvin – I drove to the airport and bought a ticket to Thailand via London. But they reacted pretty fast. I'd already boarded the plane. Did you know that?'

'No.'

'They thought I was running away because I was guilty,' Hjaltalín went on in a thin, rasping voice. 'That if I wasn't guilty, I'd never have tried it. But I was running away because I'm innocent. Running away from this. This cell. All this bullshit. I wanted to die in peace. That's . . . all.'

'You told the police it was a coincidence that you were heading to Thailand just after Sigurvin had turned up. Does that sound plausible to you?'

Hjaltalín closed his eyes. 'I'm not lying to you, Konrád. I've never lied to you about this business.'

'Yeah, right.'

The police handling the original investigation had discovered that Hjaltalín found it extraordinarily easy to twist the truth; so much so that he was almost a pathological liar. Time and again he had pulled the wool over their eyes, only to be caught out in a lie. He had frequently implied one thing, only to contradict himself by stating the exact opposite shortly afterwards. Instead of regarding lies as a serious matter, he had used them to delay and obfuscate the inquiry into Sigurvin's disappearance.

'I'm sorry you're so ill,' Konrád said.

'Thank you.'

'Did it seem like a wise idea to drag yourself all the way to Asia, given the state you're in?'

'I was going to look into alternative cures over there. I'd found a doctor who . . . But of course, you don't believe me, do you?'

'Why did you want to see me?'

'You understand me.'

'I'm not . . . I don't think anyone can understand . . .'

'Have you any idea what it's like, Konrád, to be locked up like this in my condition?' Hjaltalín opened his eyes again. 'Can you even begin to imagine what it's like?'

'No,' Konrád said. 'I've never experienced anything like that.'

'It's dogged me all these years. That case. Ever since I was a young man. All because I allegedly threatened Sigurvin. Because I allegedly shouted at him in a car park and some police inform-ant pretended he'd heard what I said.'

'Right.'

Hjaltalín rested his gaze on the ceiling again. 'The doctors say I shouldn't talk too much. I'm supposed to spare my voice as much as I can. The cancer has spread. They didn't think it would but it has.'

'Don't you think this would be a good moment to relieve your conscience? In case you take a turn for the worse.'

'Relieve my conscience? How? I didn't do anything. And I know you believed me. You were the only one who had doubts. You had your doubts all along.'

The witness, a repeat offender, had provided a description of the man in the car park and that description had fitted Hjaltalín. But when the police went round to see him, Hjaltalín had claimed not to have been in the car park with Sigurvin or to have made any threats. He was asked if he wanted to rule out the possibility that he was the man the witness had seen by taking part in an identity parade. Without a moment's hesitation, he said: 'Of course.'

'That's him,' the repeat offender had said, the instant he laid eyes on Hjaltalín in the line-up.

'Are you sure?' he was asked.

'Yes.'

'You don't want to take another look? We've got plenty of time.'

'No, that's him,' said the witness.

Hjaltalín hadn't been allowed to go home. Instead, he had been taken to the cells after his statutory phone call to a lawyer. He had protested at this treatment, pointing out that he'd come into the station voluntarily and that the whole thing was a terrible mistake. The witness was adamant, however, and provided an exact time for the altercation between the two men. Hjaltalín was asked where he had been during the relevant period. He said he couldn't remember. When the question was subsequently put to him again and he was asked if he could provide an alibi, he had given them the name of his girlfriend, saying that they'd been at his place together. The police had got in touch with the girl straight away and Konrád had interviewed her at the police station. She worked in one of Hjaltalín's clothes shops and had been seeing him for a while. Although she confirmed her boyfriend's story, Konrád had detected an underlying nervousness. He'd reminded himself that she hadn't been expecting to be interviewed at the police station on Hverfisgata about the high-profile missing persons case, possibly even murder, that was all over the papers, TV and radio. She'd had no previous run-ins with the police either, and it was clear from her confusion that she hardly knew what had hit her. But there was something else going on there. The elastic hairband she kept twisting between her fingers. The way she avoided eye contact and kept her gaze fixed on the door, asking repeatedly if they were done. The embarrassed smile. After two hours of questioning, Konrád had succeeding in prising out of her the admission that although she had been at Hjaltalín's place, she had

gone out at the same time as him. She had no idea of his movements after that. The timing was consistent with the alleged
encounter in the car park. Hjaltalín had called and asked her to
say that she'd been with him all evening – in case anyone ever
asked, which he said was unlikely.

'When?' Konrád had demanded, his eyes on the elastic band
the girl was fidgeting with.

'When what?'

'When did he call and ask you to do that?'

'Er, several days later.'

'After the search for Sigurvin had begun?'

'Yes.'

'Are you sure? Was it after the search had begun? This is very
important.'

'Yes, it was after everyone started looking for him.'

'Where did he say he was going?' Konrád asked. 'Where was
Hjaltalín going that evening?'

'To meet a friend.'

Konrád stared at her. 'A friend?'

'Yes.'

'Sigurvin?'

'I don't know. Some friend. I didn't hear properly.'

The significance of the fact that Hjaltalín had asked his girlfriend to lie for him *after* the search for Sigurvin had begun wasn't
missed by his lawyer. He demanded that his client be released
from custody on the grounds that Hjaltalín had suspected he
would be blamed for Sigurvin's disappearance, because of their
previous dealings and the bad blood that was known to exist
between them. In other words, he had acted to protect himself.
Admittedly, it had been a clumsy, foolish reaction, but only human

and understandable in the circumstances. If Hjaltalín had asked the girl to lie for him *before* Sigurvin's disappearance had been discovered, that would have been different. In that case, the assumption would have been that he'd had prior knowledge of Sigurvin's fate.

The girl was able to give them a fairly precise time frame and, going by what she said, it was perfectly possible that Hjaltalín could have gone straight to Sigurvin's office and met him there. At this point, Hjaltalín had altered his story. He now remembered having encountered Sigurvin in the car park, but claimed that afterwards he had gone to see a woman whose identity he couldn't reveal because she was married.

Konrád stared at the Bible lying on the desk in the cell, and wondered if Hjaltalín had been reading it and whether he knew the words of the gospel of St Luke, chapter sixteen, verse ten: 'Whoever can be trusted with very little can also be trusted with much, and whoever is dishonest with very little will also be dishonest with much.'

'I read it every day,' Hjaltalín said, following Konrád's gaze. 'I take great comfort from it.'

7

Hjaltalín appeared to have fallen asleep. His eyes were closed and his breathing had slowed. Konráð sat quietly beside his bed, reflecting that the man couldn't have long to live. He looked so weak, and the pallor of his almost chalk-white skin seemed a clear sign that his illness was gaining the upper hand.

'Are you thinking back to those days?' the threadbare voice whispered, though Hjaltalín didn't open his eyes. 'I often relive what it was like in prison. It wasn't a good time.'

'You seemed to take it in your stride,' Konráð said. 'They want to know how you transported Sigurvin's body to the glacier. You were arrested two weeks after he vanished, which would have given you ample time to dispose of him.'

Hjaltalín opened his eyes and contemplated the ceiling for a while. Then he pushed himself upright, very slowly, until he was sitting on the edge of the bed. He buried his face in his fingers for a moment and groaned, then rubbed a hand over his hairless scalp and looked Konrád in the eye.

'I've never set foot on a glacier in my life,' he whispered weakly. 'You have to stop this, Konrád – you and your mates in the police. I haven't got much time left.'

'You used to own a four-by-four.'

'So did everyone else. The police can't do this to me. You were supposed to solve the case, Konrád. Look what you've done to me. You might as well have killed me. I haven't had a proper life since then. Everyone looks at me like I'm a murderer. They all think I killed him. They stare at me and . . . What do you think it's been like, Konrád? What do you think it's been like, having to live with this? This hell on earth. It was your job to find the person who did it, you useless shit. How could you have been so fucking useless? You were all useless, the whole lot of you. A bunch of fucking losers.'

Seeing how exhausted Hjaltalín was, Konrád endured his tirade in silence. He felt sorry for the sick man. Knew what a tough time he'd had ever since he was first arrested on suspicion of murder.

'The woman you said you were with – the married woman you refused to name . . .'

'She's not important.'

'Because she never existed,' Konrád said. 'Why do you persist with this bullshit? You fell out with Sigurvin; you threatened him, followed him and spied on him, waited for the right moment, then attacked him up by the tanks on Öskjuhlíd.'

Hjaltalín shot him a glance. 'You said you believed me.'

Konrád rose to his feet. He could see no point in prolonging this encounter. 'I said I wasn't entirely sure. I shouldn't have said that. And you shouldn't have taken it seriously. You're still the only person in the picture. Nothing's changed. And your extraordinary attempt to flee the country has done nothing to help your cause.'

'But you said it.'

Thirty years ago, Hjaltalín had told Konrád repeatedly that they should direct their attention elsewhere. But the police had reckoned that they'd exhausted all other avenues. All the evidence pointed to Hjaltalín. Once, after a long day, Konrád had been so tired and out of sorts that he had raised the possibility, in Hjaltalín's hearing, that the man could in fact be innocent; that maybe CID hadn't done enough to investigate other lines of inquiry. Hjaltalín had seized on this.

'Why did you summon me?' Konrád asked now. 'You have nothing to say. You've got absolutely nothing to offer but the same old crap.'

'You're the only one I can get through to. I know you. We sometimes used to talk about other stuff apart from bloody Sigurvin.'

'That was a long time ago.'

'I thought we were friends.'

'You were wrong about that.'

'Oh, really?'

'Yes, I'm afraid so. We're not friends and you know it. I have no idea what you're trying to achieve but . . .' Konrád broke off, seeing from Hjaltalín's face that he'd hurt him.

'You . . . you think you're better than me?' Hjaltalín croaked. 'When you couldn't even solve the simplest bloody cases.'

'Look, let's just call it a day. I hope you're not in too much pain and that you recover your health. And I'm sorry to see you in such bad shape, but there's nothing I can do for you. Sadly. So . . .'

'Is that prick Leó still in the police?'

'Leó?' Konrád was wrong-footed. 'Yes, why?'

'He was an evil bastard. Did his best to break me down. Kept going on and on about me being a liar. Saying I was guilty.'

'You called most of us evil bastards.'

'Not you.' Hjaltalín gave Konrád a long, searching look, his limpid blue eyes like oases in the desert of his haggard face. 'I was thinking about your old man before you got here.'

'You're not seriously going to start on that again?'

'They told me he was no angel. Remember? They said he was a real scumbag.'

Konrád smiled, determined not to rise to this. Hjaltalín had sometimes tried to drag his father into it when he was being interviewed at Sídumúli Prison. Someone had leaked the story to him, and after that Hjaltalín wouldn't stop needling Konrád about it.

'Nice how you've always taken such an interest in me,' Konrád said drily.

'You must have been shocked,' Hjaltalín said. 'It must have hit you hard. Were you close? Or was he a total shit like they said? The cops at Sídumúli, your mates – they said he used to knock your mother about. Is that true? Did you watch?'

Konrád didn't answer.

'They said he was a bastard.'

'Don't bother your head about him,' Konrád said.

'They said he probably deserved to be stabbed. Do you think he deserved it? Because of your mum?'

'What are you trying to do, Hjaltalín?'

'I'm hoping you're not like him. I'm hoping you're not a piece of shit like him.'

'Right, I'm off,' Konrád said, preparing to make a move. 'I can't be bothered to listen to this any more.'

'What do you say to that, eh? Could anyone escape unscathed from contact with a man like him? From a background like that? Are you sure there isn't a bit of him in you? A bit of a devil?'

'Goodbye.'

'You never found out who killed him, did you?' Hjaltalín persevered. Clearly he had no intention of letting Konrád get off so lightly. 'You must have been burning for revenge afterwards. So what happened when you got no answers? Did you lose interest? Didn't it matter to you any more? Wasn't he worth it? A lowlife scumbag like him.'

Konrád refused to let the other man's needling get to him.

'Was that it?' Hjaltalín went on. 'That he just wasn't worth it?'

'I'm going to hit the road,' Konrád said. 'You're talking a load of shit like you always did.'

'You're my friend, Konrád. Oh, I know you deny it and you don't want to be and you fight it, but you're my only friend in this whole shitshow. You always were. You understand people like me; people like me and your dad. I'm not perfect, I admit it. But I didn't kill Sigurvin. It wasn't me!'

Exhausted by this speech, Hjaltalín sank down on the bed, but clearly he wasn't finished with the subject of Konrád's father, because he started asking again if Konrád had inherited his dad's vicious side. In the end, Konrád had to repeat his threat of walking out. At that point, Hjaltalín relented.

'I want to ask you to do something for me,' he whispered. 'In case I don't have much time left. I want you to find the person who did it.'

'They reckon they've found him.'

'It wasn't me,' Hjaltalín repeated, his voice cracking with the strain. 'I'd never go anywhere near a glacier, Konrád. Ask anyone. Never in a million years.'

'You could have got someone else to do it for you,' Konrád said. 'Someone you'd dragged into the mess.'

Hjaltalín didn't answer. The police hadn't yet been able to establish whether Sigurvin had died *in situ* on the glacier or been dumped there after his death, though the former possibility was considered unlikely. Sigurvin hadn't been known for his interest in the great outdoors or shown any enthusiasm for trips on the country's ice caps, and no equipment had been found in his possession that pointed to that kind of hobby. Like many people in Reykjavík, he had owned a pair of skis but only used them on the slopes at Bláfjöll, just outside the city limits. He'd had a jeep too, but it wasn't specially modified for travelling on ice, and he'd never owned a snowmobile. The alternative appeared much more likely: that Sigurvin's body had been transported to the glacier after he was killed.

'Why Langjökull?' Konrád asked now. 'Surely you could have found a better place if you wanted to get rid of him. Ice doesn't destroy evidence, it preserves it. And it preserves bodies. I've seen Sigurvin. It's like he's been dead no time at all. The glacier didn't destroy him – quite the reverse. It's like time has stood still for thirty years.'

Hjaltalín smiled dully. 'Please, will you do it for my sake?'

'I've left the police,' Konrád said. 'I came here because you insisted and I was curious to see if you'd changed at all. But it was a total waste of my time.'

'I want you to clear my name once and for all,' Hjaltalín said, his voice so faint now that it was almost inaudible. 'Can't you see the state I'm in? Look at me! I want you to clear my name. Please! I didn't lay a finger on him. You lot couldn't pin it on me at the time and you can't do it now either. I didn't take him to the glacier. That was someone else. It wasn't me.' Hjaltalín reared up a little, his pale eyes fixed on Konrád. 'It wasn't me!'

'Goodbye.'

'If you ever find him, make him pay,' Hjaltalín whispered, slumping down again. 'Will you do that for me? Will you make him pay for what he's done to me . . . ?'

It was a relief to get back outside into the open air. Konrád had been filled with a growing sense of unease in the cell, and Hjaltalín's sickly white face had done nothing to lessen it. He had delivered his report of their meeting to the waiting detectives, before leaving the building. Afterwards, he drove unhurriedly home, deciding to take the roundabout route via Selfoss rather than returning over the Threngsli pass. The weather was bright and sunny on the grassy lowlands around the River Ölfusá. But soon enough he was ascending the hairpin bends into the mountains again, passing the eternal columns of steam rising from the Hellisheidi geothermal power station, then on through the volcanic wastes until at last the city opened out below, surrounded on three sides by blue sea. Yet the landscape passed in a blur. All Konrád's thoughts were taken up by the memory of his visit: the feeble voice, the stamp of death on Hjaltalín's face, the reply of the prison officer when Konrád asked if Hjaltalín read the Bible.

'Never seen him open it,' the officer had said, in direct contradiction of Hjaltalín's own claim. 'He said it didn't help.'

Konrád was still brooding on the visit when he got into bed not long after midnight. It started to pour with rain outside as if the heavens had opened. He had no idea who had been responsible for telling Hjaltalín about his father's murder, back when he was detained in Sídumúli Prison thirty years ago. Hjaltalín had started asking Konráð about it, hesitantly at first, but the longer he was in custody, the more he pestered him, until in the end they could hardly meet without him bringing up the subject of Konráð's father. He had found his jailer's Achilles heel.

'Why do you think he was killed?' Hjaltalín used to ask. 'Haven't you ever tried to discover the reason, since you joined the police? What was your relationship like? Was he a good father? Did he treat you better than he did your mum?'

Konráð had tried to ignore his questions, but eventually he had given in and provided Hjaltalín with a brief account of his father's murder, in the hope that it might help to loosen the prisoner's tongue. Konráð had been eighteen at the time of his father's death. He told Hjaltalín that his old man had been stabbed twice with a knife, and that neither the killer nor the weapon had ever been found. The murder had been all over the papers at the time and Konráð had read the coverage obsessively. But when Hjaltalín kept pushing for more information, like how Konráð had felt or why his parents had been separated at the time of the murder, Konráð had clammed up. By then, Hjaltalín's time in custody was drawing to an end.

'And then you go and become a cop yourself,' Hjaltalín had said to him when he was released. 'The son of that man. Isn't there something warped about that? Does it add up?'

Konráð turned over restlessly, trying to banish these thoughts. But when he finally dropped off, sleep didn't bring him any relief. Instead, he dreamt of Hjaltalín's ashen face and pale blue eyes and woke with a gasp in the middle of the night, sweating and filled with that sick feeling of unease.

Shortly after their meeting at Litla-Hraun, the Supreme Court ruled that the police had no grounds to detain Hjaltalín in custody.

Two weeks later, Konrád learnt that he had died in the oncology ward at the National Hospital.

Hjaltalín had gone to his death, insisting to the last that he hadn't killed Sigurvin.

8

A series of deep autumn depressions had lined up over the Atlantic and were now advancing relentlessly across the country, bringing rain, gales and plunging temperatures. Konrád had discovered when he retired that the days seemed to stretch out twice as long, not least when summer gave way to autumn. Life acquired a strangely timeless quality. Minutes expanded into hours as time meandered along at its own sweet pace, freed from the fetters of habit. No longer measured off in shifts, lunch breaks, overtime, supper time, meetings, coffee breaks, working days, holidays, weekends. All these were wiped out, to be replaced by one never-ending Saturday. It was as if his life had been transformed into a perpetual holiday.

Now and then he would go for a meal at his son's house and sit with him for part of the evening. He read newspapers and books, surfed the net, went to museums and galleries, watched films and plays, and hung around in second-hand bookshops, doing all the things he'd persuaded himself he didn't have time for while he still had a role to play in society. He often felt like a tourist in his own city, and sometimes found he had blundered into one of their groups – in a museum, perhaps, or on his way down Skólavördustígur. All of a sudden it would dawn on him that everyone around him was speaking Swedish. He had twice been addressed in French as he was queuing at a restaurant. That's what he got for wandering about town during the day, when all normal people were at work.

Time was mainly measured in seasons now. Konrád was happiest in spring, when the days began to lengthen, the sun rose higher in the sky, trees and grass awoke from their long hibernation, migratory birds began to return to Iceland's shores, and human life shook off its winter torpor. He and Erna had always loved to travel around the country in the summer holidays and had a number of favourite places. One of these was the campsite at Thakgil, which nestled at the mouth of a dramatic gorge in the foothills of the Mýrdalsjökull ice cap in south Iceland, not far from the notorious volcano Katla. They used to try to go there every summer. He had never liked autumn, when the sun sank ever lower in the sky and gales whirled the dead leaves through the streets. As for winter, it was a time of stasis, when everything went into suspension, waiting for the return of the sun.

Yet another autumn depression was passing over, battering them with high winds and heavy rain, when Konrád took a seat in Marta's office at the police station on Hverfisgata, to ask her about Hjaltalín's last hours of life. He had, after some reflection, rung her to see if they could have a quick meeting. She had agreed immediately. Konrád hadn't come into the station much since retiring and there were a number of new faces he didn't recognise. The old ones greeted him warmly, though, shaking him by the hand and asking how he was doing, telling him that society was going to the dogs, but then that was nothing new.

Marta was the wrong side of forty, plump, with a large head and dark eyes and hair. She'd never been interested in clothes, going in for an unvarying uniform of shapeless trousers and shirts, and her hair was usually a mess. It was almost unheard of for her to put on lipstick or perfume. She had lived for years with a woman from the Westman Islands, but ever since that relationship hit the rocks she had been alone. To her colleagues in the police, she was invariably known as Smart Marta.

'They were buried a week apart,' Marta commented, handing him a coffee in a plastic cup. 'Hjaltalín and Sigurvin. Ironic, don't you think? One died recently; the other thirty years ago.'

'You didn't tell me Hjaltalín was ill,' Konráð reproached her.

'No, maybe I should have. Did it bother you?'

'He didn't look good.'

'We weren't to know he had so little time left.'

'Did you find anything useful on the glacier?'

'No. Not a thing. I reckon they're going to close the inquiry for good.'

'Hjaltalín never confessed?'

'Nope.'

'Then why do you want to close the inquiry?'

'Not my decision. I expect they think we've done enough – the guys upstairs, I mean.'

'He asked me to find the murderer.'

'He never gave up, did he? What did you say?'

'I said I'd retired.'

Svanhildur had told him confidentially that Sigurvin's death was the result of head trauma, as her preliminary findings had suggested. His nails were clean and neatly cut and he had recently visited a barber. His internal organs were thawed before they could be examined but, even so, Svanhildur's fingers had got so cold during the post-mortem that she'd had to keep a bowl of tepid water beside her to warm them. The stomach contents indicated that Sigurvin had eaten shortly before his death; a burger and chips, probably at a fast-food place. Nothing was found in his pockets except his house keys and wallet. The assumption was that, after leaving work and having the altercation in the car park, he had gone home, changed out of his suit into more comfortable clothes, then got back in his car and gone to buy a meal, before driving up to the hot-water tanks on Öskjuhlíd. When the appeal for information had been at its height after his disappearance, the police had paid particular attention to checking if he'd been seen at a variety of possible locations, including burger bars and petrol station shops, but no sighting had ever been confirmed.

The original investigation into Sigurvin's background had failed to unearth any bad habits or underworld connections to drug smugglers, debt collectors or thieves, let alone to hardened criminals. He had run his company successfully and employed a sizeable staff, all of whom had spoken well of him as a boss and owner. The reason for Sigurvin's presence by the hot-water tanks on Öskjuhlíd was unknown. At the time, the tanks, which had formerly supplied geothermal hot water to the city's homes by the power of gravity, had been taken out of use. Empty and crumbling, they had served as a playground for the local children, who scrawled graffiti over their walls and clambered inside them or were even, in some cases, foolhardy enough to climb up to the top.

'So,' Konrád said, 'Sigurvin must have met a person, or persons, unknown by the old tanks and got a lift with him or them to the glacier – if that's where he was killed?'

'Yes, except he wasn't wearing protective gear. In fact he wasn't dressed for the outdoors at all,' Marta pointed out. 'Which means the person with him would have had to lend him some clothes, then take them off his body afterwards, which seems a bit far-fetched.'

'OK, so it's February when Sigurvin vanishes but he isn't warmly dressed. He's wearing a shirt and a lightweight jacket. In other words, he's not expecting to be outdoors for long.'

'No,' said Marta. 'And he's wearing trainers, which means he can hardly have been intending to get out of the car. Though, having said that, the weather on the evening he was last seen wasn't that bad here in Reykjavík. It had snowed heavily after New Year, but that was followed by a spell of milder temperatures before it started freezing again. At the time of Sigurvin's disappearance, the streets were bare of snow, as I'm sure you'll remember.'

'Could he have been taken to the glacier by force? He gets into a jeep and next thing he knows he's being carted off to Langjökull? A struggle ensues, during which he's hit over the head. Or did he go voluntarily?'

'The post-mortem indicates that he was taken there after he died. Rigor mortis was setting in and his tissues had begun to show signs of deterioration.'

'But why the glacier? What's on Langjökull? Why does he take Sigurvin there?'

'Hjaltalín? I haven't a clue.'

Konráð shrugged, defeated. He recalled the moment they found Sigurvin's car. Shortly after it had been advertised as missing, a report had been received of a red Jeep Cherokee parked on Öskjuhlíd. Konrád often thought about that jeep because he'd had a hankering for one himself; it was the perfect size and he admired the design, the interior and the fact it had gears on the steering wheel. He'd never have gone for a red one, though, had he been able to afford it; definitely a white.

In those days the tanks had been approached by a gravel track, and the jeep had been found abandoned at the end of this. The police had conducted an exhaustive search for Sigurvin on the wooded slopes of the hill and in the surrounding area, with the help of dogs, but to no avail. There had been countless wheel marks on the gravel track and in the vicinity of the tanks, and casts had been made of some of the marks closest to the jeep. But there had been no signs of a struggle near the vehicle, and the gravel had been too hard for any footprints. The police's job hadn't been helped by the fact the area was popular with kids, as well as a much-visited viewpoint offering a 360-degree panorama over the city, from the distant Snæfellsjökull glacier, rising out of the sea to the west, to the mountain ranges of Hellisheidi and Bláfjöll to the east, the looming bulk of Esja to the north and the Reykjanes Peninsula far away to the south.

'Did you send anyone to see Hjaltalín in hospital?' Konrád asked. He finished his coffee, reflecting that it hadn't improved much since his day.

'No,' Marta said. 'His health underwent a rapid deterioration in custody and he was admitted to hospital almost immediately after his release. His doctor hadn't expected things to progress that fast.'

'He must have got a nasty surprise when Sigurvin turned up after all these years,' Konrád remarked.

'Yes, you'd think so.'

'Still, you wouldn't have known it when I met him. He just lay there in bed, looking calm and stoical. Mind you, I suppose he had other, more serious things on his mind, given the state of his health.'

'He didn't have anything new to say, then?'

'No, he just kept banging on about being innocent.'

'Are you going to do anything about it?'

'I can't "do anything about it",' Konrád protested. 'I don't have the authority.'

'He asked you to help him.'

'True.'

'And?'

'There's no "and". You tried to talk to him yourself, didn't you? Did you ask him about Sigurvin's car keys?'

'He said he didn't know anything about them,' Marta said. 'Did you ask him?'

'I didn't know they were missing. Svanhildur was still examining the body when I went to see him. Sigurvin had his house keys and wallet in his pocket but not the keys to his jeep. Don't you find that strange? Who had his car keys?'

Marta shrugged as if it was pointless asking her.

'The whole thing's so sloppy,' Konrád said. 'Like the job was only half finished.'

'I've never in my life come across a more obstinate bastard than Hjaltalín,' Marta said, after a moment. 'He knew what was going to happen when we let him go; he knew he was dying.'

'He still denied having laid a finger on Sigurvin,' Konrád said, 'though he had nothing to lose any more.'

'Flatly denied it to the very last,' Marta said, crumpling up her coffee cup and chucking it in the bin.

9

Konrád's son Húgó, an orthopaedic consultant at the National Hospital, was forever jetting off to international conferences, accompanied by his wife, who had a shop in the Kringlan centre. Konrád and Erna would often babysit their two lively grandsons, who had always been devoted to them. The twins were twelve now, and although they said they were perfectly capable of looking after themselves, there was no way they could actually be trusted to do so. In their parents' absence, Konrád had brought them to stay with him for a few days, promising them a trip to the cinema. They chose the film, an abysmally bad thriller that Konrád hadn't even heard of, in which some glitzy Hollywood star mowed down a host of enemies.

Having the boys to stay was a pleasant change from the usual monotony of his life and he did his best to treat them, though he suspected their parents already spoilt them rotten. The last thing he wanted to do was interfere in his grandchildren's upbringing, but he couldn't help raising his eyebrows over the demands made on the poor kids, whose week seemed to be booked solid with extra sports coaching, music lessons, art courses and countless other extracurricular activities.

'Ambition will be the death of that lot,' was his sister Beta's verdict whenever the subject came up in conversation.

Konrád had driven the boys to school that morning, then picked them up from their guitar lesson before taking them to the cinema. The guitars were in the boot of his four-wheel drive, and when they got home that evening he asked the boys to show him what they could play. But they begged to be excused, saying it was boring enough having to do the lessons. Instead, they commandeered the television in the sitting room with their game console, and after that they were lost in a world of their own until bedtime. Since it was a Friday and they had the whole weekend ahead, Konrád allowed them to stay up as late as they liked. Sometime after eleven, though, Húgó called from Gothenburg and ordered him to send the boys to bed. He obeyed.

Clearly, the body in the ice had been discussed at the boys' house.

'Granddad,' one of the boys said as he laid his head on the pillow, 'did you know the dead man they found on the glacier?'

'No.'

'Dad said you knew him,' the other boy objected, his eyes still bloodshot from all the on-screen slaughter.

'I didn't know him personally but I knew who he was.'

'Dad said you searched for him for years and years. When you were a cop.'

'That's right.'

'But you never found him.'

'No.'

'Why not?'

'Because he was hidden on the glacier. That was a terrible film you tricked me into seeing.'

'No way! It was awesome,' the twins protested. 'Totally kickass.'

'You're idiots,' Konrád said, smiling to himself as he pushed the door to.

He could hear them giggling as he tidied up in the kitchen before going to bed himself. Just as they'd finally quietened down, there was a faint tapping on the front door. At first he thought it was the autumn wind rattling the letterbox, but then he heard another light knocking, louder this time. He wasn't expecting anyone. Beta could be trusted to drop in at all hours, but she would march in armed with her own set of keys and would never tap politely like that. It could hardly be a salesman. Konrád made a habit of buying lobsters and dried fish from door-to-door salespeople, but they would never dare to disturb him at this time of night.

He went to the front door, opened it and saw a woman of indeterminate age standing on the step.

'I saw a light on,' she said. 'Could I possibly speak to you for a moment?'

She came across as shy and diffident. 'Timid' was the word. Konrád assumed she was going to try to sell him something, like a newsletter or a lottery ticket, and was tempted to send her packing, but there was something so pathetic about her that he didn't have the heart to be rude. He took in the cheap clothes hanging off her thin body: the faded jeans, brown fake-leather jacket and purple jumper. She was wearing a black headband over her ears.

Under it her hair was thick and blonde, and her face was pretty, though age and experience had etched soft wrinkles in her skin, pursing her lips and deepening the pouches under her eyes.

'Sorry,' she said, 'for disturbing you like this.'

'What are you selling?' Konrád asked. 'It's very late. You do realise that?'

He scanned the parking area to see if she was alone. There had been a few occasions when men Konrád had crossed paths with in the line of duty hadn't been content with swearing at him down the phone but had turned up outside his house after work, with a confused idea of getting something straight. Usually drink had played a role. It hadn't led to any trouble, though. Konrád had always managed to calm the visitor down, if he was agitated, or else listened patiently to his bullshit, if the guy was in the mood to rant, before sending him away without taking any further action.

'Oh no, I'm not selling anything,' the woman said. 'I wanted to talk to you about my brother. If I could come in for a moment?'

'Your brother? Do I know him?'

'No,' the woman said. 'No, I don't think so.'

'Should I know you?'

'No.'

'Then why do you want to tell me about your brother?'

'Because of something he saw when he was a boy. By the tanks on Öskjuhlíd.'

10

The unknown woman whispered these last words so quietly that Konrád could barely catch them. He stared at her, instantly grasping what she meant by her reference to the tanks on Öskjuhlíd: the old hot-water tanks where Sigurvin's jeep had been found. The woman avoided his eyes, as if she had said something shameful. There was an interval of silence, broken only by a noisy car driving past. Konrád was sure he had never seen this woman before; she couldn't have been on their radar during the original inquiry.

'I take it you're referring to the Sigurvin affair?' he asked warily. 'When you refer to the tanks?'

'Sorry to come round at such a stupid time.'

'Don't worry about it.'

'Could I come in?'

'Please do.' Konrád opened the door wider and ushered her into the hall. 'I didn't mean to leave you standing out there in the cold like that. I'm just not used to getting visits so late in the evening.'

He glanced at his watch. It was midnight. The woman edged her way into the sitting room, still shy and diffident, gazing around her at the paintings on the walls and the shelves full of books.

'Have a seat,' Konrád said. 'Would you like a coffee, maybe? Or something else?'

'I wouldn't mind a coffee,' the woman said. 'My name's Herdís,' she added, holding out her hand. 'You wouldn't have a shot of something to put in the coffee, would you? I'm a bit chilly. There's quite a northerly blowing out there.'

'Sure, can do,' Konrád said.

The woman perched on a chair in the sitting room and continued to study her surroundings, while Konrád put on the coffee and dug out the bottle of vodka he kept in one of the kitchen cupboards along with the gin and the rum. He himself drank only in moderation, and then mostly red wine. He poured a generous splash of vodka into a cup, feeling puzzled by this unexpected visit. It was a mystery to him why she should have come round to see him in the middle of the night rather than going to the police. He guessed she must think he was still working on the inquiry. His name had been quite prominent in the coverage of the original investigation, when he'd had to take the role of police spokesman at times. On his way back to the sitting room, he checked on the boys, who turned out to be sound asleep, and firmly closed the door to their room.

'Yes, it's turning chilly,' he remarked as he sat down and handed the woman the cup.

She took it. As the coffee wasn't very hot, she finished it in one gulp and handed it straight back.

'Like another?' he asked.

Herdís nodded. Konráð went into the kitchen and fetched the coffee pot and the bottle, placing both in front of the woman. She poured a tiny splash of coffee into her cup, filled it up with vodka, drained half in one go, then finished it. Konráð waited patiently.

'He was only nine,' she said, once she had thawed out a bit. 'We were very hard up. We lived in a tiny basement flat in the Hlíðar area and used to play outside all day long. We'd hang about in the streets or kick a ball around in the park at Klambratún or go onto Öskjuhlíð. The hill was a brilliant playground for us kids. You know . . . the wartime bunkers left over from the British occupation, the quarry and the woods. It was . . . And the hot-water tanks at the top of the hill . . . it was like this magical world.'

'I remember the tanks well,' Konráð said. 'They used to be white. Bit of an eyesore towards the end. Always were, I suppose.'

'Yes. They were torn down not long afterwards to make way for the new tanks with Perlan on top.'

She spoke very quietly and seemed keen to make a good impression, though she couldn't hide her craving for the vodka. Konráð guessed she was around forty, but she could have been older. The fingers clasping her cup were bony; the nails rough, with black dirt underneath.

'He was only nine,' she said again.

'What was it he saw?'

'He had no idea it might be important. Not at the time. He didn't know anything about the case – about Sigurvin and the police investigation. He didn't know about any of that. He was only a kid. It wasn't until much later that he heard about it and realised that what he'd seen might have had something to do with it. He started reading up on the background, to find out more about the case. By then he was nearly thirty and it was years since that night by the tanks – so long that he thought maybe he'd dreamt or imagined it.'

'What does your brother do – for a living, I mean?'

'He used to work on building sites. As a labourer. But he wasn't always in work. He's . . . he used to drink a bit. But Villi was a nice guy.'

Herdís grimaced as if pushing away an unpleasant thought.

'Are you younger than him?' Konrád asked.

'Yes, by two years.'

She began to tell him about herself and her brother, still in that low, faltering voice. About the basement flat in the Hlídar area on the slopes of Öskjuhlíd, where they had lived with their mother, who worked in a shop and found it hard to make ends meet. Their parents had split up and they rarely saw their father, who had moved to another part of the country. There were only the two of them; they didn't have any siblings. Neither got on well at school and both left as soon as they could. While still very young, Herdís had shacked up with a man in a rented flat on Hverfisgata, while her brother had gone to sea. He hadn't taken to the fisherman's life, though, so he'd got a job on land instead. He'd lived alone and partied hard.

Her brother couldn't remember exactly when he'd first heard about Sigurvin's disappearance but his interest had been sparked by an Icelandic true-crime documentary on TV, which had made a big deal about the fact that the victim's car, a red jeep, had been found up by the tanks on Öskjuhlíd. Scenes from the story were dramatised and a red jeep was superimposed on photos of the hot-water tanks as they used to be, back before the new ones were built and topped by the futuristic glass dome known as Perlan.

'It triggered a memory,' Herdís said. 'About things he'd never connected before. This was about twenty years later.'

'That's quite a long time,' Konrád said. 'For a witness statement.'

'He was so desperate to talk about it that he told me and loads of other people too. But, all the same, he found the idea of getting mixed up in an old criminal case a bit embarrassing – stupid, you know. He couldn't be sure he was right either. I encouraged him to tell the police anyway, so he went and talked to one of your lot, but the man thought it was all too vague to take seriously. Apparently they'd had hundreds of tip-offs that hadn't led to anything. Villi reckoned his would end up in the same pile.'

'Do you know who he spoke to at the police station?'

'No, he didn't say.'

'What was it he saw?'

Herdís glanced at her empty coffee cup as if trying to decide whether to have another. Konrád watched her wrestle briefly with her conscience before making up her mind and helping herself to more vodka, not bothering with any coffee this time. She knocked it back in one.

'Sorry to barge in on you like this,' she said, replacing the cup on the table. 'I didn't mean to come round so late . . . I was . . . it's just I had to have a couple of drinks first.'

'You needed a bit of Dutch courage?'

'I suppose.'

'Why didn't your brother come with you?'

'I saw the news about Langjökull and felt I had to talk to someone. It made me think about my brother so much. And someone said you were the person who knew most about the case.'

'Of course there's no reason why you should be aware of it, but I've left the police,' Konrád told her. 'I've retired. I could point you and your brother to the people who are dealing with the case today. They'd be pleased to hear from you.'

'You never found the person who did it.'

'We thought we knew who it was,' Konrád said. 'But he always denied it.'

'That Hjaltalín?'

'Your brother's not with you?'

'No.'

'They'll probably want to talk to him again,' Konrád said. 'The police, I mean. I could go with him this time.'

'Yes,' Herdís said slowly. 'Except it's too late.'

'Too late?'

'You can't go anywhere with him.'

'Why not?'

'Villi's dead,' she said. 'He died in a car accident.'

Konrád could sense her distress.

'He was only thirty-four. He . . . he would have been forty this year.'

'I'm sorry to hear that,' Konrád said. It sounded inadequate. He groped around for some way of offering more sympathy. 'Terrible things, car accidents.'

'It all came back to me when the body turned up on the glacier,' Herdís said. 'Villi's story about the man he saw by the tanks on Öskjuhlíd – the man who threatened to kill him.'

11

The boys spent a lot of time playing on Öskjuhlíd that winter. They had watched the building of the new bowling alley overlooking the Valur stadium, and used the construction site as a fort, skirmishing with swords and shields among the grey concrete walls and steel reinforcement bars. Now that the alley had opened, they hung around inside, watching people bowling, and if anyone had money they would have a go on the arcade games or buy themselves chips with ketchup. When they got tired of that, they would go down to the old quarry or walk out to Nauthólsvík Cove to watch the kayakers or the occasional weirdo swimming in the sea.

That February evening Villi was alone. He looked in at the bowling alley and watched the players for a while but, having no real interest in the sport, he didn't stick around long. His mum had warned him not to be late because kids his age weren't allowed out after eight o'clock, and it was already after the curfew when he left the flat. He wandered up the hill, hardly aware of his surroundings, in low spirits because his handball team, Valur, had just lost an important game. The cold didn't bother him as he was warmly dressed in a thick anorak, woollen hat and gloves. Seeing the hot-water tanks in the moonlight, he headed towards them. He didn't mind being alone. Although he had good friends and liked nothing better than playing with them, he was also perfectly content with his own company.

The tanks loomed against the sky like the towers of a deserted castle, wide-bellied and obsolete. They were marked down for demolition, to make way for a modern geothermal heating system. The old tanks, eight of them, formed a circle on the crown of the hill, and it was possible to walk between them into a central space, floored with concrete and littered with scrap metal, such as the wreck of a stolen bicycle that was now beyond repair. Each tank had a ladder attached, leading to the roof, but the lowest rung was more than two metres off the ground, which meant another ladder was needed to reach it. The boys had been resourceful enough to acquire one and some of them had climbed right to the top. Villi had once gone all the way up himself but was terribly afraid of heights and wouldn't ever want to do it again. The tank had a sloping roof and he'd had the horrible sensation that he was constantly sliding down it. Some of the other boys, who didn't suffer from vertigo, had strutted around on top, walking along the very edge or sitting there with their legs dangling in the air. A few even jumped between the tanks, but he would never in his life dare to do that.

Crude graffiti had been sprayed all over the blank canvas provided by the walls, including a clumsy drawing of a cock, which always made the boys giggle.

Villi walked into the circle formed by the tanks and lay down on his back in the middle, gazing up at the sky. He glimpsed the moon in the gap between the huge, dark shapes and watched as it gradually passed out of sight, while the big revolving light on top of one of the tanks appeared and disappeared in turn. His mum had told him it was a beacon for planes landing at the domestic airport on Vatnsmýri, at the foot of the hill. Its green and yellow beam sliced through the night above the city with a slow, steady rhythm, round and round, like the slightly fast second hand on a clock.

He lay there for a while, then thought he should probably be getting back before his mum grew worried and came out looking for him. She'd had to do that more than once and was always complaining about his absent-mindedness, calling him a real 'space cadet', a term he didn't really understand. He knew his teacher had told his mum that he didn't pay enough attention in class. His mum tried to help him with his homework and he did his best, but school bored him rigid and he couldn't see why he had to spend all his time learning stuff he didn't have the slightest interest in.

He was brooding on this problem when, out of nowhere, there was a sound of footsteps right next to him. He leapt to his feet. A man he'd never seen before, with long hair and a small ring in one ear, was standing in front of him, looking angry.

'What are you doing, messing about here?' the man said roughly, as if his anger were directed at Villi, though Villi had never done anything to him.

'Nothing,' Villi said.

'Get lost,' the man ordered. 'Piss off!'

'OK,' Villi said, careful not to provoke him, though he felt he had every bit as much right to be there as the man did himself.

Then, without warning, the man lunged at him and grabbed his arm.

'If you tell anyone you saw me, I'll track you down and kill you, do you hear me?'

Villi didn't dare say a word.

'Do you hear me?'

Villi nodded.

'Now get lost,' the man said, letting him go.

Villi stumbled away, badly frightened. As he darted out from between the tanks, he spotted the man's car, a big off-road vehicle, parked in the lee of a small concrete hut that had once housed the control centre for the geothermal heating system. It occurred to him that the man must have arrived before him or he would have heard the engine.

He hurried away, repeatedly snatching glances over his shoulder, terrified that the man would chase him. The last thing he saw before breaking into a run was the headlights of another car as it drove up to the tanks, illuminating them for a moment, before it disappeared from view behind the concrete hut.

Herdís finished her story. Konrád had been forced to lean towards her as she spoke because her voice was so low that it was a strain to catch what she was saying. It didn't help that his hearing was going and he was too stubborn to do anything about it. After a few moments' silence, he asked if he could offer her anything else to drink. She shook her head.

'I shouldn't have come round so late,' she repeated.

'That's all right,' Konrád said. 'Don't worry about it.'

'I don't usually do things like this.'

'I'm sure you don't.'

'I've been thinking about it so much since that man's body was found in the ice.'

'That's understandable.'

'I felt like I had to do something about it, in memory of Villi. I was his little sister and he was always so good to me. He was one of a kind, was Villi. A wonderful brother. He'd been trying to stay off the booze at the time of his accident. It was the middle of winter, there was a whiteout and the roads were icy, and somehow Villi got hit by a car. The driver never came forward, just made off. And there were no witnesses, so we never found out who it was.'

'Was that ... Vilmar, wasn't that his name?' Konrád asked, suddenly realising that he had in fact heard of her brother. He remembered the hit-and-run; remembered a man dying and the search for the driver who'd fled the scene. A highly unusual incident for Reykjavík. It had happened on Lindargata, near the city centre, a place Konrád knew well as he had lived there as a boy.

'It was terrible for a lovely bloke like him to lose his life like that,' Herdís said. 'Absolutely terrible.'

'And you said he told lots of people his story?' Konrád asked. 'When the memory of it came back to him?'

'Yes, he did. After watching that TV programme, he realised what he'd seen might be important and he started talking about it to anyone who would listen.'

'Who was the man on Öskjuhlíd?'

'He never knew. Villi was only nine at the time and the news about the missing man completely passed him by, like I said. It never occurred to him that his experience could have had anything to do with Sigurvin vanishing. But he never forgot the man who scared him that night. Once he started thinking about it, he remembered the handball game earlier that evening. He could remember which team Valur had been playing, so it was easy enough to look up the old match reports. It turned out the game had taken place the evening Sigurvin went missing.'

'I see.'

'But I . . .' Herdís broke off.

'What?'

'Sometimes I find myself thinking maybe Villi's death wasn't an accident. I mean, why didn't the driver help him? Why didn't he stop?'

'The weather conditions were very bad,' Konrád pointed out. 'You said so yourself. Visibility was poor. It's possible the driver thought he wasn't badly hurt, even though he'd been clipped by the car. If I've remembered right, that was one theory at the time.'

'Well, the more I think about it, the clearer it seems to me that he *meant* to kill Villi.'

'And you think it's connected somehow to Sigurvin?'

Herdís nodded. 'I wanted to ask if you could find the man who ran Villi down,' she said. 'Your case has been reopened and I can't help feeling Villi's part of it somehow.'

Konrád was still wondering how to answer this when Herdís abruptly rose to her feet.

'I've kept you long enough.'

'The police may want to talk to you,' Konrád said, standing up as well.

'That's all right, as long as they keep quiet about it. I don't like the idea of any fuss.'

'I don't think you need worry about that. Did your brother tell you anything else about the man?'

'Only that he had long hair and a small ring or stud in his ear, and that he was very scary and sinister.'

'Did Villi know who Hjaltalín was?'

'Yes, later, when he began to make the connection.'

'Was it him?'

'No. It was a totally different man.'

'Are you sure?'

'He was sure.'

'What about Sigurvin? Could it have been him?'

'No, it wasn't him either,' Herdís said. 'Villi was positive it wasn't either of them who threatened to kill him.' She stood there in silence for a few moments, her eyes lowered. 'I just find the whole thing so unbearable,' she said at last, 'that I wondered if you could help me. If there might be some way of tracking down that driver and . . . and finding out what really happened. You know, whether it was an accident or he . . . deliberately set out to kill Villi.'

12

The following day Konrád met up with Marta. He invited her for a Thai meal in the Skeifan retail park, preferring to meet her on neutral ground rather than constantly going into the police station as if he were still working there. While they were eating, he reported what Herdís had told him about her brother – both what Villi had witnessed by the tanks on Öskjuhlíd and how he had died in a hit-and-run. Marta listened in silence.

'It's not much to go on,' she said when he'd finished, trying to put out the fire in her mouth with the help of rice and a sip of water. She was a big fan of spicy oriental food and liked to boast about the fact. As usual, she had ordered one of the hottest dishes on the menu, and her forehead was beaded with perspiration.

'Well, I think it's significant,' Konrád said. 'The story could be relevant to Sigurvin's disappearance.'

'We can't interview the witness.'

'No, that's true.'

'What sort of people are they?'

'Just ordinary types,' Konrád said. 'Decent people. The sister made a good impression on me. She was clear and knew exactly what she wanted to say. She came forward on behalf of her brother because she still misses him.'

'She's not making it up?'

'I find that extremely unlikely.'

They were trying to keep their voices down, as the restaurant was busy. It was justly popular for the quality of its cooking. Konrád had always had a lot of time for Marta, ever since she'd joined CID as a young woman. She'd been a good colleague because she never got carried away but approached each case with a cool head, taking her time, and as a result she rarely put a foot wrong. Once she had acquainted herself with all the details of a case, she would home in unerringly on the essentials and it took a lot to deflect her from her course.

'What's new about it?' she asked dismissively. 'We've always suspected that someone – i.e. Hjaltalín – picked Sigurvin up in a car by the tanks. A man with long hair? Where does that get us?'

'I remember at one point we thought Sigurvin might have gone up to Öskjuhlíd to get a breath of fresh air and clear his head. That maybe he'd bumped into one or more individuals who attacked him. If the boy's story is to be believed, it's possible that this man was waiting for Sigurvin and took him away in his car. He had what the boy referred to as an off-roader.'

'The boy didn't see Sigurvin,' Marta pointed out.

'No, and the man he met wasn't Hjaltalín either.'

Marta went on shovelling down her food.

'Hjaltalín had a good head of hair,' Konrád remarked. 'When we first arrested him, he had a mullet, long at the back and bushy on top.'

'A mullet? God, that was a terrible fashion.'

'You're telling me.'

'Like so much else in the eighties,' Marta said.

'Anyway, Villi was sure it wasn't him.'

'Isn't it more likely he just invented the whole thing? You know how stories grow up around cases like that. There are always all kinds of rumours. And what's an off-roader to a nine-year-old boy? Aren't all jeeps off-roaders?'

Marta wiped the sweat off her forehead with her napkin. Her face looked puffy. 'This isn't bad,' she said.

'Why not just admit that it's got you beat?'

'This? This is nothing.'

'I don't believe he invented it,' Konrád said, abandoning the attempt to wind her up, as he knew she'd never admit to being defeated by a curry. 'When the boy was older, he made the connection between what happened to him and Sigurvin's disappearance, and reckoned he'd witnessed something important.'

'OK, I get that, but it's weak at best. Hjaltalín's still my man.'

'You mean you're not going to do anything about it?'

'It's useful to know but . . .' She shrugged.

'We have a new witness,' Konrád said. 'That's got to mean something.'

'That's not true, Konrád, and you know it. The witness is dead and may not have been particularly reliable either. He was a kid when it happened. And only remembered it years later.'

Konrád made a face. He had to admit that Marta had a point. He'd asked Herdís if her brother had been able to remember the colour of the vehicle he saw on Öskjuhlíd, but its appearance had been too hazy in his memory; lost in the mists of time.

'Sometimes I think we must have made some fundamental mistake during the original inquiry,' he said.

'Hjaltalín had a Ford Explorer, if I recall correctly,' Marta said, ignoring his remark. 'And a second car, a Nissan Sunny.'

Konrád looked at her without speaking. Eventually he replied: 'If the boy was right, there was another man, not Hjaltalín, up by the tanks the evening Sigurvin vanished. I don't think we – by which I mean you – can ignore that fact. I think you should at least bear it in mind.'

'I have to say, I'm pretty sceptical about this, Konrád, but I'll talk to the woman who visited you. No problem. We're still receiving all kinds of tip-offs about Sigurvin, believe it or not.'

'She even thinks, or suspects, that her brother's death, the hit-and-run, could have had something to do with the case.'

'OK, OK, I'll hear what she's got to say.'

'Can you actually taste anything?' Konrád asked.

'Sure, it's delicious, though maybe it could be a bit hotter,' Marta said, wiping away a drop of sweat that was trickling down her nose.

After his lunch with Marta, Konrád took a short drive out to Seltjarnarnes, the westernmost tip of the peninsula on which Reykjavík was built. He parked on the road leading to the golf course and sat in the car for a while, his eyes on the shore ridge in front of him, remembering the last time he had come here with Erna. There was no lunar eclipse now. The heater creaked a little as it pumped hot air into the car. It was bitterly cold outside. Konrád gazed over at the isthmus at Grótta, where the lighthouse had been guiding seafarers safely through the dark for more than half a century.

Marta's reaction hadn't been particularly encouraging, but Konráð could understand that. When all was said and done, Villi's story didn't add much to their theories, and yet to him there was something fresh and exciting about it, something that stirred up the dust in the lumber room of his mind. Admittedly, Villi had only recalled the incident a long time afterwards but, nevertheless, it meant they had a new witness in the bizarre mystery that Konráð had thought he would never have to wrestle with again.

Hjaltalín had been wrong when he said that Konráð had believed him. The case had been discussed from every possible angle, but they had never managed to find any incriminating evidence against Hjaltalín. In fact, evidence of any kind had been extremely thin on the ground. They had no murder weapon, no body. The search of Hjaltalín's home and workplace had brought nothing to light. The two men's quarrel could have been the motive the police were looking for, if Sigurvin had in fact been murdered, but Hjaltalín's persistent denial, in spite of his long spell in custody, had cast doubt on the value of that theory.

Hjaltalín had appeared to cope extraordinarily well with his detention. Many people were badly affected by being kept in solitary confinement. There were examples of prisoners suffering a complete breakdown in a matter of days, but Hjaltalín's time in custody had seemed to make no impact on him. He had stuck to his guns throughout, steadfastly insisting that his conscience was clear.

The only thing of interest that had occurred during his detention was his attempt to develop a personal relationship with Konráð and turn him into his confidant, eventually going so far as to refuse to speak to anyone else in the police. Konráð hadn't liked that at all. He'd felt a strong antipathy for the man, which made him reluctant to meet him more than absolutely necessary. Nor did he approve of giving in to a prisoner's demands like that.

It was true that over time Konrád had begun to have his doubts about the case they had built up against Hjaltalín, but he had kept his misgivings largely to himself. Once CID began to focus their sights on Hjaltalín, the scope of the investigation had gradually shrunk until it was almost entirely concentrated on him. They had been pretty certain that Sigurvin had been killed the evening of the two men's quarrel, as nothing had been seen or heard of him since.

Konrád gazed at the lighthouse as if it could guide him onto the right course, as if he were a sailor lost at sea. Then he set the car in motion again and continued on his way, further out along the peninsula, into his last memory of Erna.

13

Hjaltalín's ex-girlfriend still worked in retail, but these days she ran her own womenswear shop in partnership with her sister. They had emerged relatively unscathed from the financial crisis, without too many debts, and had rented a sizeable space in the Smáralind shopping centre while prices were low. They had bought the clothing concession from a man who had gone spectacularly bust, which was hardly surprising given his four-hundred-square-metre house, his three SUVs, and his overdue loans for shares he had bought in various banks and businesses that had played a part in Iceland's overseas expansion.

The ex-girlfriend, whose name was Salóme, must be fifty now, but age had treated her kindly. Although Konrád hadn't seen her for years, he recognised her immediately, as she stood talking to a customer, by her head of thick, dark, shoulder-length hair. She was dressed in black trousers and a white top, and wore a string of pearls round her neck. Once a ballerina, she still carried herself with a dancer's grace.

There were two other customers in the shop, waiting to be served. Konrád took his time, examining the merchandise and watching Salóme serve the women, who seemed to be looking for good-quality clothes that weren't too expensive. They stole sidelong glances at him, probably assuming that he was after something for his wife. Or mistress. Finally, only Konrád was left and Salóme came over. He saw that she had placed him, remembering him only too well from the investigation.

'Your people have already talked to me,' she said. 'What is it now?'

'You mean the police?'

'Yes, of course I mean the police, who else?'

'You remember me, then.'

'Konrád. Yes, I remember everything. I thought it was all in the past and then they go and find that man on the glacier. It feels as if I'll never be free of it.'

'I've left the police,' Konrád told her.

'Oh,' Salóme said, 'then what are you doing here?'

'Old habits die hard,' he said, trying for humour. It was met with a stony reception.

'Excuse me, but if you've left, is it any of your business?'

'Like you said, it feels as if I'll never be free of it.'

'I know, believe me, but . . . the thing is, I'm not actually obliged to talk to you, am I?'

She looked at him, her brows raised in enquiry. It was clear she would rather Sigurvin had never been found and that the case had remained closed. All she wanted was to be able to get on with her life without any further disruption from the events that had shaped it so decisively thirty years earlier.

'I didn't even know what they were talking about,' Salóme continued at last. 'Are you going to start asking all the same questions again too?'

Konrád shook his head. She had grown in self-confidence over the years and bore little resemblance to the young woman who had sat in his office on Hverfisgata more than three decades ago, fiddling with an elastic hairband and claiming that Hjaltalín had been with her the evening the witness saw him and Sigurvin having a row in the car park.

'I know you didn't think much of me as a witness,' she said, as if reading his mind.

'You told us you and Hjaltalín had been together all evening.'

'Yes. And you know what? I can't be bothered to go into all that again. It was bad enough having to talk to that policewoman.'

A customer came into the shop and Salóme went to serve her. She was a middle-aged woman in search of a coat and possibly trousers. Salóme assisted her without being pushy but the woman couldn't find anything suitable and left.

'You also told us you didn't know anything about the woman Hjaltalín claimed to have been with,' Konrád said, continuing from where he'd left off. 'He never revealed her identity and we just took it for granted he was lying to us.'

'I know nothing about her,' Salóme said. 'I always doubted she ever existed. Hjaltalín couldn't open his mouth without lying. It was one of the first things you learnt about him. The truth was some kind of joke to him; he would just invent stuff to suit himself. Not just about Sigurvin, but all the time. He told me endless lies. It was his nature. Then, next thing I knew, I'd started lying for him too.'

'You split up after that?'

Salóme gave him a look as if she was considering whether to go on answering. But she hadn't minded Konrád, not like some of the other detectives who had kept pestering her with the same questions back in the day.

'It was over as soon as he said he'd been with another woman,' she said. 'I wanted to be shot of him and the whole mess – the lies, the police. We hadn't been together that long when it happened. He was . . . he wasn't a total bastard, you know. Far from it. He could be very considerate and kind and loving, in spite of everything. It was just . . . all that tough-guy posturing got a bit wearing. But I never really believed he'd be capable of hurting anyone.'

'You told me at the time that he had a short fuse; that he had trouble controlling his temper but that he'd never laid a hand on you.'

'He never did. He could get incredibly angry, but probably no more than anyone else.'

'Did he ever get in touch with you later, after it was all over? In the last few years, for instance?'

'No, he didn't,' Salóme said. 'And I never spoke to him again. I sometimes thought about him and felt a bit sorry for him, but we never had any contact.'

Radio music was playing softly from the small speakers in the ceiling. The shopping centre was fairly busy, with people buying things or just browsing and letting themselves dream.

'Remind me,' Konrád said. 'What kind of car did you have back then?'

Salóme thought. 'Some crappy Japanese job. It belonged to my mother actually, but I was always driving it.'

Konrád noticed a young woman come into the shop. Salóme didn't pay her any attention.

'Since Sigurvin turned up on the glacier,' he went on, 'people have supplied the police with a few new details, including the information that Sigurvin may have got into another jeep, not his own – an off-road vehicle.'

Salóme stared at Konrád. 'And?'

He shrugged. 'Apparently the driver had long hair and possibly an earring.'

'Hjaltalín never wore an earring,' Salóme said flatly.

'Do you remember anyone else in your circle who owned an off-roader or had access to one?'

'No,' Salóme said, without even needing to think.

'Or any men who wore an earring?'

'No.'

'No one at all?'

She shook her head.

'You said you were at your mother's the evening Sigurvin vanished; you went round to hers straight after leaving Hjaltalín and stayed over that night.'

'I was still living at home,' Salóme said. 'The police know all this.'

'I understand your mother's dead.'

'Yes, she died three years ago.'

The young woman came over to Salóme. 'Do you work here?' she asked bossily.

Salóme looked at her. 'Yes, just a moment,' she said. 'Are we done here?' she asked Konrád.

'Yes, we're done,' he said, and Salóme turned her back on him and asked the young woman how she could help.

14

That evening Konrád went round to Húgó's for supper. His son lived in an attractive terraced house in the new suburb of Grafarvogur, with his wife, Sirrí, and the twins. As usual, the boys were delighted to see their grandfather, who read them stories and poems when he babysat them and told them properly hair-raising ghost stories before bed. Konrád's daughter-in-law was less than thrilled about this, as he tended to get carried away. Recently she had thrown a fit when she and Húgó had come home to find the three of them watching a film on TV and the boys in a state of wild overexcitement and terror. The film had been *The Exorcist*.

'I've had it up to here with this!' Konrád had heard Sirrí saying angrily to Húgó.

His son was an excellent cook and had made a delicious Spanish pork dish that Konrád, who was starving, wolfed down. The twins reported various things that had been happening in their lives since they'd last seen him, then, getting fed up with sitting at the table, they went off to play. Sirrí owned a beauty shop and was forever dropping the names of local celebrities who came in. Konrád didn't recognise many of them, though he gathered that her regulars included a well-known lifestyle guru. Worse than this, though, was the way Sirrí liked to put down her husband when she'd had a bit to drink. She did so subtly, and it had never led to any kind of row in company, but Konrád and Erna used to feel uncomfortable, noticing the sly digs. Húgó, a man of moderation in everything, got annoyed when she drank and avoided alcohol himself except with meals. Konrád didn't know if the marriage was happy, but Húgó never complained.

Sirrí was in the middle of telling them about a visit the lifestyle guru had paid to her shop, during which he had said he was blown away by her display of a new range of French cosmetics, when Konrád's phone rang. Seeing from the screen that it was Marta, he smiled at his son and daughter-in-law, and rose to his feet, saying he had to take this call but he would only be a minute.

'I thought you'd retired,' Marta snapped.

'Retired?'

'Oh, come on,' Marta said. 'She rang us – Hjaltalín's ex-girlfriend – to complain about being interrogated by a man who's supposedly left the police. She wanted to know if she could expect any more visits like that.'

'Calm down, it's your own fault.'

'*My* fault?'

'You were the one who dragged me into this,' Konrád said. 'It wasn't my idea to go and see Hjaltalín at Litla-Hraun. I told you I'd retired.'

'Have you been talking to many other people?'

'No.'

'Did you get anything new out of her?'

'No, nothing.'

'You can't just start investigating the whole thing again off your own bat,' Marta said. 'It's totally unacceptable. Surely you can understand that? You have to leave it to us.'

There was a lengthy silence. Konrád was thinking hard about whether to take the next step. He had been expecting to have this conversation with Marta sooner or later, and had been wondering how to bring the subject up. Since the opportunity had landed in his lap without his having to make the first move, he decided to go for it.

'What am I to tell Herdís, then?' he asked.

'Herdís who? What are you on about?'

'The sister of that boy on Öskjuhlíd.'

'What about her?'

'She asked me to help, for her brother's sake. I agreed to do it.'

'What kind of nonsense is this?'

'It's not nonsense. I'm doing it for her. You can hardly forbid me to talk to people.'

'What? Don't tell me you're going to . . . to start playing the private detective? Is this some kind of joke?'

'Private detective?' Konrád laughed. 'I'm going to do her this one favour and that's it. Did you talk to her, by the way?'

'Yes, and I have to say that what she's claiming is very tenuous. Very tenuous indeed.'

'Well, I find her convincing and I'm going to help her.'

'Her? You're doing this for no one but yourself, and you know it.'

'Think what you like.'

'You can't withhold information from us if you dig something up. You can't just decide to investigate it yourself. You're retired!'

'If I come across something juicy I'll let you know,' Konrád said and ended the call.

'Is everything OK?' Húgó asked, when he returned to his seat.

'Fine, it was just Marta.'

'Anyway,' said Sirrí, who had broken off her anecdote about the lifestyle guru until Konrád got back. He noticed she had a glass of wine in her hand. She now embarked on a seemingly interminable story about the guru and their friendship and his opinion on various topics, about which they thought *exactly* the same. Konrád kept losing the thread, preoccupied by his conversation with Marta, but he nodded and tried to smile in the appropriate places, though he hardly took in a word she said.

Later, father and son sat alone in the sitting room, chatting about the English football, which was as boring in Sirrí's opinion as lifestyle gurus were in theirs. She had gone off to talk to someone on the phone.

'What did Marta want?' Húgó asked once they'd run out of things to say about the football. He was named after his maternal grandfather, and was a tall, slim, handsome man, with a dependably level-headed approach to life.

'It was about Sigurvin.'

'Don't tell me you're up to your neck in the investigation again?'

'Hardly. I'm just keeping an eye on their progress.'

'You must have got a shock when he turned up.'

'You can say that again. I wasn't expecting it. I didn't think Sigurvin would ever be found.'

'Perhaps that's what you were hoping: that he would never turn up.'

Konrád looked at his son. 'I was sick to death of that case,' he said. 'And now I'm being sucked into it again. Maybe I shouldn't have gone to see Hjaltalín in prison.'

'You couldn't have done anything else.'

'No, maybe not.'

'You've never been able to shake it off.'

'It would be good to get to the bottom of it once and for all,' Konrád admitted. 'We're long overdue some answers.'

15

The succession of autumn depressions relented, the sun came out and Konrád tried to make the most of the mild days by going for long walks in the Ellidaár Valley. He wasn't as agile as he used to be and seemed to be stiff all over these days, with aches and pains in his joints, legs and back. Apart from that, though, he was in rude health and rarely suffered from any ailments. He took one pill a day for his high cholesterol but that was it.

On one of these walks he phoned Svanhildur.

'Do you have any more information about the blunt instrument used on Sigurvin?' he asked. 'Have you any idea what it could have been?'

'A length of piping or a bar, maybe; something heavy – possibly a small crowbar. Something that would rust, anyway. We found particles in the wound along with other trace elements and dirt which we're still analysing. He was struck twice; it wasn't an accident. He didn't trip over anything. Someone hit him over the head with the intent to do damage. Haven't you asked Marta about this?'

'No,' Konrád said. 'The blows were both to the back of his head, you say?'

'Yes. It's easy to imagine the attack taking him by surprise. Someone must have crept up behind him. I didn't find any signs that he'd tried to defend himself, and there were no other wounds on his body. He seems to have been very healthy, as you'd expect of a young man.'

'Any explanation for why he was taken up to the glacier? I mean, what would someone gain from that?'

'Is it a worse hiding place than any other?'

'Well, we certainly missed it.'

'Are you going to keep avoiding me forever?' Svanhildur asked, as Konrád was on the point of hanging up.

'I don't know,' he said. 'We're talking now, aren't we?'

'Not about what matters.'

'I don't think I'm avoiding you.'

'You've been doing that ever since she got ill,' Svanhildur said. 'Don't you think it's gone on long enough?'

'I should have told her about us.'

'How would she have been better off?'

'I don't know, but *I'd* feel better,' Konrád said. 'I should have told her about us but I didn't. I didn't and then it was too late.'

Their conversation ended there and Konrád carried on walking through the green oasis of fir and birch woods between the rocky courses of the two rivers. Earlier that day he'd had an errand to run in the city centre and had stopped off at the National Hospital, where he'd spoken briefly to the hospital chaplain, the last man Hjaltalín had talked to before he died. Konrád knew and liked the chaplain, who had comforted him and Erna when Erna had taken a turn for the worse. He knew all about Konrád's involvement with Hjaltalín too, and said he'd been half expecting him to drop by.

'How are you, by the way?' the chaplain asked as they took a seat in the hospital corridor.

'I'm fine, thanks,' Konrád said. 'Trying to stop myself getting too bored, you know how it is.'

'That's good,' the chaplain said. He was fiftyish, with a serene manner and a low, soothing voice that he never saw any reason to raise. 'You probably want to know something about Hjaltalín. Or am I jumping to conclusions? You haven't suddenly developed an interest in God, have you?'

Konrád smiled. They had once had a rather one-sided discussion about religion. Konrád, an atheist who knew his Bible, regarded God as an utterly absurd concept and had said that he didn't believe in the Creation and found the Holy Trinity of God, Christ and the Holy Spirit incomprehensible at best. 'Who is this Holy Spirit anyway?' he'd asked. 'Wasn't he invented at some synod? By a conference, basically! Hold up your hand all those who want the Holy Trinity!' Konrád had been angry at the time. The short, stocky chaplain, whose name was Pétur, hadn't tried to argue with him.

'He never confessed,' Konrád said now, after a brief silence. 'But I wondered if he'd said anything at the end. I went to see him in prison, you know, a couple of weeks before he died.'

'So he told me.'

'He didn't look well.'

'No, he went downhill very fast. But he didn't blame the police for that. Hjaltalín was touched that you'd looked in on him, by the way. He mentioned that.'

'I asked if he wouldn't like to tell us the truth, in the circumstances. Pointed out that he had nothing to lose. But it didn't work.'

'Naturally, I'm sworn to silence about what passed between me and Hjaltalín,' the chaplain said, 'but if that's what you're after, I can tell you that he didn't budge from what he'd said before.'

'Did he bring up the case at all?'

The chaplain thought for a moment. 'He wasn't particularly preoccupied with that, to be honest. We talked about other things.'

'Nothing about the glacier? The married woman? Öskjuhlíd?'

The chaplain shook his head.

'Did he have many visitors?' Konrád asked.

'No. His parents are dead and his sister lives abroad. She couldn't get here in time, sadly. She came to the funeral, though, then went back home. I wasn't aware of any circle of friends. In fact, he gave the impression of being rather alone in the world, as if he'd been abandoned. I don't know if people had turned their backs on him because of the business with Sigurvin.'

'It's possible,' Konrád said.

'The evening – or night – before he died . . . it had completely slipped my mind . . .'

'What?'

'. . . I was going to look in on him but there was a woman I hadn't seen before sitting by his bed. I didn't actually get more than a glimpse of her. She had her back to me and seemed reluctant to attract any attention. She didn't say hello and Hjaltalín gave me a sign to show he wanted to be alone with her. When I went past shortly afterwards, she'd gone. I asked if she was his sister but he didn't want to discuss it.'

'What did she look like?'

'I couldn't really see. As I said, she had her back to me and was trying to be inconspicuous. But I do know it wasn't his sister because she arrived shortly after Hjaltalín died and was upset that she hadn't been in time to see him while he was alive. I admit I was a little curious about the woman who'd visited him – we priests are only human, after all – so I asked the nursing staff responsible for Hjaltalín, but it turned out they hadn't noticed her. It was very late in the evening when I saw her but I asked around the next day and that's what they told me. No one had seen her. She can't have stayed long.'

'Was she Hjaltalín's sort of age?'

'I simply can't say. Like I explained, I only caught a glimpse of her.'

'Wealthy-looking? Poor?'

'Neither. Just a very ordinary woman. Quite small, with a dark coat, I think, and dark hair under the kind of headscarf women used to wear years ago. I didn't like to stare, and Hjaltalín clearly wanted to be left in peace, so I made myself scarce.'

'You were the last person to see Hjaltalín alive?'

'Yes.'

'And he didn't confess?'

'No. He closed his eyes and died. He was very stoical towards the end. Of course it must have come as a bad shock when he learnt about his cancer, but I think he'd become resigned to it. From what I could tell, anyway. He didn't express any regrets or repentance for anything he'd done, if that provides you with a clue.'

'Was he religious?'

'In comparison to you, yes.'

Konrád returned to the present and the Ellidaár Valley, pausing to survey his surroundings. There was a fine view over the city and the mountains to the north, and he stood there for a while in the autumn sunshine, drinking it in. Nearer at hand, he could see a steady stream of traffic on the Breidholt road. As a true Reykjavík boy, Konrád couldn't think of anywhere better to be when the sun was shining.

His thoughts drifted back to the hospital and his conversation with the chaplain.

'Do the police know why he was taken to the glacier?' the chaplain had asked as they were saying goodbye.

'No. I don't work for them any more – I don't know what they're thinking.'

'But you haven't quite put the case behind you?' the chaplain said.

'I have.'

'Then why are you asking me all these questions?'

'I . . . Hjaltalín's been on my mind a bit,' Konrád said. 'I wanted to know if he'd said anything. This was only meant to be a chat – I didn't mean to interrogate you. I hope it didn't come across like that?'

'Hjaltalín didn't absolve you,' the chaplain said, 'if that's what you're after.'

'No,' Konrád said, 'I didn't expect him to.'

16

When she'd notified the police about her brother, she'd had her whole life ahead of her. Naturally, she'd been anxious about his unexplained absence, but her manner had been smiling and friendly in spite of that. She wasn't to know then that she would spend the next three decades living in the shadow of his disappearance. Now, with a good portion of her life behind her, Konrád thought he could see how much the loss had left its mark on her.

Her name was Jórunn. Konrád, who hadn't seen her for years, noticed the stamp of tiredness on her face, like a visible reminder of the hard times she had endured. There was no trace of her former smiley manner. These days her friendliness was more guarded. She told him that, grateful as she was to fate for making the glacier return her brother, she had found it hard to deal with the accompanying media storm. It had been bad enough having to cope over the years with the steady flow of conspiracy theories in the papers, with all the new rumours, old photos, and endless rehashes of the events surrounding the case. She had soon stopped answering the phone to the press, and suffered agonies every time the case was brought up, until in the end she had stopped following the coverage altogether. She'd been forced to go ex-directory as well, to avoid all the phone calls from drunk, obnoxious strangers claiming to know exactly what had happened.

Brother and sister had been close, which had made it easy for her to answer questions about Sigurvin's private affairs during the original inquiry. She and Konráд had always got on well. She'd had full confidence in him, knowing in her heart that he was doing everything in his power to solve the case, so when he asked if they could meet up now that her brother had been found, she readily agreed. Marta had been to see her twice and asked her repeatedly about the glacier, but Jórunn, as astonished as everyone else by the fact her brother's body had been found there, was unable to provide any new insights.

'I heard you'd retired,' Jórunn said as she invited him in. She lived alone, never having married or had children, and Konráд wondered if her brother's disappearance had played its part in this.

'That's right, I have. But the situation's rather unusual.'

'It certainly is. As no one knows better than you.'

'It must have come as a shock.'

'Yes. It was . . . surreal somehow, when it finally happened. I didn't think it ever would and had long ago accepted the fact. Accepted that he was dead and that I'd never find out what had become of him. Then this.'

'What was your first thought when you heard about the glacier? What was the very first thing that came into your mind?'

'I don't know. What did you think?'

'That we should have done better,' Konrád said. 'That we must have cocked up badly and missed some vital clue. That we should have found him long before this.'

'I always felt you were doing your best.'

'It wasn't enough. We . . . we messed up somehow.'

'I was astonished, of course,' Jórunn said. 'What on earth could Sigurvin have been doing up there? But when I heard he hadn't gone to the glacier voluntarily, I immediately thought whoever did it must have been experienced at travelling on ice. No one would go up there unless they knew what they were doing. Marta told me the police have been devoting a lot of energy to examining this angle but that they haven't uncovered any leads yet. Of course, all sorts of people travel on glaciers – nowadays, anyway. Tour operators. Mountaineers. Fishermen. Skiers. Walking groups. The Icelandic Touring Association. The Útivist Club. All of them.'

'The search and rescue teams . . .'

'Yes, of course. Aren't they always having to rescue people from the ice caps?'

'Did nothing at all occur to you in connection with Sigurvin?'

'No. I've been racking my brains ever since but I can't think of anything.'

'He never mentioned anything about a glacier trip?'

'No. Not that I remember, anyway.'

'Did he have any friends or acquaintances we weren't aware of, who were interested in that sort of thing? Who were into travelling in the interior or mountaineering?'

'I don't think so. Sigurvin never wanted to set foot outside Reykjavík,' Jórunn said. 'He had no interest in travelling round Iceland. Going abroad was what he enjoyed. We weren't well off as kids, so when Sigurvin got rich, he wanted to make the most of it, and one of the ways he did that was by taking foreign holidays.'

Konrád was aware that brother and sister had grown up with a single mother who had died some years after her son vanished. They had been desperately hard up when they were young; so poor, in fact, that their mother could barely put food on the table. A relative had taken pity on them, though. He had a small wholesale business and saw to it that both kids continued in education: Jórunn went to the Reykjavík Sixth-Form College, Sigurvin to the Commercial College. They were both diligent and Sigurvin was particularly resourceful, providing them with a small income from mowing lawns and other odd jobs. He had got his driving licence as soon as he was old enough and started working for his relative. Whenever he saw a chance of making a few extra krónur, he would leap at it. And once he reached adulthood, it seemed he had never been short of money again. Konrád had talked to the relative during the inquiry and he had spoken well of Sigurvin and mourned his loss, while describing him as very money-minded. It was a description that stayed with Konrád because it fitted the impression other people had given of Sigurvin, though they hadn't put it quite as tactfully as the kind-hearted relative. Sigurvin had been motivated by a desire to get rich. He'd enjoyed racking up a profit.

Jórunn had once told Konrád that her brother had always taken good care of their mother, as well as being generous to her. Yet he could also be tight-fisted and had been very insistent that people should stick to contracts. He had been terribly hurt when Hjaltalín started accusing him of dishonesty, of ripping him off and deceiving him, and the more Hjaltalín had raged, the more Sigurvin had dug in his heels. Jórunn didn't know how things had got so bad between them. But the fact was, her brother could be unreasonable. She'd asked him once why he and Hjaltalín couldn't just find a solution that would make them both happy. He'd retorted that he'd behaved honestly when he'd bought Hjaltalín out; there'd been no cheating or machinations behind the scenes, and it wasn't his problem if Hjaltalín felt he'd done a bad deal.

'Tell me something,' Konrád said now, after they had been chatting for a while. 'Hjaltalín received a visit in hospital shortly before he died. A woman was seen sitting by his bed. Do you know anything about that?'

'No.'

'It wasn't you?'

'Me?'

'You didn't go to see him?'

'What for? I had absolutely nothing to say to that man.'

'No, of course,' Konrád said, dropping the subject. 'It must have been someone else.'

'Sigurvin was a good guy,' Jórunn said after a long pause. 'He didn't deserve what happened to him. No one deserves a fate like that.'

'That's true.'

'I always felt he was like the Boy Scout he'd once been,' Jórunn said. 'Eager to help. A sweet person. A lovely man, brother and son.'

'Was Sigurvin in the Scouts?' Konrád asked, pouncing on this detail. He didn't remember having heard it before.

'Not for very long. He was bursting with enthusiasm when he joined but I don't think that lasted more than a year or two.'

'No longer than that?'

'No. He soon got bored and quit.'

'How old was he?'

'Ten or twelve. He can't have been much older than that.' Jórunn's head drooped. 'I'm glad he's been found,' she said. 'The uncertainty about what happened . . . it's been eating away at me all these years. Not a day's gone by when I haven't thought about him and . . . you can't imagine how much . . . what a huge relief it is that he's turned up at last.'

17

The old man leant on his Zimmer frame, shuffling along the corridor to his room in the nursing home with Konrád at his side. He had been sitting in the canteen over a meal of poached haddock and potatoes when Konrád disturbed him. They had never exactly been good mates. In the old days Konrád had sometimes handled his convictions for theft, forgery and smuggling booze. The man had drunk heavily at one time and ended up on the streets, but had managed to haul himself back up again. After that he had joined a Christian congregation, started attending meetings and promised to clean up his act. It was then that he started working for Sigurvin's company. He had driven a delivery van and done whatever jobs were required and, as far as Konrád could discover, he'd been well liked. But after Sigurvin's disappearance the company had undergone a number of changes, and in the end he'd handed in his notice and gone to work for the City Council instead. He'd had his fifteen minutes of fame as the key witness in the Sigurvin affair, but the attention hadn't been welcome and he often used to say that he wished he'd never heard a damn thing that evening.

His name was Steinar and he had aged a great deal in the intervening years, but despite his failing health, he was willing to talk and his mind proved as sharp as ever. He'd recognised Konrád immediately and knew that he'd come to ask him yet again about the altercation between Hjaltalín and Sigurvin in the car park.

'I've been half expecting you,' Steinar said, once they reached his room. 'Seeing as they had to go and dig him out of the ice.'

He put aside his walking frame and dropped heavily onto his bed. His clothes – a shirt with a faded pattern, and worn Terylene trousers – appeared to be several sizes too big for his shrunken frame. He hadn't shaved in a while and his hair, which had once been thick and bushy, was now thin and grizzled and flecked with dandruff.

'Couldn't the poor sod have been left in peace?' Steinar asked, stroking a hand over his few strands of hair as if smoothing them from habit.

'I'm sure some people would have preferred that. I wondered if it had jogged your memory at all when it turned out that Sigurvin was on Langjökull.'

'I'd stopped thinking about that business altogether,' Steinar said, 'so it gave me a bit of a jolt when I heard on the news that they'd found him.'

'To be fair, I don't think anyone had been expecting to find him up there.'

'No. You cops weren't clever enough to spot that,' Steinar said, with a hint of schadenfreude. 'Are the police investigating the whole thing all over again?'

'I've retired from the force,' Konrád said. 'I'm just curious on my own account, so you're under no obligation to tell me anything unless you want to.'

'Retired? That old, are you?'

Konrád nodded.

'Next thing you know, you'll be moving in here yourself.'

Konrád had sometimes wondered if he would end up in a home and found the idea distinctly off-putting. He noticed that Steinar shared his room with another man. Konrád couldn't imagine what it would be like having to live out your last years with no privacy. Even the prisoners at Litla-Hraun got cells to themselves.

'You never know,' he said with a smile. 'Look, I'm aware you must be sick of being asked the same old questions, but now this new information has come to light, I thought it would be good to hear what you had to say.'

'But what's it got to do with you – if you're retired?'

'I worked on the case for a long time,' Konrád said. 'Maybe it's my hobby. I don't know. What was the first thing that came to mind when you heard about the glacier?'

'That Hjaltalín had done a bloody good job of hiding him. And that it must have taken some doing.'

'Do you remember any talk at Sigurvin's firm about glacier trips? Was there someone who enjoyed travelling in the highlands or on the ice caps? Or who had an off-roader designed for that kind of thing? Or any clients who turned up in that sort of vehicle?'

Steinar thought about it, scratching his head.

'No, I can't say I do. But then it's hardly fair to ask me all these years later. I can't say I remember any blokes with big jeeps in

Sigurvin's circle, but of course I didn't really have any contact with him. I got the job through a cousin of mine who knew the foreman. I hadn't been working there long when it happened.'

'You weren't going to report it at first – the row you overheard.'

'I'm no snitch. What those men did was none of my business. Nothing to do with me.'

Konráð remembered Steinar's first interview as a witness. It turned out that the anonymous tip-off the police had received about Hjaltalín quarrelling with Sigurvin had come from Steinar's live-in girlfriend. He had told her what he'd witnessed, adding that he wanted to stay well out of it. His girlfriend had ignored his objections, though she was careful not to betray his name during the phone call, saying only that he worked for Sigurvin's company. After that, tracking him down was easy. Konráð, knowing Steinar and his shady past, noticed that he was jumpy when he talked to him, as if keen to get the interview over with as soon as possible. Konráð told him that, according to information the police had received, Hjaltalín had been overheard making threats against Sigurvin, and was Steinar aware of this? The police had been tipped off by someone who wanted to remain anonymous. Steinar pretended to know nothing about it but later confessed to another detective, Leó, telling him exactly what he'd heard and seen in the car park.

Since Steinar's reliability as a witness was in doubt, the police had looked into the possibility that he might be trying to get himself off the hook by lying about Hjaltalín. At one point he was even a suspect, but his girlfriend provided him with an alibi, claiming she was with him on the evening and night that Sigurvin had vanished and, besides, he had no obvious motive to kill his boss or wish him any harm. Nevertheless, he had been the last person, apart from Hjaltalín, to see Sigurvin alive, and had been guilty of withholding important information, which made the police suspicious.

Steinar was grilled repeatedly about why he hadn't gone to the police immediately after Sigurvin was reported missing. He replied every time that he had wanted to avoid exactly the kind of interrogation he was being subjected to now. Anyway, he'd known that because he had form, they'd suspect him of having an ulterior motive. He was afraid the police wouldn't believe him and might even think he had harmed Sigurvin himself.

He was made to attend an identity parade and quickly picked out Hjaltalín as the man who had quarrelled with Sigurvin in front of the offices. He seemed confident and stuck to his statement throughout the inquiry. According to Steinar, that evening in the car park had been the first time he'd laid eyes on Hjaltalín.

'I asked you about Öskjuhlíd at the time,' Konrád said now, his eyes resting on the walking frame by Steinar's bed. 'Maybe it's unfair to make you try and remember it so many years later. But do you recall anything about the men's cars?'

Steinar thought. 'No, I can't say I do.'

Konrád cleared his throat. 'What kind of car did you yourself drive at the time?'

'Me?' Steinar said. 'You don't still think *I* bumped him off? I didn't own a car. I was sometimes allowed to drive one of the delivery vans home, but that was the only vehicle I had access to.'

'I don't think any such thing. I was only asking.'

'I didn't like the way you lot used my testimony to hound that bloke,' Steinar said, his voice suddenly weary. 'I knew I should never have talked to you. That bitch, ringing you like that. That bloody bitch.'

'There's no need to talk about her like that,' Konráð said reprovingly. 'We'd have found you anyway.'

'I doubt it.' Steinar snorted. 'I very much doubt it.'

Neither of them said anything for a while. Instinct told Konráð that Steinar was withholding something. A member of staff he'd met in the corridor had said that the old man never got any visits, just sat in his room and didn't mix much with the other residents. His health had declined rapidly over the last few weeks and they couldn't be sure how long he had left.

'Is Le— Is Leó still in the police?' Steinar asked after a long silence.

'Leó? Yes, he's still working. Why do you ask?'

Steinar scratched his white stubble, looking frail and hollow-cheeked.

'Oh, I don't know. By the way, about my old girlfriend . . . I don't know why I called her a bitch. Maybe there have been enough lies.'

'What do you mean?'

'Leó never told you?'

'Told me what?'

'How he treated me?'

'What do you mean? How did he treat you?'

'Oh, it doesn't matter. It was nothing. Forget it.'

'What did he do?'

'No, it doesn't matter,' Steinar repeated, raising a hand to his chest. 'It was nothing. I'm tired. I need to lie down.'

'Steinar . . . ?'

'I'd like you to go,' Steinar said. 'I'm not up to this. I can't be doing with this any more. Please, just leave me alone.'

Konrád helped him to lie down on the bed, then said goodbye. On his way out, he let the staff know that the old man had been complaining of feeling tired, and they promised to keep a careful eye on him.

18

Herdís rang Konrád the next day, wanting to meet up, and asked if he could come and see her at the Krónan discount supermarket where she worked. He decided to pick up a few groceries while he was there: bread, milk, coffee and other basics. Herdís spotted him out of the corner of her eye as she was serving at the till, asked a colleague to relieve her, and came over. It was lunchtime and there were few other customers on the vast shop floor.

'That cop was all right, that Marta,' Herdís said as they shook hands.

'Yes, she's pretty good,' Konrád said. 'You've spoken to her then? Where do you keep the olives in this barn?'

'Come with me,' Herdís said, and he followed. 'I got the feeling she didn't really buy it, though.'

'No, Marta always takes a bit of time to digest things.'

They entered a long aisle containing Italian goods – pasta, tinned tomatoes and sauces – and Herdís pointed out the olives. He selected a jar of large green ones and put them in his basket.

'I need porridge oats too,' he said. 'I've no idea where anything is: I've never been in here before.'

'I wanted to let you know,' Herdís said, setting off again, 'that I bumped into one of Villi's old mates here and we got talking. It turns out Villi told him what happened that night by the tanks and he remembered that he'd been up there himself around the same time and noticed a big off-roader parked nearby.'

'An off-roader?'

'Yes. He mentioned that specifically. It wasn't your ordinary jeep; it was one of those super jeeps, with the huge tyres. Villi told him it could have been the same car he saw.'

'And this was around the same time, you say?'

'Villi's mate saw the car a bit before he did. He knows that because he was at a junior-league handball game at the Valur indoor court then went up to the tanks afterwards with some mates. He could remember the game and looked it up to see what date it was on. Turns out it was at the beginning of February.'

'The car was that memorable, was it?'

'Yes. He started thinking about it when Sigurvin turned up on Langjökull. According to him, a super jeep like that could easily have been used for glacier driving.'

Konráð put a packet of rolled oats in his basket.

'Good. I might have a word with the guy,' he said. 'I'm asking around a bit about the case. It won't stop bugging me, so I've been talking to a few people and gathering information, telling them it's on your behalf. I just wanted you to know. Are you OK with that?'

Herdís stared at him. 'On my behalf?'

'I tell them I'm looking for answers about what Villi saw – and that I'm doing it for you. That's my excuse.'

'I asked you to find the person who deliberately ran Villi down. Isn't that an even better excuse?'

Konrád sat in his kitchen late that evening, when peace and quiet had settled on the neighbourhood and most people had gone to bed. Despite the late hour, he opened a bottle of wine Húgó had given him, hoping that a glass or two would help him get to sleep. Not that it really mattered. His internal clock was so messed up that day and night had ceased to have much meaning for him.

The light was on over the kitchen table, but apart from that the house lay in shadow. Konrád smoked a cigarillo, going over the conversation he'd had with Hjaltalín in prison for the umpteenth time.

'Is it because of him?' Hjaltalín had asked, trying to stay on the subject of Konrád's father.

'What?' Konrád had said. 'Is what because of him?'

'That you joined the police?'

'I have no idea what you're on about. As usual.'

'Are you sure?'

'Yes, I'm sure,' Konrád had said. 'I didn't come here to talk to you about my father. He's absolutely none of your business and never was.'

'So you're not trying to compensate for what he was like?'

Konrád hadn't bothered to answer that.

'Isn't that what it's all about, Konrád? Aren't you trying to be a better man than him? Isn't that why you joined the police? Isn't that why you're this sad-sack failure of a cop?'

'Fuck off!'

'You must take after him in some ways. He's part of you, after all. But in what way, I wonder? How are you alike? Inherit some of his nastier traits, did you? Your dad's vicious side, perhaps?'

Konrád took a mouthful of wine and at that moment his phone started ringing. It was Steinar's nursing home to tell him that the old man had been admitted to hospital following a heart attack and that he was asking to see Konrád.

19

Steinar had been rushed to the National Hospital after being found lying in the corridor of the nursing home. He'd been suffering severe chest pains and was about to call for help when he collapsed. A member of staff had found him and raised the alarm, and now he was in intensive care. The only thing he had asked for was to see Konrád, but Konrád was warned that he couldn't stay with the patient more than a few minutes. It was touch-and-go whether he would survive the night.

Steinar opened his eyes after Konrád had been standing over him for a while. It took the old man a moment or two to recognise him. Then a faint smile twitched at the corner of his mouth before his eyelids drooped again.

'I don't want to take it to my grave,' Steinar murmured, so quietly that it was hardly more than a breath.

'What?'

'Luckily, that Hjaltalín was never convicted, and now the poor man's dead, so . . . And then the body turning up like that . . . it's been preying on my mind ever since I saw the news.'

'What has? What are you talking about?'

Steinar opened his eyes again and looked at Konrád. 'That Leó was a piece of work. When he used to nick you in the old days . . . the bloody sadist. He wasn't above knocking you about a bit. He kicked me so hard once I could hardly walk for days. Shoved my head down the toilet too. But maybe you knew about that. Maybe you were no better yourself.'

'I'm not like Leó.'

'I don't give a . . . shit,' Steinar whispered. 'He can't touch me now. The whole thing was his idea.'

'What was?'

'He threatened to frame me for the murder. Said I didn't have an alibi. And I was shit-scared because of my . . .' Steinar's eyes closed again. He was so weak that Konrád knew he shouldn't stay with him much longer. After a moment, the old man struggled on, his voice a hoarse whisper: '. . . my past. I knew he could make trouble for me. He was sure Hjaltalín was guilty and that all they needed was to get a conviction in the bag. That's what he said: "in the bag".'

'Then what happened?'

'I saw them arguing in the car park – Hjaltalín and Sigurvin. That's no lie. And Hjaltalín was pretty worked up, like he was ready to go for Sigurvin.'

'But . . . ?'

'But I didn't actually hear what they said.'

Konrád stared at the old man. 'What do you mean?'

'I never heard Hjaltalín shout that he was going to kill Sigurvin.'

'What are you saying?'

Leó was a thickset man in his early sixties, with white hair and a neatly trimmed goatee, regular features and small, flinty grey eyes that never missed a trick. He was a well-regarded figure in the force, with a reputation for caring about his fellow officers and being dedicated to improving their welfare. He and Konrád had worked together a great deal at one time but their friendship had long ago cooled.

'I don't have to listen to this bullshit,' Leó said, turning to open the door and walk out. He had been on unpaid leave for some time as the result of a drink problem.

'For Christ's sake, stay where you are!' Marta barked. 'And you shut up, Konrád.'

'That poor old bugger Steinar's completely lost his marbles,' Leó said. 'I can't understand why you'd listen to a word he said.'

He addressed this remark to Marta, as if Konrád weren't in the room.

'You know what this means, Marta,' Konrád said. 'If what Steinar said is true, none of the investigations this man has been involved in can be taken at face value. Not a single one. Ask yourself, what else has he lied about? What evidence has he planted? What other witness statements or confessions has he extracted by force or threats?'

'Shut the fuck up,' Leó snapped.

'Shut up yourself,' Konrád retorted.

'Steinar's . . . he's telling lies about me,' Leó said. 'Come on, it's obvious. And it wouldn't be the first time either. He's got it in for me, that's why he's saying it. I don't understand why we're even discussing it.'

'But why?' Konrád asked. 'Why would he do that when he's dying? If he wanted to get you into trouble, why wait all this time?'

'Hjaltalín always denied having threatened Sigurvin in the car park,' Marta said, her eyes resting on Leó.

'Well, what else would you expect?' Leó said. 'Of course he did. You can't be serious? He'd hardly have admitted threatening to kill a man who'd vanished straight afterwards.'

'Leó organised the whole thing, right down to the smallest detail,' Konrád said. 'He used us. Used me. And I don't suppose for one minute that it's the only time he's done something like that. If it wasn't for him, we could have pursued a different line of inquiry.'

'I cannot believe this,' Leó said. 'It's total crap. If we have to listen to every lowlife who tries to get one over on us, we might as well shut up shop.'

'You should take a formal statement from Steinar before it's too late,' Konrád said. 'Get it documented, signed and –'

'Yes, right. That's the problem,' Marta interrupted. 'No can do, I'm afraid. He died last night, shortly after you left him.'

Leó uttered a bark of laughter. 'A visit from you was obviously the last thing he needed,' he said to Konrád. 'You must have bored him to death.'

'Hjaltalín spent months in custody because of you.' Konrád rose to his feet and walked right up to Leó until their faces were almost touching. 'He went through hell thanks to you. You're a disgrace to the police. You always have been.'

'You prick,' Leó said, shoving him away. 'Are we done?' he asked, turning to Marta. 'I very much doubt the old man said those things about me. It's just Konni here putting lies in his mouth to get at me. He's the one who's a disgrace. I've had it up to here with this shit.' He tore the door open and charged out, slamming it behind him.

'He's right, you know,' Marta said. 'Steinar could have been lying about him, or you could be making it up to get back at Leó.'

'Marta . . .'

'I'm not saying that's what happened but it's going to be difficult to prove otherwise now the old boy's gone and died on us.'

'Leó coached the witness, threatened him and made him believe he'd heard something he hadn't,' Konrád said. 'There should be an internal inquiry into his past cases to find out what else he's been up to.'

'Yes, but that's not going to happen,' Marta said, 'and you know it. Not based on the word of one old man who's no longer here to tell the tale. It's not enough. Not nearly enough.'

Konrád shook his head.

'I got those recordings for you,' Marta said.

'Recordings?'

'From the hospital.'

21

Marta brought out the CCTV footage from the National Hospital, which she had requested in the hope that the woman who'd visited Hjaltalín had been caught on film. But since the chaplain's description hadn't been very detailed, Konráð didn't know what to look for apart from a woman on her own in the vicinity of the oncology ward. There were a lot of cameras, as it turned out, both inside and outside the hospital, but at least they had a fairly precise time for the visit. The woman had been sitting with Hjaltalín late in the evening, when the hospital was at its least busy. As the chaplain had mentioned, the nursing staff had been unaware of her presence. The woman hadn't spoken to anyone at reception, just slipped unobserved into Hjaltalín's room, sat there for a while, then left as unobtrusively as she had arrived. Hjaltalín had waved the chaplain away when he came to the door.

'He didn't want the chaplain to see who was visiting him,' Konrád said, fast-forwarding through the footage from the camera covering the rear entrance and the ambulance bay.

'Why do you think this woman's important?' Marta asked for the second time. She had got hold of the CCTV recordings at Konrád's request – albeit reluctantly, because she still wasn't happy with the idea of him carrying out his own private investigation and interfering with the work of the police. But they were old colleagues and Marta could see that there might be something to be gained from Konrád's efforts.

'I've already told you. Hjaltalín's alibi was that he'd been with a married woman when Sigurvin vanished. It could be her.'

'Wasn't that his big lie?'

'He's not the only one who lied to us,' Konrád said, thinking of Leó.

'And you believe they've been in contact with each other since then?'

'Why not?' Konrád said. 'Or, alternatively, maybe their relationship ended years ago but she wanted to say goodbye to him.'

'And to thank him? He went through hell to avoid naming her.'

'Exactly. To thank him for everything. She owed it to him.'

Konrád studied Marta as she sat at her computer, looking heavy-eyed. She belonged to the new generation of detectives after Konrád's, and had taken her first steps in CID under his guidance. She hadn't yet met the woman from the Westman Islands in those days, and used to say she didn't mind living alone. Konrád had been sceptical about this and was subsequently proved right when the woman moved in with her. Marta had been on cloud nine, believing she had finally found happiness, and Konrád had been sad at the way their relationship ended some years later. Marta wasn't one to complain, she had a habit of ringing him late in the evening, especially in winter, and talking at length about whatever happened to be on her mind, though she hadn't been calling as much recently. At those times he sensed her loneliness. Marta's colleagues generally had a lot of time for her, though she could be harsh and tactless in her dealings with people. One of them had said flippantly that under her rough exterior she had a heart of stone. Konrád didn't agree.

He put another recording in the machine and asked Marta how she was doing. She said she was fine and demanded to know why he was asking. Konrád said he thought she was looking tired and wanted to check everything was all right.

'Couldn't be better,' Marta said. 'It's not like you don't look tired yourself at times.'

'If you ask me, that spicy food doesn't agree with you.'

'What do you know about it? It's super healthy.'

'Has the new inquiry turned anything up yet?'

'Nothing of real interest. Anyway, I don't know if I should be sharing any details with you, seeing as you're working on it for some weird reasons of your own. It's not a good idea to take things like this personally – to let them get to you. I seem to remember you teaching me that.'

'Have you ever followed my advice?' Konrád asked.

You shouldn't take your work home with you, he had once told Marta. But they both knew that obeying the eleventh commandment of policing could be tough.

'Somehow I get the feeling I've managed better than you on that front,' Marta said.

'You think so?'

'Yes, I do.'

On the screen, doctors, orderlies and nurses walked in and out of the frame, along with paramedics and a scattering of people who appeared to be visitors.

'What's that woman got to hide?' Marta asked suddenly.

'Which one?'

'That one there,' she said, pointing to a figure standing by the lifts. 'Rewind a little.'

Konrád rewound and they watched as a woman wearing a long coat and a scarf over her head darted in through the doors and over to the lifts. She kept her back to the security camera. A moment later she had vanished into the lift.

'Is that . . . ? What's she up to?' Marta asked.

Konrád rewound the footage a second and a third time. It was obvious that the woman was trying to be inconspicuous. He got the impression she was aware of the CCTV and was keen to avoid being caught on camera.

'Can we see when she enters the building?' Marta asked.

Konrád changed the recording. Now that they had a precise time for the woman's arrival, they were quick to find the right place in the footage from the camera outside the rear entrance. They spotted the woman but, frustratingly, she kept just beyond the range of the camera until the last minute, when she dashed in through the doors with a hand over her face. It looked as if she was holding her scarf over her mouth and chin.

'Who is she?' Konrád asked.

He found the footage from the camera on the second floor, where the oncology ward was located. They watched as the lift doors opened. Two orderlies came out, followed by the woman in the headscarf, who hurried into the ward. It was eleven in the evening, around the time the chaplain said he'd walked in on Hjaltalín's conversation with the unknown woman.

'Is that the woman we're looking for?' Marta asked.

Konráð fast-forwarded. They saw no one else in the vicinity of the oncology ward until the chaplain went in.

'Isn't that your mate?' Marta said.

'Yes – Pétur. He's a good guy.'

Konráð fast-forwarded again until the door opened and the woman in the headscarf emerged into the corridor. He slowed down the playback. The woman walked over to the lifts and pressed the button, but instead of waiting she headed for the stairs instead. She kept her chin lowered to her chest and one hand over her forehead the whole time, making it impossible to see her features.

Konráð found the footage from the camera covering the rear entrance again and located the right time. They saw the woman approaching along the corridor towards the exit. She had her head bowed and was still holding a hand over her face. Then, as if startled by something, she briefly lowered her arm and the scarf fell away from her mouth and chin.

Konráð paused the frame. Gradually it dawned on him that he had seen the woman before, a long time ago.

'Is that her? Is it possible?'

'Who?' Marta asked.

'What's Linda doing there?' Konráð frowned at the screen.

'*Who?*' Marta said, straightening up in her chair.

'I don't believe it,' Konráð whispered.

'What?' Marta was growing impatient.

'Isn't that his wife?'

'Whose wife?' Marta asked, exasperated now.

'It's Linda. It's his wife! Why was Sigurvin's wife visiting Hjaltalín?'

'Is that who she is?' Marta asked, leaning towards the screen for a closer look.

'What the hell did she want from Hjaltalín?' Konrád whispered, not taking his eyes off the frozen image of the woman.

22

The following day, Marta paid Linda a visit – accompanied by another officer – to question her about why she had gone to see Hjaltalín in hospital. At first Linda wouldn't admit to having been there, but when pressed she said she'd wanted to keep her visit secret for obvious reasons, which was why she'd been trying to hide. She'd heard that Hjaltalín had been admitted to the oncology ward and wasn't expected to live, and had simply wanted to grab this last chance to ask him if he'd killed Sigurvin. That was all. She'd thought Hjaltalín would tell the truth on his deathbed. When it turned out he had nothing new to say, she had soon left. She'd been aware there were security cameras everywhere and had done her best to avoid them but clearly hadn't succeeded.

Linda begged Marta to ensure that news of her visit to the hospital wasn't leaked to the press.

Afterwards, Marta rang Konrád and gave him a brief report of their encounter.

'Was that all?'

'That was all.'

'Do you believe her?'

'Hard to say.'

'Are you having her phone records checked?'

'Yes. I'll send you the information as soon as it comes in, which shouldn't be long. It would be good if you could talk to her as well. You're our link to the case.'

'Plus, I was the one who tracked her down, don't forget.'

'Yeah, yeah, don't start getting all up yourself.'

Impatient as ever, Konrád paid his own visit to Linda that evening. She lived in a modern detached house in the suburb of Grafarholt on the eastern edge of the city. The front garden was largely paved over, with a flower bed around the edge. In the middle was a leafless bush, which looked rather melancholy in the autumnal darkness and drizzle. Linda answered the door herself. She didn't show any surprise at seeing Konrád. Although it was a long time since they had last met, she recognised him at once and was in no doubt about why he was there. It was as if she'd been expecting him and no one else.

'Is this about my visit to the hospital?' she asked, before he even had time to say hello.

Konrád nodded.

'I heard you'd retired.'

'I have,' Konrád said, 'but there are some things you can't let go of so easily.'

Linda looked at him. 'No, I suppose not,' she said. 'Come in.'

The house was homely and welcoming, with beautiful objects arranged on the surfaces and paintings hung on the walls. From the windows, the city could be glimpsed in the distance, blazing with light through the drizzle, and closer at hand was the illuminated golf course. He wondered if she played golf, given that the course was so conveniently close by, and asked her.

'No, I don't,' she said. 'My husband does. He's in Scotland,' she added, as if to explain his absence. 'On business.'

She'd got remarried fairly recently to a man who ran a small import company based in Kópavogur. She herself was a pharmacist. Before that she had lived alone for many years with her and Sigurvin's daughter. The daughter had later studied technology in Denmark before moving back to Iceland, and was now married with two children of her own. Following his disappearance, Sigurvin's share in his business had been sold for a considerable profit, providing mother and daughter with a tidy sum of money that Linda had invested wisely. Her daughter had been able to use the legacy to pay off her study loan and put down a deposit on a flat, and there had still been enough left over for mother and daughter to live in comfort, with no financial worries.

'I gather golf's a popular sport with couples,' Konráð said, without actually meaning to pry into the state of her marriage.

'Not in our case,' Linda replied. 'I've never had the slightest interest myself but Teitur's crazy about it.'

She offered him coffee or another drink of some kind and he accepted a ginger beer. They sat down in the sitting room, each determined not to make the encounter any more awkward than necessary. Linda was in her fifties, blonde, with pretty features in an oval face, her slightly plump figure dressed in a comfortable at-home outfit of loose trousers and shirt, and no jewellery of any kind.

'Your friend came to see me earlier today,' Linda said, sipping her ginger beer, to which she had added a splash of vodka. Konrád had declined, saying he was driving.

'Marta, yes.'

'She can't have been satisfied with the answers she got if she's sent you along.'

'As a matter of fact, I'm here on private business,' Konrád said. He proceeded to explain about Herdís and the mystery of her brother Villi's death.

'Marta mentioned a new witness,' Linda said. 'I wasn't aware. But people have said so many things over the years. There have been so many claims by so-called witnesses.'

'The difference is that this guy's story rings true,' Konrád said.

'I don't doubt it.'

'Also, the police asked for my help after they arrested Hjaltalín and I regard that deal as still valid.' He smiled.

'All right, what do you want to know?'

'Why did you go to see Hjaltalín?'

'I've already told your friend. I went to ask if he had anything he wanted to get off his chest before he died. He didn't. And that was that. I only stayed with him a few minutes.'

'You wanted to know if he'd killed Sigurvin?'

'Isn't that obvious?'

'And he denied it, as always.'

'Yes.'

'Wasn't he surprised to see you?'

'Surprised? Maybe. A bit. I suppose it was ... well ... it was a bit unexpected.'

'You went to a lot of trouble to avoid being recognised.'

'You can hardly be surprised about that, in the circumstances.'

'Of course not,' Konrád said. 'I'm far more surprised by the fact you went to see him at all.'

'Well, I was just seized by this . . . this need. I don't know what it was. I needed to see him before . . . before . . .'

'Did you have any other contact with him before he died? Before visiting him in hospital?'

'No, none.'

'You never heard from him?'

'No. Then one day I learnt that he was dying.'

'As you're well aware, and as Marta no doubt reminded you, Hjaltalín didn't have a confirmed alibi for the evening of Sigurvin's disappearance. He claimed to have been with a woman whose name he couldn't reveal because she was married and he wasn't prepared to expose her. He stuck to that story all these years, right up until he died. I went to see him after Sigurvin was found in the ice and he was still protesting his innocence, still trotting out the same feeble alibi. To tell the truth, I almost began to believe him.'

Linda took another sip of ginger beer.

'It wasn't until I saw the CCTV footage from the hospital that it dawned on me,' Konrád went on. 'It had never occurred to me before and I can understand why. Because it's not immediately obvious.'

'What?'

'I don't believe you suddenly felt an overwhelming need to go and talk to him on his deathbed,' Konrád said. 'I don't believe you were looking for answers at all.'

'Oh?'

'No, I think it's more complicated than that.'

Linda took another sip of her drink. Apart from that, she was perfectly composed. But then, Konrád remembered, she'd always had an air of calm self-possession.

'What are you implying?' she asked.

'Hjaltalín received a few calls on his mobile while he was in hospital, and made a few himself. But two of the calls he made went through the hospital telephone system. Maybe his battery had run out of juice or he suspected his phone was being tapped by the police. But he obviously didn't have the same concerns about the hospital phone. Or perhaps he was so desperate to get in touch with you that he took the risk. One of the calls was to his sister in America. The other was to this house.'

Linda didn't react.

'That was the day before you went to see him.'

She remained silent.

'It was Hjaltalín who got in touch with *you*, wasn't it?' Konrád persisted. 'It was the first time in thirty years that you'd heard from him. He said he was dying and wanted to see you.'

Linda regarded him impassively.

'Hjaltalín was a born liar but he wasn't lying about one thing,' Konrád said. 'He *was* with a married woman that evening after all, and now I find it a bit easier to understand why he never admitted who it was – regardless of what happened.'

He saw that Linda's eyes had filled with tears. But she didn't move, just sat very erect in the armchair, trying to give the impression that Konrád's words hadn't got to her.

'You'd already moved out of Sigurvin's place by the time he went missing. But you weren't formally divorced, were you? You were still married.'

Linda nodded, her lips a tight line.

'We thought of you as divorced, so it never occurred to us that you were a married woman. Besides, you were with your sister that evening. I had to look it up. But I couldn't find any confirmation of that. I don't think your sister was asked to corroborate your alibi because no one ever suspected you of any wrongdoing. But then the inquiry was pretty chaotic during those first few days.'

Konrád leant forwards.

'I'm right, aren't I?' he said. '*You* were the married woman – the woman whose identity Hjaltalín would never reveal.'

23

Linda stood up. She put her empty glass down on a small sideboard and went into the kitchen, returning with a tissue to dry her eyes. When she sat down in her chair again, she had recovered her composure a little.

'I thought the police would never find out,' she said at last. 'I should be grateful. It's been torturing me all these years.'

'Hjaltalín told us so many lies,' Konrád said. 'There was no way of knowing when he was telling the truth. We did everything we could to discover your identity, but he clammed up and refused to say another word. We never found any trace of a married woman in his life. I don't think it ever occurred to anyone: Sigurvin's wife.'

'I could hardly believe it when he used me as his alibi, after all he'd said about how vital it was that no one should get wind of our relationship.'

'He was desperate. By the way, you took a risk when you paid him that visit in hospital.'

'I know.'

'But you thought it was worth it, in spite of that?'

'We cut all contact after Sigurvin went missing, and never met or talked to each other again,' Linda said. 'We just behaved as if our affair had never happened. It was very hard at times. I never dared to get in touch with him, though I longed to. The danger of discovery was too great. And the years went by . . . But seeing him in hospital, seeing him lying in bed, looking so frail . . . it was a terrible shock. I hardly recognised him.'

'Apparently he went downhill very suddenly.'

'Yes. He just seemed completely done for.'

'Why did he get in touch?'

'To say goodbye, I suppose.'

'What did you two talk about?'

'Very little,' Linda said. 'When the time came, we had so little to say. But it was good to see him and sit with him for a while and . . .' Her words died away.

'Had you been seeing each other long before Sigurvin vanished?'

'Several months.'

'Was that why you and Sigurvin split up? Because you'd got involved with Hjaltalín?'

Linda nodded. 'Partly.'

'He didn't know the reason?'

'No,' Linda said. 'He didn't know about Hjaltalín, but our marriage just wasn't working. I think we'd have separated anyway.'

'Was that why you started seeing Hjaltalín? Because your marriage wasn't working?'

'You could say that.'

'Where did you two meet up?'

'Here and there. At his place. At my place. We kept it very quiet. We used to find small guesthouses outside Reykjavík. In Borgarnes. Selfoss. No one took any notice of us and we kept ourselves to ourselves. Sigurvin was often abroad, which made things easier.'

'But why? Why did you cheat on him?'

'How can I explain?' Linda said. 'Sigurvin and I were all washed up. And Hjaltalín understood me. He used to comfort me. Cuddle me. Show me affection.'

Konrád waited in silence for her to go on, and soon she was telling him how she had first got to know Sigurvin at the Commercial College. She'd told Konrád some of it during the original inquiry, but now she had the benefit of maturity and bitter experience. Sigurvin had been a real go-getter, she said, and she'd been attracted by his self-confidence. It hadn't hurt that he was good-looking too, and always seemed to have plenty of cash. They hadn't even been twenty when they got together, and he had all these plans for how he was going to get rich. He had no intention of continuing in education, and told her she needn't study pharmacology unless she wanted to. But she was more academic than him and had always wanted to go to university, to be independent.

She hadn't paid Hjaltalín much attention at college until he and Sigurvin started plotting various business ventures together. They had a lot in common. Both were keen to make money and felt out of place at school. Hjaltalín never finished his course. Then Sigurvin persuaded him to go shares in the fishing venture as almost equal partners. Sigurvin owned the controlling share in the company, but only by a small margin, and as time went on he wanted more. The three of them used to spend a lot of time together in those days. Although Hjaltalín had plenty of girls, he'd always fancied Linda. She'd known instinctively, and one evening he came right out and told her.

'That's how it started,' Linda said, 'some time before he and Sigurvin fell out. I don't really know what made me take that step. I suppose my relationship with Sigurvin wasn't great. And Hjaltalín knew what he wanted and how to get it.'

'Was he trying to avoid Sigurvin? Was that why he agreed to sell his share when Sigurvin wanted to buy him out? Because of your affair?'

'I suppose so. That must have played a part.'

'He reckoned he hadn't been paid a fair price,' Konrád said. 'He believed Sigurvin had shafted him.'

'Hjaltalín was incredibly angry,' Linda agreed. 'He had a temper on him but his moods didn't usually last long. He was spitting mad about that, though. Still, the fact we were cheating on Sigurvin helped to calm him down a bit, because he felt guilty about it. We both did. We weren't bad people, you know.'

'Did Sigurvin ever find out about your affair?'

'No. Not as far as I'm aware.'

'You knew Hjaltalín was seeing Salóme?'

'Their relationship wasn't going anywhere,' Linda said. 'He was planning to break up with her, but then Sigurvin went missing and you know the rest.'

'Why didn't you tell us about your relationship?' Konrád asked. 'Wouldn't that have been easiest?'

'Hjaltalín said that, if we did that, the police would be sure he was involved in Sigurvin's disappearance. He was convinced of that. He got off because no one knew about us. I'd have been dragged in too. We'd probably both have been convicted. We'd have sworn we were together when Sigurvin vanished but no one would have believed us. We'd have been given life sentences. That's how he saw it. He was very panicky by then and said people kept telling lies about him and that the police were almost certainly behind it. Like that witness – the one who supposedly heard him threatening to kill Sigurvin. He said it was a total fabrication and he was sure the police had made it up. That's what he said. He didn't trust anyone and he warned me that they'd be completely ruthless about using our affair against us.'

'He certainly didn't trust anyone,' Konrád said, thinking about Steinar and Leó and wondering if he should tell her what the old man had claimed. But he decided to leave it for the moment.

'He didn't dare tell the police about our affair. He knew it would only be used against him, and that more lies would be told about him. He was absolutely paranoid by then, seeing conspiracies on every side.'

'So he wasn't just protecting the married woman; he was trying to save his own skin as well?'

Linda nodded.

'I reckon Hjaltalín was right, you know,' Konrád said. 'Right to keep quiet about you two, however much grief it caused him. He got away with it. News of your affair could have been decisive in swinging the case against him.'

'That's what he always believed.'

'He endured all that time in custody without changing his statement. You must have been proud of him. It's no joke being locked up in solitary like that.'

'Proud? I wasn't proud. I felt terrible knowing that he was in prison and I couldn't do anything about it. Absolutely terrible. But what was I supposed to do? It had been his idea. I was frightened. Should I have run to you and told you everything? What would have happened then? Would we have been convicted? What would have happened to my daughter? Who was supposed to look after her? We hadn't done anything. Hjaltalín was with me that evening. I'm not lying, I don't have any reason to. He was with me.'

'Do you know what they were quarrelling about in the car park?'

'Money. Hjaltalín wasn't happy about the way things had gone, but he'd never have killed anyone for cash.'

'Did anyone else know about your affair?'

'No. No one. We were incredibly careful.'

'So you're the only person with this new version of what happened.'

'Yes.'

'You both lied,' Konrád said. 'To Sigurvin. To the police. You withheld important information from us. You say it was to prevent suspicion falling on the two of you. Other people might take a less charitable view and say that it was because you were responsible for killing your husband.'

Linda stared at Konrád incredulously. 'We didn't do it.'

'We only have your word for that.'

'Now you can see why Hjaltalín didn't want to tell you,' she said, raising her voice for the first time. 'However much trouble he was in. It was exactly because of this. Because the police would have immediately suspected us and started inventing lies about something we never did.' She glared at Konrád. 'We . . . we cheated on him – we had that on our consciences. We cheated on him and it was awful, but that was all. We didn't do anything else.'

24

Olga was irritable and inclined to be snappish when Konrád dropped in to see her the following day. Nothing had changed. She had worked for the police archives for many years, was nearing retirement and had always been extremely prickly. As she stood at her desk, she reminded Konrád inescapably of one of her filing cabinets, with her short, dumpy figure, extremely broad in the beam, supported on sturdy legs. She had always been an eccentric character, possessed of the kind of temperament that made people go out of their way to avoid her. But, over the years, Konrád had managed to penetrate her protective shell, and towards the end of his time in the police they had developed quite a good working relationship. That didn't prevent her from being abrasive, though, and putting up obstacles when he asked her to help him look up the traffic accident in which Herdís's brother, Villi, had died.

'I thought you'd retired,' she huffed. 'So why do you want to know about it? What's it got to do with you?'

'His sister asked me to look into it.'

'Is she some girl you're messing around with?'

'No, she's a woman who came to me for help.'

Konrád knew there was a reason why she had immediately assumed he must be involved with a girl. According to Marta, Olga was worse than ever these days because her husband had finally reached the end of his tether and walked out on her. They'd been married for thirty years when, out of the blue, he'd announced to her and their two daughters that he'd had enough and was leaving. He didn't give any explanation but Olga had quickly found out that he'd moved in with another woman – 'some skinny little cow,' as she put it – and was behaving as if he had never known his ex-wife. Konrád searched around for some way of expressing solidarity with her plight.

'How are you?' he asked cautiously.

'Oh, don't pretend you haven't heard,' she snapped.

'I'm not, I . . .' Konrád had been about to offer her his condolences, but stopped himself because no one had died and he didn't know any appropriate greeting for the newly divorced.

'He was always a stupid sod,' Olga said, which Konrád assumed was a reference to her ex-husband.

He had met the man occasionally at work socials, where they'd chatted a bit, and although he didn't really know him, he'd felt sorry for him having to live with such a gorgon. Now it was Olga he pitied, though he couldn't help wondering if her husband's departure wasn't partly her fault. Not that he would ever dare express such a thought.

'Are tongues wagging upstairs?' she asked.

'No, not at all,' Konrád assured her. 'But then I'm hardly ever there. I'm glad to have left, to be honest.'

'Those German tourists succeeded where you failed,' Olga said, with ill-concealed glee. 'Bet that pisses you off, doesn't it? Frankly, I always thought you lot were bloody useless not to be able to find the man. But, of course, you know that. I've given you enough grief about it in the past.'

'Yes, right,' Konrád said, careful not to rise to this.

'I can't let you have any files, Konrád,' Olga added, and he realised, with a sinking heart, that she was in her most obstructive mood. 'You know that. You're not in the force any more and we can't go opening up the archives to any Tom, Dick or Harry who wanders in off the street.'

'I know that,' Konrád said. 'Actually, what I wanted was to ask whether *you* remembered the hit-and-run. It's so rare for drivers to flee the scene like that and even rarer for them never to be traced or to come forward of their own accord.'

He had gone online and scrolled through the old newspapers that had covered the accident, finding press photos of the scene, showing a knot of people standing around the ambulance and police cars in the blizzard.

'You're referring to the incident in which Vilmar Hákonarson was killed after being hit by a car? In the winter of 2009?'

'That's right,' Konrád said.

'It wasn't your case. You were on leave, weren't you?'

'Yes.'

'The state of you back then.'

'I know.'

'If I remember right, the accident occurred on Lindargata in the early hours of the morning, during a snowstorm,' Olga said, and he was relieved that she didn't go into the reasons for his being on leave at the time.

'That's right,' Konrád repeated.

'Vilmar was on his way home alone after a night out. He was blind drunk. Judging by the amount of alcohol in his bloodstream it's surprising he was even capable of walking out of that bar. He died from a head trauma and internal bleeding. Have I got that right?'

Konrád nodded.

'They calculated directions and distances and Vilmar's weight. There was a whiteout that night, which made it impossible to measure any braking marks or make a cast of the tyre tracks, since they were buried immediately. In addition to that, the area had been trampled all over by people gathering at the site of the accident. There were no witnesses. The man was believed to have been lying on the pavement for some time before he was discovered – if memory serves.'

'Was there any indication that he had been deliberately knocked down?'

'Deliberately?' Olga frowned and pondered this idea for what felt like a long time. Then she shot Konrád a look, but there was no gleam of pleasure in her eyes now. 'You've got me curious,' she said. 'As far as I can remember, they did consider that possibility but nothing came of it.'

'It would be interesting to know.'

'Wait here,' she said, and went and fetched the files.

There were two folders, and before she knew it she was poring over their contents with Konrád, going through the post-mortem report, sketches of the scene, calculations of the vehicle speed, speculation about its model and total mass, information about

Vilmar's weight and general physical condition, including his blood alcohol level, as well as the weather report for the Reykjavík area that night, precise details of the conditions at the scene of the accident, level of visibility, and finally the names of witnesses interviewed by the police, including those from the bar where Villi had gone on his final bender.

'According to their calculations, it was a large, heavy vehicle,' Olga said. 'Not your average family car.'

'Hang on,' Konrád said, leafing through the post-mortem report. 'The vehicle caught him fairly high up, on his hip and abdomen, and the impact was pretty violent. His pelvis and four ribs were broken – they believe as a result of being struck by the car. Then he received a severe blow to the head when he hit the ground.'

'Like I said, they tried to measure the brake marks,' Olga replied, reading from another report. 'But the conditions made it impossible. They couldn't see any sign that the driver had stopped and got out to see if Vilmar was OK, but then the scene had been trampled all over in the interim. The driver must have carried on, and there's some speculation that the poor visibility might have prevented him from seeing the victim.'

'He can hardly have failed to feel the impact, though,' Konrád said. 'He must have known what had happened.'

'Especially as they say it must have been a large vehicle,' Olga said.

'Like a four-by-four? Or a van?'

'I assume so,' she replied.

'Did the police talk to anyone who had been with him that evening?' Konrád asked. 'Anyone who was drinking with him at the bar, for example?'

Olga turned the pages. 'Here's the name of a friend of his, Ingibergur. He said he was out with him that evening.' She carried on turning the pages. 'It doesn't look as if they got much information out of him, though,' she said. 'I expect he was pissed out of his skull as well.'

25

His name was Ingibergur, known to all as Ingi, and he was the last member of Villi's circle of friends to have seen him alive. They had become good mates while working together on building sites. It was crazy how busy they were in those days, Ingibergur said, reminiscing. Whole new suburbs of houses, terraces and blocks of flats had appeared in a matter of months. Retail outlets had sprung up everywhere, many of them in vast hangars on the outskirts of the city. The housing developer they worked for hadn't been able to keep up with all the invitations to tender for new projects, large and small, and was permanently short of labour. He'd been forced to deal with an agency that provided him with foreign workers, and at one point Ingi and Villi's crew had spoken four different languages, which had led to problems at times. They had been the only ones who spoke Icelandic.

Ingi and Villi were both single, around the same age, and shared an interest in sport. Ingi, who had grown up in one of the more easterly suburbs, supported Fram, the arch-rival of Villi's team, Valur, and their friendship had got off to an unpromising start when Ingi joined the crew and immediately started bad-mouthing Valur. The team had performed disappointingly the previous summer and had dropped to the first division. But as Fram weren't on particularly good form either, Villi had no problem answering back. He was forever referring to the history of the clubs and claiming that Valur had a far more impressive record than Fram. Ingi rejected this claim as absurd and started listing examples of Fram's glorious past. This had caused friction between them at first, but they soon began to see the funny side of their rivalry and discovered a common enemy in the KR club from the west of the city, which they never tired of trashing. Before long, they were going to games together, or to sports bars to watch live match broadcasts and down lager and schnapps until the early hours. That was another thing they had in common: their ability to put away booze.

The alcohol affected them differently, though, making Ingi silent and withdrawn, reluctant to talk to anyone, while Villi, in contrast, became very chatty, overcoming his natural shyness to strike up conversations with other customers in the bar. He knew all the regulars and would greet newcomers like old friends. As the evening wore on Ingi would tag along, silent and unsmiling, not speaking unless directly addressed, and even then not saying much. Once, when someone asked Villi what was up with his companion, he had joked that Ingi was his 'silent partner'.

One evening late in November, he and Ingi had gone to the sports bar as usual, to watch a Spanish-league game. They had arrived early to secure a good table and had it to themselves until the place began to fill up and they were joined by three other fans. Soon the bar was packed and the game began. It was a lively, entertaining match, which generated a happy buzz in the bar. The two friends got chatting to the men sitting next to them, and all agreed that Barcelona had the edge on Real Madrid.

Once the game was over, people started drinking up and going home – calling out goodbye and thanks to the barman, zipping up their jackets and bracing themselves to face the Arctic conditions outside. The wind had picked up during the evening and was now gusting hard, driving thick curtains of snow across the city. But Villi and Ingi weren't bothered, since they weren't going anywhere. Before long they were alone at their table and Ingi had reached the morose stage.

Customers were still drifting off home, and Villi, who had drowned his shyness, started scanning the emptying seats. A handful of women had come to watch the football and a couple were still sitting at the bar. Since they were the same sort of age as the two friends, Villi started giving them the eye and nudging Ingi. But Ingi merely glanced over and shrugged. Just as Villi rose to go and talk to the women, they got up, one kissed the barman goodbye, and they plunged into the storm outside.

Villi went over to the bar anyway to get in another round. As he was waiting, Ingi saw him say hello to a man sitting there and make some remark – about the match, no doubt. The man obviously wasn't averse to being disturbed and they got into conversation. Ingi, meanwhile, remained at their table, hunched over his beer, darting occasional glances at his friend. Then his attention was caught by three women who tumbled in through the door as if blown in by the wind, dusting off the snow and laughing. He hadn't seen them there before and they behaved like it was their first time, looking around curiously and making their way over to the bar where they ordered drinks – colourful cocktails rather than beer – before taking a table at the back, as if they wanted to be left in peace. Ingi was no womaniser. He'd once had a girlfriend but she hadn't stuck around long. He thought about going over and joining them. He had drunk enough by now to get beyond the shy stage, but something still held him back. He didn't know what to say, and didn't want to come across like some creep who'd only gone over to bother them.

After a while, having finally thought of something to say, he stood up and went over. But just as he reached their table he lost his nerve, swerved at the last minute and brushed past them. They didn't give him so much as a glance. Unable to return to his own table for fear of looking like an idiot, he pretended he'd meant to go and sit in the corner, and plonked himself down with his glass, his heart pounding.

Maybe he was drunker than he'd thought. He had no idea how long he sat there, but he vaguely recalled the barman bringing over another two beers for him during that time. When, belatedly, he rose to his feet, swaying, and looked for Villi at the bar, his friend was nowhere to be seen and neither was the man he'd been talking to. Ingi reeled over to the bar and clambered onto a stool, then slumped forward on the counter and fell asleep. He woke to find the barman and another man lifting him up and helping him outside. They were closing. He left the building, still half asleep, and barely even registered the snow as he had the wind behind him all the way home. He could remember next to nothing about his walk.

*

After finishing his story, Ingibergur stroked his beard, then took another sip of beer.

'Villi must have thought I'd left,' he told Konrád.

'And you never saw him again?'

'No.'

26

They were sitting in the same bar as the two friends had been drinking in the evening Villi was killed. It was still run as a sports bar, though it had changed hands three times in the intervening years, but there were no games on at this time of the afternoon in the middle of the week, and the place was quiet, with only a few souls occupying the tables. Soothing music was playing from the speakers on the ceiling. There was a clinking as the barman lined up clean glasses under the counter.

Ingibergur was halfway down his third beer. He had red hair, a ruddy complexion, and a coarse beard that he kept stroking as he talked. He still worked on building sites, he said, having been taken on by a contractor three years previously after a spell of unemployment. He had also done a stint work-ing on the construction of sports facilities in Akureyri for several months, but hadn't got on with the harsh northern winters.

It was Herdís who had put Konrád in touch with Ingi. She knew the name of the building contractor her brother had worked for; and, although he'd subsequently gone bankrupt, he remembered Villi and Ingibergur well. He'd directed her to another contractor, who said he thought Ingi was in Akureyri, and gave her his unlisted phone number. When Herdís called it, Ingi had answered after three rings. It turned out he was back in Reykjavík.

Ingibergur told Konrád he'd gone over that evening so many times that much of his and Villi's last trip to the sports bar was indelibly imprinted on his memory. Certain details, like the final score in the match or what they'd been talking about beforehand, were crystal clear, but most of what had happened after his failed attempt to approach the three women was hazy.

'I should never have gone over to talk to them,' he muttered into his glass, as if still troubled by guilt at having abandoned his friend.

'But you didn't talk to them, did you?'

'No, I lost my nerve. I took a seat in the corner over there,' Ingibergur said, pointing. 'Sat there drinking while Villi was talking to that bloke. I was . . . pretty wasted, to be honest.'

'Villi too.'

'Yes, he was. They did a blood test.'

'He was pissed out of his mind,' Konrád said, to ease Ingibergur's conscience. 'What can you tell me about the man he was talking to?'

'Nothing,' Ingibergur said. 'I didn't get a good look at him. He was hunched over the bar. But I do know that I didn't recognise him and I don't think Villi did either. It wasn't someone who worked with us or anything like that. Just some bloke at the bar who Villi got talking to. He was like that, Villi. He could chat to people when he'd had a bit to drink. But I think I've already told you that.'

The barman who'd been working that night hadn't been able to give the police a very detailed description of the man who'd been talking to Villi, though he had noted that he wasn't a regular, and that he'd been wearing a bulky anorak, like most of the other customers, because of the weather. Some had taken their coats off but he hadn't. He'd been wearing a baseball cap too, so the barman had never got a proper look at his face. The police had appealed for information about the man, on the basis of the few details Ingibergur and the barman had been able to provide, but no one had come forward.

'I know you've heard these questions many times,' Konrád said, 'but do you think they could have left together?'

Ingibergur had often wondered about this over the years, and wished he could recall the evening more clearly, especially towards the end. But he couldn't. He didn't know what had happened to his friend. He had been totally unsuspecting, as he was blown home by the blizzard, that Villi was lying in a pool of blood on Lindargata.

Ingibergur shook his head.

'Did they have an argument?'

'I don't know what they were talking about.'

'Is it possible he was trying to sell Villi something? Dope, for instance?'

'I don't know. Villi wasn't into drugs. So . . . I hardly . . . I don't . . .' Ingibergur trailed off.

'Is it possible they could have fallen out, even if it didn't turn into a shouting match? Could Villi have pissed him off somehow?'

'Why do you think the man in the bar knew something? He was just a stranger.'

'I know, but I'm grasping at straws here,' Konrád said. 'That's the worst part – we've got so little to go on. This man might be able to help fill in the picture if only we could track him down. He won't necessarily know anything, but I think it's important to talk to him anyway.'

'Is Villi's sister still trying to find out what happened?'

'Yes.'

'She was very nice to me when she called.'

'Is there any reason why she wouldn't have been?'

'She's never blamed me for anything,' Ingibergur said. 'It was his idea to go to the bar.' He paused. 'Then he goes and gets himself killed.'

'The man he was talking to was wearing an anorak,' Konrád said. 'Did you notice any logo on it? Or on his baseball cap?'

He had phoned the bartender and put the same questions to him. But the man had served more customers than he could count that evening, as he had on so many others, and had long ago stopped noticing individuals. As far as he was concerned, they'd just morphed into one seething mass of people who didn't want to be kept waiting and had to be served as fast as possible. Besides, he'd been playing online poker in the quieter moments, so his attention had been taken up with that.

'No, no logos,' Ingibergur said. 'He was older than us. At least, that's the feeling I've always had. The dour type. I don't think he had much to say for himself; he just listened to Villi talk.'

'Why didn't you go and join those women?'

'I just changed my mind.'

'Yes, but why?'

'I . . .' Ingibergur hesitated.

'What?'

'I recognised one of them,' he said. 'She was in my class for the last two years of school. Helga. I recognised her as soon as they came in and I was going to say hello but . . .'

'You couldn't do it?'

'No. I . . . I changed my mind.'

Konrád gazed over at the corner where the chicken-hearted Ingibergur had sat that evening seven years ago. 'Villi must have told you about Öskjuhlíd,' he said.

'Loads of times,' Ingibergur replied. 'He was always banging on about it. But then of course you used to run into all sorts on Öskjuhlíd in the old days.'

'Yes, indeed.'

'Like the gays,' Ingibergur said. 'They used to hang out there.'

'So you remember the talk about the gay men on Öskjuhlíd?' Konrád prompted. 'From when you were a boy?'

It had been rumoured that gay men used Öskjuhlíd for their encounters. The police had considered the question of whether Sigurvin might have been cruising there, though he wasn't known to be homosexual. But his sister had dismissed the idea as absurd, and said there was no way he could have been picking up men on Öskjuhlíd – that was crazy. Konrád had sometimes wondered if there might have been other people hanging around the tanks that night who hadn't dared come forward because it had been so much tougher in those days to be gay.

Ingibergur drew a deep breath. 'It might never have happened if I'd been with him,' he said in a low voice.

'Did you usually go back to his place after your trips to the bar?'

'Sometimes,' Ingibergur said, his voice dropping until Konrád could hardly hear him. 'Sometimes to mine. We'd listen to music. He was a good mate. I . . . I was really sad about losing him. Still am.'

'It's tough, losing a friend,' Konrád said. 'I can hear how much you miss him.'

'I still think about him all the time,' Ingibergur said. 'I miss him like hell.'

27

Húgó dropped round that evening with the twins. Their mother was entertaining her women friends and Húgó had taken the twins to a burger joint before stopping off at their grandfather's place on the way home. Konrád was delighted to see them, as always, and joked around with his grandsons before giving them some chocolate ice cream he had in the freezer.

'How are you doing?' his son asked. 'Still obsessing over Sigurvin?'

'No, not really. I've just been looking into a couple of things since he turned up,' Konrád said, switching on the coffee machine. 'I have to amuse myself somehow.'

'You refuse to let it go, you mean,' Húgó said. 'You're determined to find out who put him there.'

'I try not to get bored, is all I meant.'

The boys had sat down in front of the TV with their ice cream and found a film to watch. Húgó left them to it. They could be boisterous at times, especially when visiting their grandfather, who had a habit of winding them up. Anything that calmed them down was a bonus.

'Aren't you just bored and missing work?' Húgó asked.

'No, I'm not.'

'You did when you were sacked.'

'I wasn't sacked,' Konrád protested. 'I took a year out.'

'You didn't take a year out, you were sent on leave. You're still in denial. It's unbelievable.'

'All right, I was sent on leave,' Konrád said. 'Why bring that up now? What's it got to . . . How's it relevant?'

Konrád fetched their coffee, a little taken aback at the turn the conversation had taken. He didn't know why Húgó had brought it up. The fact was, he'd been sent on unpaid leave a month or two before Villi was killed in the hit-and-run. That was why he knew so little about the case. He'd blotted his copybook and for a while it had looked as if he wouldn't be reinstated, but it had been sorted out in the end, thanks largely to Marta.

Konrád handed Húgó his coffee. In looks, Húgó took after his mother's side of the family, which was lucky for him.

'Of course it's relevant,' Húgó said. 'You and Mum. The old Sigurvin case. You were a real mess at the time.'

'It was a difficult case, Húgó. Honestly, I don't know what good it does to rake it up.'

'Then why not leave it alone? You're not in the police any more. It's none of your concern.'

'I don't know. It was a big part of my life. Cases like that, they stay with you. I can still make a contribution. Besides, Hjaltalín wouldn't talk to anyone else. He was the one who dragged me back into it.'

'In spite of everything?'

'Yes, in spite of everything.'

'I imagine Sigurvin's body reappearing like that must have stirred up a lot of ghosts, a lot of uncomfortable stuff you've maybe tried to forget. Then all of a sudden it's brought up to the surface and you have to start processing it all over again.'

'I'll survive. There's no need to worry about me.'

Húgó picked up the wedding picture of his parents from a nearby table. It had been taken outside Háteigur Church immediately after the ceremony. Konrád was wearing a borrowed dinner jacket and Erna a beautiful bridal gown, and they were smiling into each other's eyes.

'It's been nearly six years,' Húgó remarked.

'Yes. Six years.'

After Húgó had left with the boys, Konrád picked up the picture and contemplated it. He hardly recognised the young couple on the church steps. Hardly remembered those days. Him tall and lanky, with long hair. Her wearing her hair down, with a white ribbon round her head, and heavy make-up. He had been twenty-six; she'd been a year older. It had been a beautiful summer's day, the last weekend in June, and their smiles conveyed the certainty that they would be together for the rest of their lives. The news at the time had revolved around fishing treaties and the hay harvest. In the outside world, the usual wars had been raging. They had already lived together for several years, as had been the fashion in those free and easy times, and on the morning of their wedding day he had watched her sleeping until he could no longer resist it and had woken her with a light kiss. Then they had lain in bed and laughed over all the fuss involved in preparing for the ceremony. In those days it hadn't been the norm for young people to get married, let alone to have a church wedding, but they had decided to go for it, however bourgeois it seemed. He had actually gone down on one knee to propose. He had suggested they elope and find a country church where they could get hitched, just the two of them, but she had been afraid of disappointing her family.

'Always thinking of others,' he whispered to the picture.

He heaved a sigh and into his mind came a line from a popular song that he suddenly remembered had been played at their wedding reception; a poignant tune that reached him like a whisper from a long-ago summer's evening:

> *the trial of many an aching night*
> *is to suffer and endure . . .*

28

Konrád rarely spoke of his father to anyone, but he made an exception for Eygló. She had worked as a psychic for a while, just like her father before her. Konrád had met her when he was looking for answers about his father's connection to a crime dating back to the Second World War. The victim, a girl called Rósamunda, had been found murdered behind the National Theatre. When the hunt for her killer was at its height, her parents had attended a seance hosted by Konrád's father, at which Eygló's father had acted as the medium. During the seance he had claimed that he sensed Rósamunda's presence, but one of the other participants had suspected foul play. It transpired that Konrád's father had gathered information about Rósamunda's parents before the meeting and passed it on to the medium. The pair were found guilty of fraud and deception over a long period, and were accused of having deliberately set out to profit from the parents' grief and desperation for answers. Not long ago, Konrád had immersed himself in the details of Rósamunda's case, which had taken place in 1944, the year he was born, and it had turned out to involve soldiers from the American occupation force, leading members of Icelandic society, and residents of the Shadow District.

The one time they'd met, Eygló told Konrád that several months after his father was stabbed to death outside the abattoir, her father, the medium, had taken his own life. She had never received any explanation for this. All she would say was that Konrád's father must have had something on her dad, which he'd used to blackmail him into colluding in their scams. Because her dad had told her he was coerced into taking part in that seance. And he'd described Konrád's father as a bad character. When the two men died in 1963, the war had long been over and so had their fake seances, but Konrád knew his father had associated with some dodgy types and he wanted to find out if there was any chance he could have returned to his old bad habits and started holding seances again.

All this had gone through Konrád's mind when Hjaltalín raked up the subject of his father during their meeting in the prison cell and asked if Konrád had lost interest in his father's fate, perhaps because he thought he wasn't worth wasting any time on. Although Konrád hadn't admitted as much to Hjaltalín, the truth was that he'd been quite preoccupied with his father's death in recent months. The inquiry into his murder had been fairly comprehensive by the standards of the day, yet his killer had never been found. Konrád had looked up the case files after joining the police. The conclusion had been that it was a random killing, which made life difficult for the investigators. His father was simply the wrong man in the wrong place at the wrong time. The chances were that he'd lost his temper with some complete stranger he ran into. But there didn't appear to have been any kind of struggle before he was stabbed, and the motive couldn't have been robbery as his wallet and watch were found on his body. All his known associates, many of them crooks like him, had been questioned, but nothing of any significance emerged.

Konrád himself had always sworn that he knew nothing about his father's movements that evening. His parents had divorced many years previously and his mother had moved with Beta right across the country to Seydisfjördur in the East Fjords. She'd put up with her husband's violence for years, and it had been a marriage in name only for a long time. He'd never had a proper job, drank too much and hung around with other drinkers and petty criminals. When his wife had finally had enough, he wouldn't hear of her taking Konrád: Beta could go with her, he said, but Konrád was staying with him. She was faced with an impossible dilemma but believed that in time her husband would relent and let Konrád join her. This never happened, though, despite all the trips she made to Reykjavík to visit her son and try to persuade her husband to come to his senses and stop using their boy for revenge.

The evening his father died, Konrád was out on the town with his mates. By then he had dropped out of school, started drinking hard and become involved in petty crime. He had done a few jobs for his father, like selling stolen goods and distributing contraband – both from the American base at Keflavík and from the cargo ships – and on one occasion he had broken into a shop selling watches with a mate but ended up fleeing the scene without bringing away any loot. He was on the fast track to ruin, mixing with the wrong company, and deep down he'd known it.

'You must have been shocked,' Hjaltalín had said to him in that prison cell, but that was an understatement. It had been like a punch in the guts when the police broke the news and manner of his father's death to him. Konrád felt as if the shock waves from that evening had been reverberating inside him ever since.

Eygló had been reluctant to meet Konrád when he rang this time but, after repeated requests on his part, she had finally agreed to have lunch with him at a restaurant in the city centre. She turned up punctually, dressed in black as she had been at their first meeting; petite, only a little younger than Konrád but looking good for her age. Her face was as smooth as if she'd never known a day's worry in her life. They shook hands, two strangers linked by a pair of old conmen.

'Do you really think you can dig up anything new on your father after all these years?' Eygló asked, having chosen the plaice from the menu. Konrád ordered the same, remembering how quick she was to get to the point – no beating about the bush.

'A while ago someone asked if I'd forgotten him,' Konrád said. 'Asked if I felt he wasn't worth wasting my energy on. I have to say, I was a bit taken aback. But I have less to do these days and maybe it's taken me all these years to get to the point where I want to know more about my father.'

'He was a deeply unpleasant man,' Eygló said, 'according to Engilbert, my dad. But then you can't have failed to be aware of that. Men like your father make enemies.'

'I believe the police talked to everyone who knew him, as well as a whole load of people who didn't, but nothing doing. I don't really know where to begin looking into his death, so it occurred to me to start with you. Last time we talked you said you reckoned my dad had something on Engilbert.'

'Yes. I also told you that I didn't know what it was.'

'Do you think they'd started working together again?'

'I can't believe that.'

'Why not?'

'Because Dad loathed your father. He thought he was an absolute shit and didn't want anything more to do with him.'

'Is that what he told you?'

'Yes.'

'So how come he was talking to you about my father?'

'He never used to, but one time he and my mother had a fight and your father's name came up – and my mother started ranting about what a bastard he was. Afterwards, I asked Dad who she'd been talking about, and he told me he'd got into bad company when he was younger and had let himself be talked into doing things that he deeply regretted later.'

'Did he tell you what those things were?'

'No. What makes you think they'd started working together again? What evidence do you have for that?'

'Just some stuff I found among my father's papers after he died,' Konrád said.

'What stuff?'

'Some articles about notorious fake mediums and how they'd been exposed. Stories about fraud. Accounts of the Ether World.'

'The Ether World?'

'Yes.'

Eygló gave Konrád an appraising glance. He had noticed before how wary and suspicious she was by nature.

'Was his interest in the Ether World out of character?' she asked at last. 'Was it a side of him you hadn't seen before?'

'Yes, totally. The articles and stories were recent – from a couple of years before his death – and it occurred to me that he might have started messing around with spiritualism again. But I never found any confirmation of that.'

'Do you believe in the spirit world yourself?' Eygló asked. 'Or the Ether World or whatever you want to call it?'

'No,' said Konrád.

'Are you sure?'

'Yes, I'm sure.'

'Then why do I get the sense that you do?'

'Search me.'

'Engilbert respected believers,' Eygló said. 'He had compassion for people who were suffering and searching for answers. But your father didn't believe in anything. He didn't feel empathy for anyone. He mocked people who were looking for answers. How could those two men have worked together? Tell me that. How on earth did their paths ever cross?'

Konrád had no answer to this.

'My father believed in what used to be called the Ether World,' Eygló went on. 'He believed that people went there after their death, that it was as real as our own world, and that from time to time the inhabitants of the Ether World would make contact with us. His role was to mediate those contacts. To act as a channel. Your father managed to abuse that. He perverted my father's talents. I find it painful even to think about and, to be honest, I don't know what to make of you – what to make of your fumblings for the truth. I just don't know.'

29

Hurt though he was by what Eygló had said about his father, Konrád didn't bother trying to defend him. He knew it was a hopeless task, and anyway, her unflattering portrait was nothing compared to what he'd heard from other people. The only thing that surprised him was that his father should continue to evoke such strong reactions so long after his death.

He had sometimes heard his dad talk about the seances, mostly to raise a laugh or share a curious anecdote. The subject had caught Konrád's imagination, and over the years he had acquainted himself with various theories about the afterlife, including the idea of the Ether World, which was no less real to spiritualists than the world here on earth. When someone passed over into the Ether World on their death, so the theory went, their soul took with it all their human characteristics, such as their personality and memories, and these became the basis for a new existence in their 'ether body'. All that was left behind in the physical world was their earthly remains, their dead body, which without its soul was no more than a useless husk. If Eygló's father had believed in this theory, he must have seen himself as having a kind of antenna connecting him to the souls in the Ether World.

'All I'm trying to do is get a better sense of my dad,' Konrád eventually replied. 'I know he wasn't perfect – I'd be the first person to admit that – and if you can't bring yourself to talk about this stuff, I'll understand. I'm not even sure myself what I hope to achieve from my "fumblings". Maybe I'm just trying to get a better idea of who he was. I don't think I knew him particularly well.'

'Sometimes it's better to let sleeping dogs lie,' Eygló said. 'Have you considered that?'

'To tell you the truth . . .' Konrád hesitated.

'What?'

'That's exactly what I've been doing up to now – letting sleeping dogs lie. I reckon I've avoided looking into his death because I dreaded finding out something I didn't want to know. He wasn't an easy man to be around. He was mixed up in various shady activities that wouldn't tolerate the light of day. I wasn't sure I wanted to know any more about him or why he had to die like that. What if he simply deserved it? I expect you've –' Konrád broke off. 'You probably haven't got a clue what I'm talking about.'

'The difference between him and Engilbert was that my father was a dear man who would never hurt a fly,' Eygló said. 'But he was very sensitive and couldn't cope with stress. That's why he drank, I think. I've wondered for years why he killed himself. He didn't leave any explanation behind or give any hint of what he was planning to do in the days beforehand. Or write a note to my mother. Or me. We had nothing to help us understand why he chose to end it all like that.'

'Was it a spur-of-the-moment decision?'

'It must have been.'

'Had he tried before?'

'Yes, actually. Once. Many years before.'

Eygló stared at Konráð in silence and he saw that she had no intention of elaborating. Which he could understand. They barely knew each other and he could tell that she was deeply unsettled by their conversation. 'Did he work as a psychic at all after their war-time scam was exposed?' he asked.

'Yes, he did, but only on a very small scale, for a selected few.'

'And was he successful? At making contact with the . . . Ether World?'

'You can make fun of him all you like,' Eygló said, her hackles rising at what she took to be Konráð's mocking tone.

'No, sorry,' he said hastily, 'I didn't mean . . . I just don't know how to talk about this stuff. I really didn't mean to offend you. It was the last thing on my mind. I'm just not used to discussing the subject.'

'He was a genuine clairvoyant,' Eygló said. 'He gave people comfort. Don't sneer at that.'

'Last time we met you told me he'd been very shocked to hear about my father's death – about how it happened. Can you tell me more about that?'

'It was my mother who told me. She said she'd been a bit taken aback by Dad's reaction. He seemed terrified but she had no idea what of. He would hardly leave the flat unless she was with him. He kept checking that the door and all the windows were securely locked and insisted on keeping a light on, as if he'd suddenly become afraid of the dark.'

'And he only started behaving like that *after* he heard about my father's murder?'

Eygló nodded. 'My mother had the feeling he was afraid your father would come back as a ghost. That he'd start haunting him.'

'Had he ever behaved like that before?'

Eygló shook her head. 'He was very sensitive . . . weak, really,' she said. 'It didn't take much to get him into a state, and Mum said that being denounced as a fraud during the war had knocked him sideways – he'd never really got over it.'

'Because he had the gift?'

'Yes, of course, and because he didn't want to hurt anyone. He wasn't like that. He felt guilty about everything, however trivial, and always wanted to do his best.'

'Was there a post-mortem?' Konrád asked.

'No. They didn't think it was necessary. Everything happened so fast. Why would they have done one?'

'I don't know. It's just something that occurred to me. You said he used to drink. Last time we met, I think you described it as going on benders.'

'Yes, he did. Mum used to be so worried about him when he didn't get in touch for days. She thought he might be associating with people like . . .'

'My father?'

'Yes.'

'Was he drunk when he . . . had he been on one of his benders when he killed himself?'

'Yes, he'd been drinking.'

'Was it your mother who found him?'

'No,' Eygló snapped, suddenly angry. 'You want to know what happened, do you? You think it matters? You want to hear the gory details?'

'Sorry,' Konrád said. 'I didn't mean to be insensitive. I just wondered . . . I don't know how to put it . . . Did it ever occur to you that he might have suffered the same fate as my father? That it could have been a crime?'

'A crime?'

'That he'd suffered the same fate?'

Eygló gaped at Konrád and he saw that the idea had never entered her head.

'No! Of course not.'

'But if they'd started working together again,' Konrád said, 'they might have got on the wrong side of someone. My father's death might have been connected to some scam they were involved in.'

'Is that what you think?'

'They died a short time apart. Do you think their deaths could have been linked?'

'No – impossible. Impossible! Why would that even occur to you?'

'I don't have any evidence,' Konrád said. 'I didn't learn what happened to Engilbert until you and I first met. But I've been thinking about it ever since and wondering if our fathers could have been working a scam together again. I mean, it's obvious from those newspaper cuttings that my dad had been thinking about spiritualism – about the Ether World.'

Eygló sat there in silence, turning it over in her mind. What Konrád was suggesting had never occurred to her in all the years that had passed since her father's death. 'We didn't find him ourselves,' she said at last, in a low voice. 'He just turned up in the harbour at Sundahöfn.'

'How . . . ?'

'We just assumed it was suicide. Though I suppose it's possible it was an accident. He could have gone for a swim or fallen in the sea,' she said. 'In all his clothes. They didn't find any injuries on him. He sometimes used to hang out in the boats down at the harbour, when the crews had *brennivín*.'

There was a crash from the kitchen. Someone must have dropped a plate on the floor. The two of them were almost the only people left in the restaurant now that the midday rush was over.

'Did they measure his blood alcohol? I assume they must have done.'

'Yes. Like I said, he'd been drinking.'

'And he was fully dressed?' Konrád said.

'Yes.'

'Shoes and all?'

'Yes.'

'And nothing had been stolen or . . . ?'

'No. There was nothing to steal.'

They sat there for a long moment, facing each other in silence, as if time had stood still at their table.

'I can't imagine how he must have suffered,' Eygló whispered. 'It makes me shudder just thinking about it.'

30

That evening, Elísabet paid her brother a visit. She was single and had begun to look increasingly to Konrád for company in recent years. She worked in a library, and when he asked how it was going she gave her usual answer: fortunately there was enough to do. People still read books. She also volunteered at Stígamót, the counselling service for survivors of sexual abuse, though she rarely talked about that, but then she had always been unforthcoming about personal matters. She was a big woman, with raven-black hair, a face that tapered towards the chin, and sharp brown eyes above a long, pointed nose. Her clothes were designed to hide her figure: thick jumpers, as many as two or three in cold weather, thick skirts and galoshes. She had a colourful collection of woolly hats as well, and would often cram two on her head at once.

'Are they still investigating the Sigurvin murder?' Beta asked, after she had sat with Konrád for a while and was on the point of leaving. 'Are you involved?'

'I didn't intend to be,' he said, 'but I keep being drawn in.'

Hardly knowing where to begin, he told her about Villi and his sister, Herdís, and the man Villi had seen on Öskjuhlíd. The police were currently evaluating this new information. But Konrád didn't feel that his meetings with Olga and the chaplain really counted as part of the inquiry. That was just his retirement hobby. He had taken early retirement, fed up with police work, and had never felt any desire to return to his job. Perhaps it was just another sign of what had become a common theme in his life recently: he lacked purpose and resolve, which, when you stopped to think about it, was odd for a man his age. He smoked cigarillos but wasn't a smoker. He dabbled in criminal investigations without being a policeman. And, strangest of all to him, he was a pensioner but didn't feel remotely old.

Perhaps these were natural feelings for someone later in life. Konrád was one of the last Icelanders to have been born under the old Danish monarchy. The day after his birth in 1944, Iceland had been declared an independent republic in the pouring rain at Thingvellir. For a brief moment of his life, so brief it was almost immeasurable, he'd had a Danish king.

He had been a sunny-tempered child and never let it bother him that he had a slightly withered arm. His left arm had less strength and mobility than his right and appeared noticeably weaker. When he was old enough to ask about the difference, having observed that everyone else he knew had two equally strong arms, his mother had explained that it had happened during his birth. He hadn't wasted too much thought on it. Since he didn't know what it was like to have two sound arms, he had nothing for comparison. All he knew was that he was a bit different from other people. He had been teased about it when he started school but hadn't let it upset him, and since he was naturally good at PE and swimming, and took part in the other kids' playground games, the teasing soon stopped. As time went on, few people even noticed that his arm was different from any other arm that sported a hand and five fingers. Only Konrád knew how weak it was when put to the test.

His form teacher at primary school had been a God-fearing woman of around sixty, who believed in miracles and urged Konrád to pray to the Lord for healing, in case that would help. Jesus had healed a man with a wasted arm, she told him, and had broken the law of the Sabbath to do so. From what she'd said, Konrád gathered that the son of God was familiar with the problem, and that this should make it easier for him to solve it.

In contrast, Konrád's paternal aunt, a countrywoman from the north who was fiercely traditional in her beliefs and habits, said that his withered arm bore all the signs of being a mark of punishment and misfortune. Not that she thought the poor innocent child was being punished. Oh no, it had been visited upon him as a reminder of past misdeeds. And here she had flung her words at her 'no-good brother', which was her usual name for Konrád's father.

When Konrád was a boy, he had sometimes noticed a short man in an overcoat walking around town and had been told that he was a great poet. Like Konrád, he had a withered arm. He was said to have been given a tough time over it as a child, and that this might have been one of the reasons for his acid tongue and morose temperament, but that the adversity had also helped make him into an outstanding poet.

'Why are you so quiet?' Beta asked, studying her brother, who looked as though he were miles away.

Konrád decided he might as well tell her about his meeting with Eygló. Beta already knew about his theory that their father had started dabbling in spiritualism again before his murder. Konrád now told her how the medium, Engilbert, who had worked with their father during the war, had died only a few months after him, and he raised the possibility that the two conmen might have reverted to their old tricks.

'Apparently Eygló's father got into a terrible state when he heard that Dad was dead,' Konrád said. 'He wouldn't go anywhere alone and had to have a light on all the time in his flat. He became afraid of the dark.'

'I didn't think mediums could be afraid of the dark,' Beta said. 'But, come to think of it, perhaps they'd have more reason to be afraid than most.'

'I wouldn't know. Anyway, then he went and died himself, leaving no explanation.'

'Perhaps he felt it was time to experience the Ether World for himself,' Beta said drily, then added that she had to get going. She had no desire to talk about their father and what had happened to him, and still less about his fraudulent practices.

Konrád remained sitting at the kitchen table, thinking back to the days when he had dropped out of his printing course at technical college. He had been sinking ever deeper into a life of debauchery until one of his less disreputable friends, who had dropped out of the Reykjavík Sixth-Form College but still attended its social events, had taken him along to a play. And there, on the stage, Konrád saw a girl who took his breath away. Her name, he discovered, was Erna.

Much later, after his father had died and Konrád had managed to drag himself out of his feckless, drink-fuelled existence and resumed his course at the tech, she had crossed his path again, as dazzling as a ray of sunshine.

'Is it crippled?' she had asked matter-of-factly, touching his arm.

'Well, it's smaller and weaker,' Konrád replied. 'It's been like that since I was born.'

'That must be hard if you're training to be a printer.'

'I can't complain,' Konrád said. 'I don't know. It doesn't bother me.'

'No, of course not,' she replied. 'You've never known any different. Can you arm-wrestle with it?' She placed her elbow on the table.

'Are you challenging me?' he asked.

'Are you too chicken?'

That was their first meeting. Erna was a top student, who had long had her sights set on medical school and, in the event, had no problem getting in. He had never known what she'd seen in him, but he had realised from the first that she was the light of his life and all the love in his heart.

He would never have believed he could cheat on her, but that only showed how little he knew himself.

31

Konrád was getting into bed when Marta rang. He assumed she wanted to know if he'd extracted any useful information from Linda, but instead it turned out that she had an extraordinary tale to tell.

Just as she was about to leave the office, she had been told that there was a man in reception who wanted to talk to someone senior in CID, someone familiar with the Sigurvin affair. Marta had gone down and greeted the man, who seemed rather nervous, and asked what she could do for him. He had asked if they could have a word in private, so Marta had shown him into her office. The man, whose name was Egill, came across as very embarrassed. Marta was fairly used to dealing with members of the public who wanted to talk to the police about Sigurvin but then failed to provide any genuine leads. Some had developed wild conspiracy theories about the case; others were just a bit odd. Marta got the impression that Egill fell into the latter category and didn't want to waste too much time on him, as she was eager to get off home.

'It's like this,' Egill said. 'We had a new kitchen put in, my wife and I.'

What the hell? Marta thought to herself, stealing a glance at her watch.

'Nothing hugely expensive, just an IKEA job, which I fitted myself. I'm a joiner, you know.'

'Right, I see. Were you happy with it?'

'Very happy,' Egill said. He was around fifty, fleshy, with a pronounced paunch and thick, callused workman's fingers. 'The old kitchen really needed replacing and this was at the height of the boom years, when everyone had plenty of cash and you could get loans for anything you liked. Not that we ever took out a loan ourselves. A consumer loan, I mean. We just carried on driving around in our old car. A lot of people I knew were behaving like idiots, throwing their money around, taking loans right, left and –'

'Excuse me, but weren't you going to tell me something about Sigurvin?' Marta interrupted, trying not to sound too rude. 'Wasn't that why you wanted to see me?'

'Yes, sorry. I just wanted to explain. I do hope we can keep this between ourselves – that it won't have to go any further. What do you think?'

'I still don't actually know what you're talking about,' Marta said. 'And I'm not sure I'll ever find out,' she added under her breath, glancing at her watch again.

'What did you say?' Egill asked, raising a hand to his ear. 'I'm afraid I'm a bit hard of hearing. It's working with all those power tools that does it.'

'It doesn't matter. Please carry on.'

'There was just the one owner between us and him. His name was Jóhann and we bought the house from him – just gave it a coat of paint and moved in, you know how it is, but since then I've been doing the odd bit of DIY, as you do. Fridný had kept saying we needed a new kitchen, so we finally went ahead.'

'Fridný?'

'My wife.'

'I see,' Marta said.

'I'm only telling you this because he turned up on the glacier like that. Otherwise we'd probably have kept quiet. I'm quite ashamed, to be honest. It's been on our consciences – mine and Fridný's. We should probably never have done what we did but we've always taken the view that it was better not to talk about it. We've never told anyone. We . . . basically, we stole it. All of it.'

'All of what?'

'The money.' Egill shrugged as if what had happened had been beyond his control.

'What money?'

'The money we found in the old kitchen. One million in new, thousand-krónur notes. He had hidden it carefully behind the kitchen units before he went missing. It was in an ordinary plastic bag.'

'Who had?'

'Sigurvin. The man you found. We knew it wasn't Jóhann, who lived there before us – who owned the money, I mean. We asked him about it, in a roundabout way. Fridný, that is. She did it very cleverly.'

'Sigurvin? What's he got to do with this?'

'Oh, didn't I explain?'

'No.'

'He used to own our house and was living there at the time of his disappearance,' Egill said, with a hint of exasperation at Marta's failure to grasp the point.

'Sigurvin? Are you sure?'

'Absolutely. We . . .'

'What?'

'Unfortunately, we can't pay it back,' Egill said. 'It's all gone.'

Konrád listened in silence as Marta relayed the joiner's story to him and was as astonished by it as she had been.

'Are you saying that Sigurvin stashed away a million krónur in his kitchen?' he asked, stunned.

'Looks like it,' Marta said.

'But what . . . what did the couple do with the money? Did it never occur to them to hand it in? To report it? What kind of people are they?'

'The poor bloke was pretty shamefaced about it. Apparently his wife, Fridný, is mortified.'

'What did they spend it on?'

'Shares in Kaupthing Bank. Fridný had a cousin who worked there.'

'And?'

'They lost the lot in the financial crisis.'

32

Konrád parked in front of the foot clinic on Ármúli late the following day and stepped inside, straight into a waiting room where two men and a woman were sitting. He enquired after Helga and was asked to take a seat. After a while, growing restless, he picked up one of the out-of-date gossip magazines. It covered the divorce of a prominent business couple; the annual party at a media company, featuring photos of people he recognised from TV; and the opening of a restaurant offering raw food. There was also a titbit about a house purchase by an influential figure in the business world. Konrád flicked through the magazines one after the other, getting a glimpse into the lives of those in the spotlight and feeling ashamed of himself for his interest.

One by one, the customers were called, until at last one of the podiatrists came out and asked if he was Eiríkur.

'No,' Konrád replied.

'Aren't you the one with corns?'

'No,' he said, 'and I'm not Eiríkur either.'

At that moment a woman he gathered was Helga appeared, and he asked if they could have a private word. When she asked what he wanted, he mentioned a man called Ingibergur, who'd been at school with her, and a fatal car accident that had taken place several years ago in the Shadow District. Although he wasn't, strictly speaking, a police officer, he'd been given the job of looking into the accident. This piqued Helga's curiosity. It turned out that she did indeed remember a boy called Ingibergur from school. She showed Konrád into a small office.

'Plenty to do,' he remarked, taking a seat as she closed the door.

'People want their feet looked after,' she replied with a brief smile. 'Look, I don't understand how . . . why you want to talk to me. What can I tell you?'

'I don't know if you remember, but about seven years ago a man was hit by a car on Lindargata. The driver took off and the man died. His name was Villi and he was a friend of Ingibergur's. They'd been at a sports bar together that evening but had got separated. I've spoken to Ingibergur. He says he saw you at the bar that evening. You were with a couple of girlfriends. He'd been drinking and decided to come over for a chat but lost his nerve. I don't suppose for a moment that you'll remember the evening, but I thought it wouldn't hurt to ask.'

Helga watched him, her expression serious, giving every sign of listening intently. When he had finished, she asked: 'What about it?'

'What about what?'

'What's it got to do with me?'

'Do you remember that evening?' Konrád asked.

'I remember Ingibergur,' Helga said. 'But it wasn't quite like you described. Was that his version of what happened? I haven't forgotten. Ingibergur was unbearable at school, always pinching us and making sleazy comments. The evening you're talking about was my friend's birthday. The three of us went out to dinner and then on a pub crawl, and ended up at that sports bar. The way I remember it, Ingibergur was totally pissed and there was a snow-storm raging outside.'

'What about Ingibergur? What did he do?'

'He came over but we refused to talk to him, so he got angry and started calling us bitches and whores. After that we told him to get lost. I thought he might actually go for us, but instead he started puking up. There were these streams of vomit pouring out of him. He caught most of it in his beer glass but some went on the floor. It was absolutely disgusting. He was such an idiot you wouldn't believe it. Me and my friends still talk about it when we meet up.'

'He didn't mention any of that to me,' Konrád said.

'I bet he didn't. He probably doesn't even remember. He was paralytic.'

'But you do know each other?'

'Well, he was in year eight and nine with me,' Helga said, 'but I didn't really know him.'

'Do you remember anyone else who was at the bar that evening?'

Helga didn't even have to think. 'No.'

'You didn't read about the case in the papers at the time? About the hit-and-run? The police appealed for witnesses.'

'No, I wasn't aware of that.'

'There were two men sitting talking at the bar. One of them was Villi. The man he was talking to was wearing a bulky anorak and a baseball cap. I'm trying to find him. The problem is, I don't know his name and have no idea who he was.'

The door opened and one of the other podiatrists put her head in to say she'd tidied up and was going home. Helga told her she still had some things to finish and that she would close up.

'I don't remember that,' Helga said, once the woman had gone. 'I'll ask the girls in case they do, but, you know . . .'

'What?'

'I doubt they'll be able to tell you anything useful.'

33

The next day Konrád rang the childhood friend of Villi, mentioned by Herdís, who had remembered seeing a big off-roader up by the tanks on Öskjuhlíd as a boy. The man proved eager to cooperate and they arranged to meet at a little place on Ármúli where he said he often went for coffee during the day.

His name was Ingvar and he turned out to be a scrawny figure, with several days' worth of stubble and a baseball cap covering a large bald patch, which Konrád noticed when Ingvar removed it to scratch his head. He worked as a lorry driver and clearly loved to talk. He went on at length about what it was like growing up in the Hlídar area and playing on Öskjuhlíd and being a Valur fan, as well as a lot of other random stuff that occurred to him. They were sitting at a small round table, sipping their coffees. The place was cosy and quiet, as the afternoon rush hadn't yet started.

Ingvar turned out to have an extraordinary memory for trivia relating to the Valur sports club. He knew the name of every single player in the handball and football teams, going back many years. He knew all the match results since 1970, and could tell Konrád what Valur's league position had been on any given date. He knew the players' birthdays, which teams they had played for before Valur and where they had transferred to afterwards. He not only remembered all the major games but had attended most of them too, and he knew details about the minor games that even the players themselves wouldn't be able to recall. Indeed, he boasted to Konrád that he had often caught out old Valur players with questions they couldn't answer. And that wasn't all: he knew the family relationships of the main players to other sportsmen and sportswomen, right back into the twentieth century. As a big football fan himself, Konrád enjoyed asking him questions that no sane man should have been able to answer, and never failed to get a reply. Ingvar was almost as well informed about Manchester United as he was about Valur, and his specialist subject was historical match results in the English football league and the FA Cup.

This all came to light because Konrád asked when he had seen the big off-roader, and Ingvar replied that it must have been exactly a week before Villi was chased off Öskjuhlíd, because that evening he had been at a junior-league game between Valur and FH at Hlídarendi, and had seen Valur wipe the floor with the Hafnarfjördur team. He had attended the match with two friends whose names he was able to provide. He could remember the final score and who had scored the most goals, and added that it had been the eighteenth birthday of one of the Valur players.

'So you can pinpoint the exact day?' Konrád said, marvelling at the man's phenomenal sporting memory.

'Yup,' Ingvar confirmed proudly.

The three friends had been delighted with their team's victory and had been reliving the highlights of the game as they walked up the hill afterwards, revelling in the power of the scorers and resourcefulness of the wingmen. Ingvar had nicked some cigarettes from his dad and they were planning to smoke them up by the tanks.

'We thought it was cool,' Ingvar said of the off-roader. 'You should have heard the throbbing of the engine as it drove away. We didn't actually give it much thought, though. I just remembered it when I was talking to Herdís and we were discussing the body on the glacier and what sort of vehicle you'd need to get up there. Villi had mentioned it to me before he died. He remembered the details of the match that had been played at the sports hall that evening, and when I looked it up, I saw that it had taken place the same evening as Sigurvin was supposed to have vanished. It seemed like a pretty amazing coincidence to us. Of course, it was a long time ago, but I'm pretty confident of the timing.'

'Do you know the make of the vehicle you saw?'

'I'm afraid I didn't notice.'

'Could it have been a Ford Explorer?' Konráð asked, thinking about Hjaltalín's car.

'More like a Wrangler. I don't know. I reckon I'm quite good at car models, especially trucks, of course, but I didn't notice that one.'

'Was the off-roader the only vehicle parked there? Was the owner waiting for someone? What colour was it?'

'It was up by the tanks when we got there. Grey, I think. We didn't see inside, so I don't know if the driver was alone, and we had no idea what he was doing there.'

'Do you remember anything special about the vehicle?'

'Just the tyres, really. That's why it stuck in my mind. They seemed so huge. We weren't used to seeing specially equipped super jeeps like that in those days. Now they all seem to be elevated on big tyres, with a ton of extra equipment.' Ingvar scratched his head.

Assuming his memory for other details was as infallible as it was for the fortunes of Valur, Konrád thought it should be possible to rely on his testimony. 'Do you think it was the same jeep that Villi saw up there a week later,' he asked, 'when he had his encounter with the guy who threatened him?'

'He reckoned it could have been,' Ingvar said. 'But he wasn't sure. He didn't remember the massive tyres. So it's possible it wasn't the same one.'

As they carried on discussing the vehicle and its tyres, Konrád discovered that Ingvar had an unusually clear memory of that evening. This wasn't just because of Valur's victory over FH or the team member's birthday, but because his father had spotted the missing cigarettes and given Ingvar a good hiding. It was one of only two beatings he had ever received.

'I came home stinking of smoke,' he said ruefully, 'and it didn't take the old man long to put two and two together. He always knew how much he'd smoked, and had banned me from ever starting myself. He was a very careful man, my dad. Spent two years in the premier league. In football. Scored three goals too. All against Akranes.'

34

Later that day, Konrád went to see the joiner and his wife, to learn more about the fortune the couple had discovered when they finally got round to installing a new kitchen. The stash, consisting of one million krónur in bundles of thousand-krónur notes, had been wrapped in a plastic bag and stuffed into the gap between the oven and the cupboard above it, then concealed by a frontage in the same style as the cupboard doors. The bag, Fridný recalled, was from the Hagkaup supermarket chain. She seemed relieved to be able to unburden her conscience at last. The couple sat in their kitchen, looking as gloomy as if they had a death sentence hanging over them, surrounded by their attractive modern appliances and units, some fronted with glass, others with wooden doors.

'It'll be a pity if it gets into the papers,' the joiner said, still unhappily preoccupied with their reputation.

'You were aware that Sigurvin had lived here before you?'

'Yes,' Fridný said, shamefaced. 'But it could equally have been put there by Jóhann. No one ever enquired about it. So we just held on to it.'

Konrád appreciated her honesty and wondered what most people would have done in their shoes, if they were short of money and just happened to find an unclaimed fortune in their kitchen. It was as if Fridný had read his mind.

'I think most people would have kept it,' she said. 'I think they'd have done the same as us. Seriously. That's what I believe. We're no worse than anyone else, honestly.'

'You spoke to Jóhann, who sold you the house, and he'd bought it directly from Sigurvin's family?'

'Yes, I sounded him out,' Fridný said. 'It was clear he had no idea what I was hinting at. We didn't spend the money straight away, though. We kept it, because we didn't know what to do with it. Finding that bag came as quite a shock, actually. I mean, what kind of person would hide a fortune like that in their kitchen?'

'We were going to talk to the police,' Egill said, 'but somehow we never got round to it.'

'And before we knew it we'd bought shares in that bank,' Fridný said, 'and things went as they did and now we don't have a króna left.'

'Will we have to repay all of it?' Egill asked.

'Do you know whose money it was?'

'Didn't it belong to Sigurvin? Won't we have to pay back his heirs?'

'We can't be entirely sure that the money belonged to Sigurvin,' Konrád said, 'though that's probably the most likely explanation. He could have been hanging on to it for someone else, for example. Really, it's impossible to know.'

'That's exactly what the other police officer told Egill,' Fridný said, with a sigh of relief.

Konrád saw that the couple had brightened up. They had been quite subdued when he arrived and they were showing him where the bag of money had been hidden. The spot was now occupied by a state-of-the-art Italian steam oven that Egill said they never used. Fridný had protested that she used it from time to time. The oven was especially good for cooking the gammon at Christmas; it made for a lovely, juicy roast.

Konrád assumed the other police officer they'd mentioned was Marta. He told them how he himself had investigated Sigurvin's disappearance for many years but that he was no longer in the police force and that these days the case was no more than a hobby. They said they could quite understand that.

'You did the right thing to contact the police when Sigurvin's body turned up. It took courage to come forward and admit what you did.'

'We felt it was only right,' Fridný said. 'We've been feeling bad about it and I can assure you that if we found that money today we'd report it immediately. Without a moment's hesitation.'

'We're not thieves,' Egill said. 'You mustn't think that. It just happened. I mean, what else were we supposed to do?'

'You say the notes were in a plastic bag?'

'Yes,' Fridný said. 'An ordinary Hagkaup shopping bag, like I said.'

'I assume you didn't keep it?'

'No. We threw it away,' Fridný said. 'Without telling anyone.'

'What was he doing keeping so much money in the house, anyway?' her husband asked.

'Dirty money,' Fridný said indignantly. 'It's just as well it vanished when the banks collapsed.'

'Could he have been killed over it?' Egill asked. 'Is that possible?'

Konrád shrugged. He had his suspicions but he wasn't about to air them in this smart kitchen with its Italian steam oven, in the home of the couple who had lost someone else's money.

He took his leave of them and was sitting in his car again when his phone rang. He didn't recognise the number or the voice of the woman at the other end.

'Is that Konrád?' she asked.

'Yes.'

'It's Helga here. I spoke to my friend but she couldn't remember the man you were asking about.'

'I'm sorry, who is this?'

'Helga.'

'Helga?'

'You came to see me at work.'

'The podiatrist?' Konrád said hesitantly, recalling his visit to the clinic.

'That's right,' Helga said. 'Is this a bad time?'

'No, not at all.'

'Anyway, she remembers that evening at the sports bar because of the birthday, but can't recall seeing any man at the bar.'

'Oh well, that's a dead end, then. I thought it was worth trying, though. Thank –'

'But there's something else.'

'Oh?'

'She went home before us and, once we started talking about it, she remembered something that happened outside the bar. There was a man in a baseball cap, like the one you described, standing outside and talking on his phone, and what he said stayed with her because she found it so horrible – the way he said it, anyway.'

'Did she recognise him?'

'No. And she didn't remember seeing him in the bar either.'

'What did she hear?'

'She only managed to catch two words but he snarled them into the phone so angrily that it shocked her.'

'What were they?'

'Kill him.'

'What did you say?'

'"Kill him." Those were the words she heard.'

'Kill him?'

'Yes, she heard him snarl them into the phone, and it gave her such a shock that it must have stayed in her subconscious. She's never forgotten it.'

35

Three ladies of indeterminate age were sitting in the hairdresser's salon, flicking through old lifestyle and gossip magazines as they awaited their turn. The hairdresser was busy attending to two other women. One was sitting in front of the mirror with strips of aluminium foil in her hair, reminiscing about having her hair set, while the other was having her hair washed. As soon as he entered, Konrád realised he couldn't have chosen a worse time to visit. He was about to go into reverse when the hairdresser shouted: 'Are you the cop?'

'No, not any more,' Konrád said, 'but I used to be in the police. I was hoping to talk to . . . Are you Elísa?'

'That's me. Helga's friend. Are you Konrád?'

He nodded.

'She said you wanted to know about that man outside the bar.'

'That's right.'

'In connection with a murder?'

'No, er . . . there's probably no connection,' Konrád said.

'With the murder?'

The three waiting ladies' heads swung back and forth between them, as perfectly in time as seals in a water park. The woman with the strips of foil in her hair watched Konrád curiously in the mirror, while the customer whose hair Elísa was washing, frustrated by her inability to see him, was forced to stare up at the ceiling, her eyes on stalks.

'Oh, look, this is obviously a bad moment,' Konrád said. 'It would probably be better if I came back later.'

'What? Don't be shy. I was just going to take a coffee break,' Elísa said, jerking her head towards a little room at the back where he caught a glimpse of a coffee machine and a paper bag from a nearby bakery. 'Take a seat in there and help yourself to coffee. I'll be with you in a sec.'

At this, the other women all directed glares at Konrád, who responded with a friendly smile. He couldn't tell if their annoyance was because he was going to add several minutes to their wait, or because his conversation with Elísa would take place behind closed doors and they wouldn't get to hear any of the juicy details. He'd like to bet it was the latter. After all, none of them seemed to be in any particular hurry, having presumably planned to spend most of their day at the hairdresser's anyway.

Konrád took a seat. The room was tiny, with just enough space for two kitchen chairs and a small table, on which there was a pot of freshly made coffee. A calendar featuring brooding male models hung on one wall. Through the open door, Konrád could hear Elísa talking to a young woman who apparently worked with her. She filled her in on what needed to be done, then announced that she was going for a break. After this, she joined Konrád in the little room, closing the door behind her.

'Are you always this busy?' Konrád asked, to break the ice.

'Yes. They're terribly loyal, bless 'em, and they love coming here – even if it's just for a chat. There's nothing they like better than a good gossip. Helga told me you wanted to hear about the man I mentioned to her. Was he a criminal or something?'

'I don't know,' Konrád said. 'I'm trying to work out what happened at the sports bar the evening you and your friends were there, so I was very interested when Helga told me what you overheard that man saying.'

'Is it important?' Elísa asked. 'I mean, it was years ago.'

'I want to track him down if I can.'

'Did he do something wrong?'

'I don't know. I'm looking into it for a woman who –'

'Is she related to the man who was hit by a car?' Elísa interrupted. 'The Villi who Helga mentioned?'

'Yes, she's his sister,' Konrád said.

'And you think the man I saw might have run him over?'

'Did it never occur to you to connect what you heard him saying with what happened to Villi?'

'No. It didn't so much as cross my mind. Not for a second. I'm afraid I remember next to nothing about the Villi business.'

'He was knocked down on Lindargata.'

'Yes, so I hear. I vaguely remembered there had been some kind of accident when Helga told me about it but I never made the connection at the time. I have a clear memory of that evening, though, and that gross guy Helga knew who threw up in his glass.'

'You heard two words . . .'

The door opened and the young woman who worked with Elísa interrupted to ask what she'd used on Dísa's hair the last time she'd coloured it. Elísa was able to answer off the top of her head. Another woman, presumably Dísa, was now occupying the chair where the one with the foils had been sitting, and smiled sweetly at Konrád in the mirror. He could have sworn she winked at him.

'You really need to come out front,' the young woman said, giving Elísa a meaningful look. 'Things are a bit crazy out here.'

'OK, I'll be right out,' Elísa said.

The door closed again.

'You heard two words,' Konrád repeated.

'"Kill him",' Elísa said, impatiently now, as if she shouldn't be wasting so much time on Konrád. 'I heard him say it as I was hurrying past him. "Kill him."'

'What did you think the context was?'

'It sounded like he thought it was a mad idea.'

'The man you saw?'

'Yes, the man I heard talking on the phone. He spat out the words. It was like he was arguing with someone.'

'Can you guess what the whole sentence might have been?'

'I don't know. Maybe: "I can't just kill him." Or: "We can't just kill him." It sounded like he was against the idea.'

'Couldn't it have been the opposite? "I could just kill him. We could just kill him?"'

'Maybe. I suppose. He sounded kind of disgusted or angry, like he was arguing about it. Arguing with someone about what he should do.'

'And the sentence ended with those words?'

'Yes.'

'Did he see you as he was saying this?'

'No. I was past him when I heard him speaking and I looked round, but he had his back to me. I just hurried off. I don't even know if he was aware of me. It was snowing so hard and he had his head turned to the wall. I couldn't see his face. Wouldn't recognise him if I saw him again.'

36

About ten days after his father was found murdered on Skúlagata, Konrád was called in for questioning. The detective who interviewed him was called Pálmi. He was leading the inquiry and had been the first member of CID to come round to Konrád's house on that fateful evening. He had been calmly professional and treated Konrád with respect and consideration, unlike the two uniformed officers who had broken the news of his father's murder to him with such unnecessary bluntness that they'd provoked Konrád into attacking them. It hadn't helped that he'd been out drinking with his mates and arrived home considerably the worse for wear, to find the cops waiting for him outside the basement flat. The officers in question had both had run-ins with his father and hadn't appeared sorry in the least that he'd been fatally stabbed.

Nearly two weeks later, Konrád was summoned to the police headquarters on Pósthússtræti, where the duty officer told him to wait in reception until he was called. After a while, growing increasingly fed up, Konrád asked if he would have to wait much longer. The duty officer told him to be patient.

Before coming there, Konrád had seen his mother off at the central bus station. Several days before the murder she had travelled across the country from Seydisfjördur to stay with her sister in Reykjavík. While there, she had told Konrád that she'd met a good man out east and that it was unlikely she would ever move back to the city. Beta was happy in the village – she'd made friends there – and his mother expressed the hope that he might join them in Seydisfjördur. Konrád had never been over to the East Fjords; never visited his mother. When he was younger, his father had forbidden him, and by the time he was old and tough enough to decide for himself, he had lost interest in going. His mother had made a number of trips to Reykjavík, though, especially in the first years after the divorce, and mother and son had at least met up, if briefly, though his father had sometimes insisted on being present.

As the moment of parting at the bus station became drawn out, Konrád had sensed that his mother was troubled about something. Her return ticket to Seydisfjördur had originally been booked for the day after the murder, and she'd got all the way to Blönduós in the north before the bus was stopped and she was obliged to turn round and retrace the almost three hundred kilometres back to Reykjavík for questioning. Before boarding the bus east again, she told Konrád that the police had checked her alibi for the time of his father's murder. As it happened, she'd spent the entire evening with her sister and brother-in-law.

'I expect they asked you the same thing,' she said warily, once all the other passengers except her had boarded the bus. The driver was waiting patiently behind the wheel. It was as if she'd delayed to the very last second before putting her worries into words, but in the end hadn't been able to stop herself. Konrád could tell she didn't find it easy. He'd already told her he'd been out with his mates the evening his father was attacked.

'Yes,' he said. 'They did.'

'And you were with your friends?'

'Yes.'

'And that's really where you were?'

'Yes.'

'Are you sure?'

'Mum . . .'

'Sorry, dear, I know – I know you'd never do it. It's just so . . . the whole thing's so awful. It was hard enough having to leave you alone with him all those years, knowing what he was like, but then this has to go and happen. They might even try and pin it on you.'

'I'll be all right,' Konrád had said reassuringly. 'Don't worry.'

'But what do they want with you now? Why do they want to question you?'

'Search me.'

Konrád snapped out of his thoughts when the duty officer finally called for him. He followed the man into a small room at the back, where he was left to kick his heels for another half an hour before the door opened and Pálmi came in carrying a number of files, and greeted him with an apology for keeping him waiting. He put the files on the table and started leafing through them.

'How are you doing?' Pálmi asked, while he was searching for the right report.

'Were you checking up on my mum?' Konrád asked.

The detective raised his eyebrows as if surprised.

'Are you lot crazy?' Konrád added.

'It was simply part of our routine enquiries,' Pálmi said. 'Just because we talk to people and ask them questions, that doesn't necessarily mean they're under suspicion. You do realise that?'

'You should leave her alone,' Konrád said.

'Thanks for the advice.' Pálmi extracted the correct papers and laid them in front of him. 'According to your mother, you two met up in town the day your father was attacked.'

'That's right.'

'What did you talk about?'

'Nothing special.'

'Did you discuss your father?'

'No. She wasn't interested in hearing about him.'

'We understand you were involved in various criminal activities with your father, though you don't have a police record. Is that right?'

'Who told you that?'

'We've spoken to a number of people and it's come up more than once. Are you saying you didn't buy alcohol and cigarettes for him from the Keflavík airbase?'

'No, I didn't.'

'You didn't do pick-ups or negotiate a price for him on contraband from the cargo ships here in Reykjavík harbour?'

'No.'

'And you didn't deliver smuggled alcohol to individuals and restaurants in Reykjavík and the surrounding area?'

'Who've you been talking to?' Konrád demanded.

'Like I said, we've been gathering information here and there, so don't you worry about that,' Pálmi said. 'Are you also denying that you were with your father when he threatened a man called Svanbjörn, then beat him up?'

'Svanbjörn cheated him and swindled a load of money out of him. Are you seriously going to listen to a word he says? He's lucky I was there or Dad would have finished him off. Was it him who stabbed my dad? Have you asked him?'

'Why should it have been him? Because they had a fight?'

'Maybe he thought it was my dad who set fire to his place.'

'Why do you say that?'

'Just, you know. He did have a fire, didn't he?'

'Did Svanbjörn have any reason to believe your father was responsible?'

'Haven't a clue. Maybe.'

'What do you yourself know about the matter?'

'I'm sure he thought my dad set fire to his place,' Konráð said. He remembered his father coming home one evening, jubilant at having called in Svanbjörn's debt. That same evening, one of Svanbjörn's two restaurants had been set alight. His father wouldn't admit to being responsible but Konráð reckoned he knew the truth. He reckoned the debt had been collected by force.

'Why should he have thought that?'

'Just, you know ... Have you tried asking him?'

'We'll do that,' Pálmi said, making a note. 'What about you yourself? What were you doing on the day of your father's murder?'

'Me?' Konráð said. 'Nothing much.'

The police had asked him this repeatedly, but that was all the answer they had got for their pains.

'We've talked to your friends who were with you that evening, and their statements tally with yours in most details. However, the fact remains that you could have slipped away for a while without them noticing. You could also have asked them to cover up for you. They're not the most reliable witnesses we've talked to, and one of them has a police record.'

'This is such a load of crap,' Konrád said.

'What did you and your father quarrel about?' Pálmi asked.

'How do you mean?'

'What did you quarrel about earlier in the day he was found by the abattoir?'

'We didn't quarrel.'

Pálmi turned over some papers. 'We've been knocking on doors in your street, as you may have noticed, and two of your neighbours claim they heard a loud altercation coming from your basement flat a few hours before your father was found murdered.'

'They're mistaken,' Konrád said.

'Are you sure about that?'

'Yes.'

'But you were both at home at the time in question. You told us so yourself. It was the last time you saw your father.'

'Yes.'

'And everything was fine between you?'

'Yes.'

'Then who was having the row in your flat?'

'I don't know.'

'Did you and your dad often fall out?'

'No.'

'So your relationship was always good?'

'Yes, mostly.'

'Did you get fed up with running errands for him?'

'I . . . I never ran errands for him – as you call it.'

So the interview went on for two hours. Konrád stuck to his story and denied having fought with his father or taken part in any illegal activities with him. Pálmi couldn't get him to change his statement and didn't feel he had enough evidence to take the matter any further. Konrád's alibi had stood up to scrutiny. According to his mates, he hadn't left their sides all evening, and there was no evidence that they were lying to cover up for him.

'You're not really a bad person,' Pálmi said, as the interview drew to a close. 'You've had to cope in very unusual and trying circumstances. It must have been hard for you, growing up with a man like that –'

'Are we done here?' Konrád interrupted, getting up to go.

'I don't think it's done you any good,' Pálmi continued, ignoring the interruption. 'I've known boys in similar situations and they haven't been happy. I don't think anyone benefits from an environment like that, and I think you're going to have a tough time rising above it.'

Konrád stalked out of the interview room, through reception and into the street, then hurried home to the Shadow District. The detective had succeeded in finding his vulnerable spot. The fact was that the neighbours had sometimes heard him shouting at his father. Like, for example, when they'd had that row about Svanbjörn, after Konrád had told his dad he couldn't just attack a man like him, couldn't just beat the crap out of him and set fire to his restaurant. His father had reacted angrily and, before Konrád knew it, they were yelling their heads off at each other and his father was calling him a pathetic cripple and saying so what if he used to slap his mother around, she'd asked for it.

Konrád had been lying to the police when he said he hadn't been talking to his mother about his father when they met up in town that day. He had been lying when he said he and his dad hadn't quarrelled when he got home.

In the end, he had stormed out of the door, beside himself with rage and wishing his father was dead.

37

There was a meeting in progress at the Scout Hut. Konrád took a seat while he waited for it to finish. To kill time, he rang Marta, who slipped him a couple of details about the investigation as if he were still a fully paid-up member of the police.

Linda had been questioned about the cash found hidden in Sigurvin's kitchen and had sworn that it was the first she'd heard of it. She couldn't imagine why Sigurvin would have kept large sums of money at home. She had no idea if he and Hjaltalín could have been mixed up in some illegal business together and fallen out over the cash. She added that she couldn't think what Sigurvin could have been intending to use it for. According to her, neither man had been into drugs. Hjaltalín drank, at times to excess, and so did Sigurvin, but Linda didn't believe he could have been taking drugs without her knowledge. Nor could she remember him being involved in any business venture that would have provided cash on the side. News of the discovery also came as a big surprise to Sigurvin's sister, Jórunn.

Although it had all happened a long time ago, the two men's names were run by the network of police informants in the drugs world, in case either of them could be linked to old rumours about dealing. This angle had been thoroughly explored thirty years ago without producing any results, but in spite of that Marta felt it was worth trying again.

'Hello, Konni, what are you doing hanging around out here?'

There weren't many people who used Konrád's nickname. He rose to his feet and greeted the man. 'I was told you were in a meeting,' he said.

'What do I want with all these meetings?' asked the man, whose name was Hólmsteinn. He was a cousin of Erna's, a tall, handsome, dapper man who wore his age well. He had held various leadership positions in the Scouts, though Konrád was hazy about the exact titles, and he had achieved a great deal within the movement. Judging by the banter he and Konrád exchanged whenever they met at family parties, he had also been careful all his life to sleep with the window open. It was the only Scout law Konrád knew and he made a habit of teasing Hólmsteinn about it.

'But that's the Scouts for you,' Hólmsteinn said, once they were ensconced in the office. 'It's all about being part of one great brotherhood.' He jerked his chin towards the room where the meeting was still in progress. It was clear from his furrowed brow that he was rather puzzled by this visit, since Konrád had never dropped in before. Konrád's explanation that he had some questions regarding Sigurvin's time in the Scouts did nothing to lessen Hólmsteinn's astonishment.

'Actually, I'm looking into the death of another man,' Konrád went on, surveying the photos of all the former Scout Masters smiling down at him from the walls. 'You see, this woman came to me for help, wanting to know if the two cases could be linked. I agreed to try and find out. Then, the other day, Sigurvin's sister told me something I hadn't known before – that he'd joined the Scouts as a boy but dropped out after a year or so.'

'Sigurvin?'

'Yes.'

The old Scout Master swung round to the computer on the desk in front of him.

'I don't remember him,' he said. 'But that doesn't mean anything. Let's see. We digitalised all the membership lists a few years ago. I should be able to find something about him there.'

Konrád glanced at his watch. He had nothing better to do and, anyway, he always enjoyed catching up with Hólmsteinn.

The old Scout Master grew briefly earnest, explaining what an excellent preparation for life the movement was, as if Konrád were a boy applying to join. Konrád nodded to humour him. He couldn't ever remember experiencing the slightest desire to become a Scout.

'Here we are,' Hólmsteinn said, bringing his nose closer to the computer screen. 'Of course,' he said, realisation dawning, 'that's when I was in Norway. I lived there for three miserable years. Did you and Erna never visit me? I was bored out of my mind the whole time.'

'Can you see Sigurvin's name?' Konrád prompted.

'Yes, he was eleven when he joined. For many kids that's the best age to be in the Scouts, but I suppose he must have decided it wasn't for him. According to the information here, he dropped out two years later.'

'Is there any other information about him?'

'No, just that.'

'Did the rest carry on?' Konrád asked. 'The ones who started at the same time as him? Did they go on to become patrol leaders or whatever they're called?'

'Yes, there was a big intake at that time, including lots of promising lads. One of them later became a committee member, I see: Lúkas. A fine young man. I don't know if you've spoken to him. He left Reykjavík and moved east over the mountains – to Selfoss, I think. I don't know if he's still there. He might remember the boy, though. I'll print out the membership lists for you from that period. I assume it's OK for me to do that.'

'Were boys that young ever taken on glacier tours?' Konrád asked. 'Would their activities have included that sort of thing?'

'No,' Hólmsteinn said, reaching out to switch on the printer. 'Are you asking because of Sigurvin?'

Konrád nodded.

'No,' Hólmsteinn repeated. 'We didn't organise any trips of that kind. Not that I remember.'

'OK. That was all, then.'

'How are you doing, by the way?' Hólmsteinn asked.

'I'm fine.'

'You don't find retirement boring?'

'Sometimes.'

'But perhaps you haven't completely retired?'

'Oh, I have.'

'It's never too late to get involved with the Scouts,' Hólmsteinn said with a grin. 'There's always plenty going on here.'

'Thanks but no thanks,' Konrád said.

*

Konrád was initially amused to learn that the meteorologist he went to see later that day was called Frosti. His amusement quickly faded, however, when he discovered that the young man in question was not only arrogant but astonishingly unfriendly. Luckily, the meteorologist didn't recognise his name or connect it to the police, but he did start grilling Konrád about things that were none of his business, like who he was working for and why he wanted the information.

'Who am I working for?' Konrád asked, taken aback. 'No one. I'm here on my own behalf. Isn't that enough?'

'What are you intending to do with the information?' Frosti demanded bossily.

'Nothing in particular. I just need some information about weather conditions during a specific period. I didn't realise they were a state secret. Perhaps I should bother someone else with my request.'

'Weather conditions during a specific period,' Frosti echoed impatiently. 'Have you tried online? You can find information about weather conditions for every month going back to 1997. Don't you have the internet?'

'The period I'm interested in is earlier.'

'Earlier?'

'Look, do you want me to pay you? It's no problem if you do.'

'No,' Frosti sighed with a put-upon air as he sat there in his cramped, stuffy office. He started muttering about members of the public who thought they could just wander in off the street, expecting to find out anything they wanted, free of charge. 'What period are you talking about?' he asked grudgingly.

Konrád was on the verge of telling Frosti to go and stick his head where the sun don't shine, but another part of him was rather tickled by the man's grumpiness. It wasn't often that he encountered a professional who couldn't care less what other people thought of them and behaved exactly as they liked.

Konrád gave him the date of Sigurvin's disappearance and Frosti entered it into the computer.

'I could look it up in our weather logbooks but it's probably been put on the system by now,' Frosti said, more to himself than Konrád. 'You are talking about Reykjavík, aren't you?'

'Yes,' Konrád said. 'To start off with.'

'What, is there more?'

'Have you got the information?'

'Good weather for February,' Frosti said. 'Minus three, gentle wind – almost a calm, very good visibility, no precipitation. Excellent winter weather, in other words. Is that enough for you?'

'What about the Langjökull area? Could you check that for me?'

'Langjökull?'

'Yes, that day and the following one. No, let's say for the next couple of days.'

'Which stations would those be?' Frosti muttered to himself, frowning as he tried to remember the locations of the observation stations around the ice cap. After a moment's thought, he entered the information into the computer, then sighed and tutted. 'I don't know why they had to adopt metres per second for measuring wind speed,' he said suddenly. 'Why go and change a perfectly good system?'

Konrád didn't know what to say. It was many years since the new metric system had replaced the Beaufort scale in Iceland. He vaguely remembered some criticism of the decision at the time but didn't feel qualified to comment.

'Dire,' Frosti said.

'Dire?'

'Yes.'

'You mean the decision to go over to metric?'

'No.' Frosti gave Konrád a look of profound irritation. 'Conditions on the glacier were dire,' he enunciated slowly and clearly, as if talking to an idiot.

38

When he got home from his meeting with the meteorologist, Konrád prepared a simple supper for himself and opened a good Chianti, which had been one of Erna's favourite wines. He fetched the photo of their wedding kiss from the sitting room and put it on the kitchen table beside him, lighting a stub of candle in front of it. Then he put on a CD of Icelandic hits from the 1970s. As the air filled with soft music, he sat there sipping his wine.

Erna had hidden her concerns at first. She wanted to be absolutely sure before breaking the news to Konrád and Húgó. It was relatively straightforward for her to get her diagnosis confirmed, as she was a doctor with a wide circle of medical friends – including several oncologists. She went to a consultant she trusted implicitly, got a second opinion from a doctor she didn't know, then a third from an acquaintance who was a specialist. After that, she didn't bother seeking any further opinions.

Konrád hadn't noticed the change. He hadn't paid any attention when she started taking rests during the day and lost a few kilos. Didn't notice her anxious expression when he came across her alone in the bathroom or kitchen. She wasn't sure what was happening until she had seen the specialist. Once that was over and she received her prognosis, she came home, opened a bottle of wine and waited for Konrád. She had been around death ever since she started in medicine. She knew what had to be done and what she would have to endure; knew how her nearest and dearest would react, and how grief would descend on her home and the lives of her loved ones until it was all over and they would begin their new life without her. She thought about her child and her grandchildren and about Konrád, and wept quietly over her fate.

When he got home that day, Konrád realised at once that something was wrong. She was sitting alone in the darkened sitting room and asked him not to turn on the lights but to come and sit down beside her. She poured him a glass of wine and told him what was happening. She could have surgery to remove the largest tumour, could try chemo and radiotherapy, but that would only delay the inevitable. The cancer had already spread. It was already out of control.

She didn't want to give him false hope, so she stated the facts bluntly, keeping nothing back. Instead of trying to reassure him or allay his fears, she was realistic and described the situation in unemotional, clinical terms. She would have liked to spare him, but that was impossible. The sooner they accepted the inevitable, the longer they would have to make the most of the time they had left.

'We mustn't waste time on unnecessary things,' she said. 'We can't afford to.'

He wasn't able to take it in at first. He kept asking questions, demanding to know how they could cure her and what they could do; what about doctors in America, the latest research? But with every answer she gave him, the reality sunk in, until at last he was forced to confront the truth: Erna had only a few months left to live; perhaps a year, if they were lucky.

'I can't believe it,' he groaned at last. 'I refuse to believe it.'

'Darling Konrád.'

'How can you be so calm about it?'

'I've had a good life,' Erna said. 'I've got you, Húgó, the twins. I've enjoyed my job. I've got lots of friends. I've lived to a reasonable age. I would love to have twenty more good years with you but it's not to be. Really, I have nothing to complain about. It's all a question of attitude, Konrád. That's my attitude, and I want it to be yours too.'

'Attitude?' Konrád said. 'I'm just supposed to accept it, am I? You're just supposed to accept it?'

'It's the only way.'

'There must be other ways, Erna. It must be possible to beat this.'

'No,' Erna said. 'It's not. The only way you can conquer death is by accepting it.'

He often thought of the darkness in the sitting room as they'd sat there discussing Erna's devastating news, and remembered her courage as she'd tried to alleviate his grief and anxiety, as if her own feelings didn't matter. It must have been something she had learnt over the years as a doctor, in constant proximity to death. Or perhaps she had learnt it as a mother, always putting others first.

After that, everything had happened extraordinarily fast. They summoned Húgó and explained the situation to him.

Although he received the news with the cool detachment of a medical man, underneath he was shattered to hear the details of his mother's diagnosis and the fact there was no hope of a recovery.

Erna gave up work and Konrád had been close to retirement anyway, so they were able to spend all their time together. He drove her out to the countryside, where they stayed in good hotels or comfortable farmhouses. They went to places they had always wanted to see but never got round to visiting. She refused to go into one of the palliative care wards, preferring to spend her last hours at home in Árbær. Their bedroom was converted into a hospital room and Konrád and Húgó took it in turns to care for her, day and night, controlling her morphine intake so she wouldn't suffer too much.

The days of mourning following her death stretched out into weeks and months, and they taught Konrád above all just what a rock he had in his son. Although Húgó was coping with his own grief, he dedicated himself to looking out for his father, but he did so as unobtrusively as possible.

At a stroke, Konrád found himself alone at home with nothing to do. No longer working, no longer a husband, no longer supporting a family. No longer anything. In a short space of time, his life had undergone such a transformation that he sometimes felt he no longer existed. He wandered aimlessly through the rooms where reminders of Erna were all around him. All the photographs, paintings, books and furniture had belonged to her; every object evoked memories of their life together. He wouldn't have had it any other way, but as the months went by Húgó began to suggest making changes, perhaps even selling the house and starting again in a new environment. But Konrád wouldn't hear of it, and Húgó didn't raise the subject again, sensing that his father needed more time. There was no more talk of change.

It wasn't any one specific thing that got Konrád moving again, apart from the passing of time, but he slowly began to gather up the shattered pieces of his life and rearrange them into some kind of shape. The pieces didn't necessarily fit together and some of the most important ones were missing, so the picture would never be entirely whole and there would always be a large gap that could never be filled. But among the pieces a pattern began to emerge of what his life would be like now that Erna was gone. Nothing could take away the grief and loss, but he could learn to live with them. His thoughts remained inextricably tied to Erna. There were times when he forgot and picked up the phone to ring her at work, only to remember at the last minute. And in the moments when he missed her most powerfully, he could almost sense her presence and imagine what she would have to say about the matters that were troubling him. He longed to have her with him, longed to talk to her, to feel her close to him; longed more desperately than anything else to be with her, if only for one last time.

Konrád sat there staring at their wedding picture. He had a clear memory of that kiss in front of the church. Of all their kisses. He reached up into the cupboard for another bottle of wine, this time an Australian Shiraz called The Dead Arm. Erna had read about it in some gourmet magazine, and when it turned out not to be available at the state off-licence, she had ordered it specially. She hadn't been able to resist it when she discovered that the vine that produced the grapes had an unusual handicap that it managed to turn to its advantage. One of its branches would wither and drop off once the vine had reached a certain size. This had the effect of channelling more energy into the remaining branches and fruit, resulting in an unusually robust and flavourful grape.

'I just had to buy it for you,' Erna had said, laughing.

39

It had been a while since Konrád had last walked down Lindargata. Once, he had been a frequent visitor, not only because it had
been his childhood home but because there used to be a *Ríki* – one
of the very few state off-licences in Reykjavík – on the street, and
he had regularly shopped there. In those days, self-service had
been unheard of; instead the alcohol had been kept behind the
counter and the place used to be packed with a heaving throng on
Friday afternoons, before it closed for the weekend. An orderly
queuing culture was something that Icelanders knew only from
pictures taken abroad. The crowd used to spill out onto the pavement, and people would push and shove until the crush at the
counter was almost unbearable. The assistants would be flat out,
taking orders from the harried customers and dashing back and
forth with their bottles. In those days the sale of beer was illegal,
and the idea of fine wine for the discerning palate was virtually
unknown. Even if a wine culture had existed, the melee wouldn't

have allowed for any pretentiousness of that kind as closing time approached. The only demand was for quick service. 'Two vodkas!' would come a cry, and notes would be passed across the counter. 'Icelandic *brennivín*!' 'Two bottles of gin!' Notes would be waved in the air. 'What kind?' 'Any kind! And one of *brennivín*!' In comparison, the clamour of the New York Stock Exchange would have seemed positively restrained.

Konrád's first memories were of the Shadow District. The house he was born in had been torn down, like so many others from those days, as the area hadn't been spared the treacherous economic upswing of the boom years. The world of his childhood had been concreted over with high-rise apartment blocks – symbols of the financial crisis, which had been standing empty ever since, exposed to the chill northerly blasts. At the height of the bubble, these derelict blocks had been the most expensive real estate per square metre in the entire city. And now things were threatening to go the same way again.

Konrád halted by the spot where Villi had been run over, and looked down the street at the sheltered housing for senior citizens that now towered over the site where the abattoir had once stood. The area between Lindargata and the sea used to be his playground. When it snowed in winter, the kids would sledge on the mound at Arnarhóll. In summer, they would play hide-and-seek by Broadcasting House on Skúlagata, or sneak into the Völundur timber yard to climb the vertiginous stacks of wood. To him, these childhood haunts seemed no less remarkable than any idyllic valley or mountainside, just because they happened to be in the city. Whenever he walked down Lindargata he was filled with the sense of coming home from some infinitely long journey.

A stone's throw from where Villi used to live, ranks of tower blocks loomed against the sky like a forbidding wall of cliffs. The young man had only been a few metres away from his front door when the car hit him. Lindargata was a one-way street, and the vehicle had approached from the west. If the driver had been the man Villi was talking to in the sports bar, he must have lain in wait for him and seen him leaving the bar and heading home on foot through the snowstorm. He could have shadowed Villi from the city centre, his car crawling after him, probably up Hverfisgata first, then down one of the side streets – Ingólfsstræti perhaps – as Villi turned off towards Lindargata. Once he reached these quieter backstreets, Villi's pursuer must have seized his chance to stamp on the accelerator and run the young man down.

In spite of the poor visibility and the size and power of the vehicle, it was hard to credit the notion that the driver could have failed to notice the impact. No, it was much easier to believe that Villi had been deliberately knocked down. Yet the alternative possibility remained, niggling at the back of Konrád's mind: that Villi hadn't in fact been followed from the bar. That the driver, whether drunk or sober, had simply been speeding down Lindargata and, failing to spot Villi in the thickly falling snow, had collided with him, then fled the scene.

The police had knocked on the doors of the neighbouring houses in search of witnesses, but none of the occupants had been able to shed any light on the incident. It had happened in the early hours of the morning and the residents of the street had been sound asleep. No one had seen or heard a thing.

Konrád noticed a man coming along the road towards him and recognised him at once. It was one of his old playmates from the area. He hadn't seen him for years, perhaps not since they'd both been caught up in the Friday-afternoon rush hour at the long-vanished *Ríki*. His name was Magnús and they used to call him Maggi Pefsi in the old days because of his inability to pronounce 'Pepsi'. Konrád didn't know if this nickname had survived and hadn't liked to ask on the few occasions when they had crossed paths as adults. Magnús had always been amazingly stubborn. Konrád had once seen him force down a whole raw onion that the kids had stolen from the Lúllabúd corner shop, simply to win a bet of a paltry ten aurar. The clearest memory he had of Maggi Pefsi was of the tears pouring down the boy's cheeks as he chomped his way through the onion out of sheer pig-headedness.

'If it isn't Konrád,' Maggi said, holding out his hand. 'Wh . . . what are you doing in this neck of the woods?'

Konrád shook his hand. They were around the same age, Maggi perhaps a couple of years older, though he had been rather a timid, introverted character as a boy, perhaps because of his stammer. He had lived with his mother in a pretty, well-kept house on Lindargata, and still lived there now. His mother was long dead and Maggi had never married, never moved out of the area or found the right person to spend his life with. At one time he had at least made an effort to change this, but his mother had been very critical of potential girlfriends and extremely disapproving of any attempt on his part to make her share him. Despite his obstinacy in other matters, Maggi had never had the guts to stand up to his mother and so he had been left alone in the world when she died.

'You never moved,' Konrád observed.

'No, and I'm not likely to now,' Maggi said. 'Just having a look around for old times' sake, are you?'

'Yes, I suppose so,' Konrád said. 'It's a while since I've been down this way.'

'I don't know what I'm still doing here,' Maggi said, wiping a drip from his nose with the back of his hand. 'Everything else has gone, G . . . God knows. Everything except me.'

'The area's almost unrecognisable.'

'Life's pretty unb . . . unbearable here nowadays, what with the racket from the student flats they've built where the *Ríki* used to be, and those m . . . monstrosities they've built all the way down to the sea. You remember what the view used to be like, over the sound and the islands, all the way to Mount Esja? Well, that's all been taken away and those p . . . p . . . piles have been p . . . plonked down right in our faces. Who would dream of p . . . putting up walls like that to b . . . block the view for everyone else? Building high-rises at the bottom of the slope and overshadowing the entire existing area?'

'They saw it as ripe for development,' Konráð said drily.

'Well, they can get st . . . stuffed. Arseholes.'

'You're telling me.'

'It's all gone: the abattoir, the timber yard, the Kveldúlfsskáli fish-processing building, B . . . Broadcasting House, Lúllabúd and all the rest of the shops. Everything except the National Theatre, and I never go there.'

'Tell me something – do you by any chance remember an accident in this street some years ago?'

'Accident?'

'A pedestrian was hit by a car . . .'

'You m . . . mean, when Villi died?'

'Yes, did you know him?' Konráð asked, surprised.

'Not really, he hadn't lived here long. I spoke to him m . . . maybe twice. A nice lad, if that's what you're asking. The police never found the driver, did they?'

Konrád shook his head. 'You didn't see anything yourself?' he asked.

'N . . . no,' Maggi said. 'Vigga said she f . . . found him. You remember her.'

'Yes, I remember Vigga,' Konrád said, recalling the woman who used to live in a dilapidated house on the street and who had scared the living daylights out of him as a child. She used to look like a tramp with her layers of ragged jumpers, her wild mop of grey hair and the grim lines of her face that never softened. He had a feeling she'd even done a spell in the dreaded Kleppur Asylum. As kids, they had taken care never to lose a ball in her garden. At times she used to shriek curses at them if they so much as dared to walk past her house. She had even been known to stop and scold children on the pavement outside for no good reason. If a child wandered into the area selling stamps and unwittingly knocked on her door, he risked a slap and an earful of abuse. Sometimes she dragged kids inside her house to read them the riot act. All this did was turn the children in the area against her. They used to play pranks on her and torment her by breaking her windows or banging on her door and running away. Once someone had even set fire to her lean-to.

'As a matter of fact, I went to see her about something not that long ago,' Konrád said, thinking back to when he'd turned to Vigga for help over the complicated wartime case in which his father had been involved. But he couldn't remember coming across any mention of her in the police reports on Villi's accident.

'Yes, she died back in the summer, p . . . poor thing. Spent several years in a nursing home, c . . . crazier than ever.'

'She's dead is she?' It was the first Konrád had heard of it.

'It was all very low-key,' Maggi said. 'I told them at the home to get in touch with me when she kicked the b . . . bucket, because she didn't have any family of her own. So I took c . . . care of the rest, as they say. She wanted to be cremated. Her ashes are in the cremation plot in Fossvogur. Imagine living that long and still telling the world to go f . . . fuck itself. She made it to a hundred, you know.'

'Her name isn't mentioned in the police file on the accident.'

'They wouldn't have known. She didn't tell anyone. She only told me about it a c . . . couple of years ago, when I looked in on her at the nursing home and the accident happened to c . . . come up in conversation.'

'What did she say?'

'It was all very vague. I just happened to m . . . mention Villi because he used to rent the place next door to her. She seemed to remember him. Said she'd found him on the p . . . pavement. Something like that. I d . . . didn't know whether to take her seriously.'

'Then what?'

'That was it.'

'She said she'd found him on the pavement?'

'I don't remember exactly what she said but it was something like that.'

'Did she help him? Did she talk to him?'

'I couldn't get any more out of her. She was pretty confused, poor thing. Out of it, you know. She thought she was b . . . being attacked by all kinds of weird creatures that only she could see.'

'What did you and Villi talk about the couple of times you met him?' Konrád asked. 'Do you remember at all?'

'He was a Valur supporter like me. It was something about foot-ball. Nothing imp . . . important. He was a good lad. It was tragic what happened to him.'

The two old playmates stood there for a while without speaking.

'You never got to the b . . . bottom of that b . . . business with your dad, did you?' Maggi asked eventually.

Konrád looked at him. 'No.'

'Strangest thing.'

'Yes, the strangest thing,' Konrád agreed, hoping Maggi wouldn't pursue the subject.

'Did you hear about Polli?' Maggi said suddenly, a new thought occurring to him. 'He's d . . . dead. Heart attack. Mind you, he'd got bloody fat. I used to work with him at the shipyard in the old days.'

'Polli?'

'Yes, you remember him? Lost all his t . . . teeth. Claimed he'd fallen downstairs. Weren't you in the same class?'

'Yes, for one winter. Then he left. So he's dead, is he? When did that happen?'

'Ab . . . about two weeks ago. You two didn't g . . . get on, did you?'

'No.' Konrád remembered Polli all right. He'd been a thug. 'I suppose she'd have been by far the oldest resident left in the area?' he said, bringing the conversation back to Vigga.

'Yes, no d . . . doubt.'

'Vigga and I didn't exactly get on either,' Konrád remarked.

'No, she was a difficult woman,' Maggi said, sniffing loudly, and Konrád had a flashback to him as a boy, standing in a back garden on Lindargata, eating that stolen onion for a ten-aurar bet while the tears streamed down his cheeks.

Come to think of it, Konrád was pretty sure Maggi had never actually got his ten aurar.

Finally, unable to restrain himself any longer, he asked: 'Do you still drink Pepsi, Maggi?'

'What, Pefsi?' Maggi said. 'Ah, you can't b . . . beat it.'

40

That evening, Konrád found some music from the sixties that Húgó had downloaded onto a tablet for him at Christmas. While the songs echoed around the house, Konrád absent-mindedly took some bits and pieces out of the fridge and sat down at the kitchen table to eat them. He couldn't stop thinking about Lindargata, about Maggi and the other friends of his youth, about his parents and old Vigga. Lindargata was never far from his heart and, whatever happened, the world of the Shadow District would always, in some indefinable sense, be his world. The calls from the abattoir, the smartly dressed theatre guests, the smell of sawdust from Völundur, the hustle and bustle of the city centre, the sailors on the docks, it all still existed in his head – the world of his childhood, always within reach, to be revisited whenever the mood took him. It didn't matter how many high-rises they built, they would never be able to overshadow his memories.

Vigga was part of it. One winter evening, egged on by his friends, Konrád had decided to play a practical joke on her. He had crept up the icy steps to her front door, kicked it twice, then bounded back down the steps, quick as a flash, only to run slap into Vigga at the bottom. She'd been in her shed and had come round from the garden, catching Konrád in the act. He was so terrified he thought he might wet himself, thereby compounding his humiliation. Vigga had a torch in one hand but grabbed his shoulder with the other.

'You little pest!' she hissed.

He froze in terror and didn't put up any resistance as she dragged him round the back of the house, opened the shed, threw him in and locked the door. It was pitch-black inside, and fear of the dark now assailed him on top of his other woes.

'Right,' he heard Vigga say angrily outside. 'You can spend the night in there.'

Then she had left.

As a final humiliation, Konrád had felt something warm seeping from his crotch down his leg and into his shoe. He was seven years old, paralysed with fear and shaking like a leaf.

The other kids had hurried off to fetch his mother, who came and had a word with Vigga, rescued her son from his prison and gave him a long lecture about not tormenting the old woman because she had already suffered enough. She had lost her only child and, for her, life was like one never-ending attack, against which she felt she had to defend herself with tooth and claw.

'Her child?' Konrád had echoed.

'Yes, she's been unhappy ever since.'

Was it possible that Vigga had come across Villi lying in the street before another pedestrian found his body and notified the police? He had lived next door to her for a while. He'd known Magnús, from across the road, to speak to. Surely it was perfectly possible that Vigga had come outside after the accident? Konrád wondered if she had witnessed it. Seen the driver, maybe. She hadn't called the police or an ambulance. If she had, the police would have known about her. And she hadn't tried to get Villi into shelter. Konrád puzzled over the question of why, in that case, she had gone out to him.

Could Villi have died in Vigga's arms?

The alternative was that it hadn't really happened. That she had lied about it to Magnús. It had certainly escaped the notice of the investigating officers that Vigga was a possible witness. But then this didn't come as any real surprise to Konrád, since Vigga had always minded her own business and other people had given her a wide berth in return. The old woman had been capricious. It was quite possible that the police had talked to her along with the other residents in the street but that she hadn't told them. And even if she had, she probably wouldn't have been considered a reliable witness. People who didn't know Vigga generally didn't want to spend any more time with her than was necessary.

Konrád decided to call his sister. Beta answered after a few rings and he told her about his visit to the Shadow District and that Vigga had passed away.

'Oh, the poor woman's died, has she?' Beta had always defended Vigga and never taken part in teasing her. Even as a child she had felt sorry for the reclusive woman and had tried her best to stop the other kids from picking on her.

'There's a chance she may have been the last person to see Villi alive – you know, the man I told you about the other day.'

'The one who was knocked down on Lindargata?'

'That's the one. It seems she may have seen what happened and gone out to him. At least, she told Maggi she'd found him on the pavement. You remember him – Maggi Pefsi?'

'Maggi? Does he still live there?'

'Yes. He stayed in touch with Vigga. The old girl would have been well into her nineties at the time.'

'Does he believe that Vigga witnessed Villi being hit by the car?'

'She could have done.'

'So she might have seen the person who did it?'

'It's possible, but you know what she was like – not quite all there.'

'Vigga was OK. She was always nice to me, even if she made you wet yourself with fright.'

'She locked me in her shed,' Konrád pointed out.

'Wasn't that Villi full of conspiracy theories about the Sigurvin case?'

'Yes, and he told them to anyone who would listen. He was a witness. Not a particularly good one, but a witness all the same, and if he was rattling on about what he'd seen to complete strangers in sports bars, it could well have had repercussions.'

'Are you suggesting that someone implicated in Sigurvin's disappearance could have run him down?'

'That's what I've been wondering,' Konrád said, 'though I doubt we'll ever know.'

'Wouldn't that be a sign of desperation? Resorting to something that drastic?'

'Yes, I imagine you'd have to have tipped over the edge to do something like that.'

'It's not exactly healthy having a death on your conscience.'

'No, quite. Keeping a secret like that for thirty years must take a lot of energy and would probably cause a lot of distress.'

'Are you hoping he'll give himself up in the end? Give in to his conscience? It wouldn't be unheard of.'

'Well, there are some types out there who'd have no problem coping with that kind of guilt. But others would be constantly tortured by it.'

'Then again, Villi's death might not have had anything to do with Öskjuhlíd,' Beta cautioned. 'You just want it to. You want to believe in a conspiracy, in tenuous links. In coincidences. Words accidentally blurted out in a sports bar that resulted in a man's death. That's how your mind works. You think like a cop.'

'Someone has to.'

The notes of the last song died away. Silence descended on the house.

'It's unbelievable how the local kids used to torment her,' Beta remarked, her thoughts obviously straying back to Vigga.

'What was it Mum said about Vigga? That she'd lost her child?'

'Yes. Mum found out about it, though I don't know how, as it wasn't like they were friends. Mum said it had been some childhood illness. That's all she knew: that Vigga had a child who died very young and the grief left her devastated. She never got over it.'

'Understandably.'

'Yes, understandably.'

41

Once they had rung off, Konrád put on more music and was just uncorking a bottle of wine when the phone rang. It was Herdís. She apologised for disturbing him at this hour and Konrád told her not to worry about it, it wasn't that late.

'I just wanted to know if there was any news,' she said.

'Actually, I was going to call you tomorrow,' Konrád said. 'Do you remember if Villi ever mentioned an old woman who lived near him on Lindargata? She was always known as Vigga.'

'Vigga?'

'A recluse. She had no family. A bit of a prickly character. I wondered if he'd ever mentioned her in your hearing?'

'Is that the old woman who was a bit odd?'

'So he did know her?'

'Not well, I think. He once told me about a woman who lived on his street who was very old. I don't remember her name. I never met her myself.'

'But they knew each other to say hello to?'

'I think so. What about her?'

Konrád described his visit to the Shadow District and what Maggi had told him about Vigga and her claim to have found Villi after the accident. Herdís listened to his story in silence. It was news to her that her brother might not have been alone when he died.

'Was it true?'

'It may have been,' Konrád said.

'Then why didn't she go for help? Why didn't she call the police?'

'Vigga was a very eccentric woman,' Konrád said. 'Things didn't necessarily happen the way she said. We can't be certain that she saw the accident or went out to Villi. But it could have happened. There's no reason to dismiss the possibility entirely.'

'So he wouldn't have died alone?'

'It's possible she was with him. It's also possible that he was dead when she found him.'

'I don't know . . . It's hard to take in, so long afterwards.'

'Yes, I can imagine.'

'Why didn't she tell someone straight away?'

'Like I said, she was a very eccentric character.'

A pause developed. Konrád knew Herdís would need time to process the news.

'There's one thing I can't stop thinking about,' she said at last.

'What's that?'

'If there was nothing more to it, if Villi's death was an accident, why didn't the driver stop and try to help him? It's weird that he didn't.'

'I know.'

'He might have been able to save him. So why didn't he?'

'Because he meant to knock him down,' Konrád said.

'That has to be the explanation, doesn't it?'

'Maybe. Maybe that's the only plausible explanation.'

Konrád poured himself a glass of wine and sipped it, lost in the reminiscences stirred up by his conversation with Maggi. Although most of the kids at school had left him alone about his withered arm, there had been exceptions, especially after he started at secondary school. And now Polli was dead . . .

Konrád had never told his father about Polli and the hassle the boy had caused him that would nowadays be described as bullying. Back then, it didn't have a name. Konrád had tried to ignore it but his tactic hadn't worked; in fact, it had had the opposite effect.

Polli had been a new boy in the dunces' class, a problem kid from Keflavík who had just moved with his parents and two sisters to a basement flat on Thingholt. He was big, strong and stupid, and soon developed a peculiar obsession with Konrád and his arm.

At first, it seemed as if Polli wanted to make friends with him, but Konrád didn't give him the chance – his gut instinct telling him that he would do better to avoid the new boy. This only made Polli more curious, if less smarmy. He blocked Konrád's way one day after school and asked if he could see his bad arm. Konrád didn't answer and was about to continue on his way when Polli shoved him into the road and asked if he was crippled in the head too. Konrád retreated before Polli's superior strength, but that was only the beginning. After that he had grown afraid of Polli, who used to tease him and call him names, or corner him and aim blows at him that Konrád was powerless to withstand. Even when his clothes were torn or he was given a bloody nose and bruises, he never complained or reported Polli; and if anyone asked what had happened, he would invent excuses. Things went on like that for much of the winter.

Konrád wasn't the only boy Polli picked on. His speciality was pulling down the weaker boys' trousers in front of everyone in the playground. Once, shortly after New Year, he managed to rip Konrád's trunks off during a swimming lesson and pushed him stark naked into the pool. Then he waved the trunks around like a trophy so everyone would see Konrád's humiliation. When no one laughed, most of Polli's glee faded and he chucked Konrád's trunks into a rubbish bin, from which one of his classmates retrieved them and handed them back to him in the pool.

And so it had continued, with blows, kicks and insults, until one day they had a PE lesson. Konrád had dawdled behind in the showers – as sometimes happened, because he loved to linger under the jet of hot water. Next minute, Polli appeared in front of him, naked, and asked if he wanted to touch his dick. Instead of answering, Konrád tried to dodge and make a dash for the changing rooms, but Polli grabbed him and started groping and rubbing up against him. Finally, Konrád managed to hit him in the face, hard enough for Polli to lose his grip, which gave him a chance to wriggle free. He was about to run out into the corridor with his clothes in his arms when the supervisor appeared in the doorway. He demanded to know where Konrád was rushing off to and why he was still messing about in the changing rooms when the others had already left, and ordered him to hurry up and get dressed. Polli didn't make a sound from the showers. Konrád said he'd lost track of time and quickly pulled on his clothes. He was still dragging his jumper over his head as he emerged into the corridor and set off for home as fast as his legs would carry him.

It was then that Konrád realised this had to stop and that only he could make it. Shortly after the incident in the showers, he sneaked to his father's toolbox, dug out a heavy plumber's wrench, weighed it in his hand and decided it would do. He walked up the hill from the Shadow District, over Skólavörduholt to Thingholt, and staked out the basement flat where Polli lived. Polli didn't emerge that evening or the following one, but the third evening – after Konrád had waited outside, shivering in the cold, for more than an hour – the door opened, and Polli came up the steps and headed over the hill in the direction of the Hlemmur bus station. It was a bitterly cold evening with drifting snow, and Polli set a fast pace through the winter darkness.

Konrád silently followed. At the top of Skólavörduholt hill, where it was darkest, he called Polli's name. The boy stopped dead and turned, looking rather nonplussed when he saw the pathetic cripple staring back at him. Before he had time to ask what he was doing there, Konrád walked up to him without a word or a moment's hesitation and, raising the wrench with his good arm, smashed it into Polli's face. The blow caught the other boy on the cheek, breaking the skin, and Polli yelped with pain. The attack was unexpected and savage, and Polli never had a chance to defend himself. Konrád followed it up with a blow to his knee, causing Polli to stumble; and before the bully knew what was happening, he had been struck again in the face, above the eyebrow. This time he fell over backwards, banging his head on the paving stones. Reacting quickly, Konrád landed a fourth blow in his enemy's face. This was the heaviest of all and caught Polli square on the half-opened mouth, breaking six of his teeth and almost knocking him out cold.

As Polli lay on the ground, barely conscious and groaning with pain, Konrád aimed a final kick at him before turning and walking calmly back down the hill to the Shadow District. Once he got home, he rinsed the blood off the wrench, dried it carefully and put it back in the toolbox. His father had once taught him two rules for winning a fight if he was faced with overwhelming odds: first, take your opponent by surprise if possible, so he doesn't know what has hit him until it's too late; second, don't show a moment's hesitation, and really make your opponent hurt.

Polli told everyone he'd fallen over when they asked about his injuries. After that, no one had any further problems with him, and he left the school that spring.

42

Konrád woke up with a headache. He had finished the bottle and opened another, smoked several cigarillos and listened to more music before dozing off on the sofa. At some point in the night he had stirred and taken himself off to bed, but hadn't been able to get back to sleep. In the end he had got up and fetched a sleeping pill, and after that he had finally conked out.

It was past midday when he drove at a leisurely pace east over the mountains to the little town of Selfoss, where he had arranged to meet Lúkas, one of the men who, according to Hólmsteinn, had been a contemporary of Sigurvin in the Scouts. Konrád had been deliberately vague on the phone when he'd explained what he wanted, just talking in general terms about old comrades in the Scouts and casually mentioning Sigurvin's name. Lúkas was surprised by the request, having heard of the case like everyone else, and invited Konrád to meet him at a cafe in Selfoss. Konrád found it in good time and parked outside. The welcoming interior was fragrant with the smell of coffee and freshly baked bread when he entered and looked around for the man he'd come to meet. It was quiet at that time of day, and a man immediately got up from one of the tables and came over to greet him.

They sat down with their coffees. Like the rest of the country, Selfoss and the surrounding district had been badly hit by the recession following the financial crisis. Unemployment had risen and many people had been struggling before tourism took off in a big way. Lúkas himself had been without work for two years and lost his house because he hadn't been able to pay off his debts. He told Konrád that he and his wife now rented a small flat belonging to a cousin of hers. He had got back on his feet, taken a course at guide school, and for some time now had been kept busy driving a tourist bus around the main sights in the south-west, like the falls at Gullfoss and the hot springs at Geysir.

Lúkas paused to drink his coffee. When Konrád asked if he could offer him a slice of cake or a sandwich, he declined. He had coarse features in a broad face and untidy light-brown hair, and wore what Konrád thought of as a typical tourist-guide uniform of thick anorak and hiking boots. Lúkas told him he'd been born and brought up in Reykjavík. It had been going to film showings at the YMCA as a boy that had led to his joining the Scouts.

Lúkas had good memories of those days and clearly enjoyed reminiscing about them. He described himself as a Reykjavík boy through and through, and said he would move back to the city like a shot if the house prices weren't so outrageous. He often had to go there for work and didn't like the commute, especially during cold spells in winter when he risked getting stuck in a blizzard on the mountain road over Hellisheidi.

'I'm with you on that,' Konrád said with feeling.

They drank their coffees unhurriedly, chatting about road conditions and house prices and what it was like growing up in Reykjavík in the old days and how the city had changed, before Konrád finally brought the conversation back to the Scouts.

'We couldn't really afford the whole uniform,' Lúkas said, smiling nostalgically. 'Those itchy green knee socks and the cap and all that. We used to march on the official First Day of Summer in April, usually in freezing weather. And for National Day on 17 June, usually in pouring rain. But it was a laugh. And the camps were fun. The people in charge were good guys too. I have nothing but fond memories of the Scouts.'

'I spoke to a veteran Scout Master called Hólmsteinn . . .'

'Oh, yes, old Hólmsteinn.'

'He told me you'd been in the same troop as Sigurvin, but that he hadn't stayed very long.'

Lúkas looked at Konrád. 'Excuse my asking, but didn't you use to be a policeman?'

Konrád nodded.

'I thought I recognised you,' Lúkas said. 'I remember you from the news reports at the time, as well as the more recent TV programmes and articles about the case. Are you still working on it?'

'No, actually,' Konrád said. 'I'm looking into another, possibly related crime,' he added, without elaborating.

Lúkas seemed satisfied by this reply. 'I do remember Sigurvin,' he said, 'mainly because of what happened to him, I expect. Like you said, he wasn't in the Scouts long but we were in the same troop, and as far as I can recall he was a nice kid. A bit shy, maybe, and I had the feeling he soon got bored of the Scouts. But he fitted in well with a group of us who'd joined before him: Gúndi and Siggi and Eyjólfur and . . . then he left and . . .'

'Did your paths never cross afterwards?'

'No, never. Next time I heard of him, his picture was all over the papers and he'd been reported missing. That business they were involved in – him and that friend of his . . . wasn't it all because of that? I've seen how stupid money can make people. We all learnt our lesson about that – the whole country.'

'You yourself continued in the Scouts?' Konrád said, not letting himself be sidetracked into talking about the crash again.

'Yes, several of us carried on and that led naturally to volunteering for the search and rescue teams later, though I didn't do that for long. Some of my mates were in the Reykjavík rescue team but I soon got work on the cargo ships and couldn't take part in any exercises. And once I'd left the sea, I moved over here to Selfoss. I was on the Scout Committee for a while, though, and I'm available whenever they have events here. I always tell them they can call on me if it's important – if they need helpers.'

'Did any of your mates get caught up in the craze for super jeeps, that you remember?'

'Super jeeps? No, not that I recall.'

'Any of them have a big off-roader?'

'Those boys? They had nothing.'

'What about later, when Sigurvin disappeared? Or even as late as 2009?'

'Well, it's possible, but I wouldn't know. Why 2009?'

'It's connected to one aspect of the case,' Konrád said. 'The rescue teams must have had those monster jeeps equipped with walkie-talkies and so on.'

'Yes, I'm sure.'

'And big aerials?'

'Yes. You need good equipment if you're undertaking search and rescue operations in the highlands.'

'And on the ice caps?'

'Sure.'

The cafe was growing busier. The two men finished their coffees and Lúkas's phone rang. A tour group was waiting for him. They parted outside and Konrád strolled down to the River Ölfusá a short distance away and stood there for a while, contemplating its turbulent grey waters. The river held a strange fascination for him. He remembered from his geography lessons at school that its main source was meltwater from the Langjökull glacier, some seventy kilometres to the north. As he stood there gazing at the glacial torrent, his mind travelled upstream into the highlands, where the secret had lain frozen all those years, and he pictured again the desiccated grin Sigurvin had worn when he finally came down from the ice cap, as though he were laughing in Konrád's face.

43

Konrád called Marta on his way back to Reykjavík, to say he needed the name of the detective who had led the investigation into Villi's death. Marta reacted irritably, demanding to know what for, to which Konrád replied vaguely that he just needed some information on one or two things relating to the inquiry.

'One or two things?' Marta said sceptically.

'Yes, just general information.'

'Like what?'

'Who they talked to. What emerged from the interviews.'

'Nothing emerged from them,' Marta said.

'I know that. Look, I just want to talk to him. Is that OK?'

'It was your mate Leó.'

'Leó? No wonder the case was never solved.'

'Oh, don't you start. Be polite to him. The poor bloke's just come out of rehab.'

'All right, keep your hair on. I only want to talk to him. How often's he been in rehab, anyway? Why should society have to endlessly waste money on useless cases like him?'

'Always the same kind heart,' Marta said sarcastically. 'Don't you dare give him any grief about his drinking.'

'I'm not promising anything.'

'That's what I'm afraid of.' Marta hung up on him.

Later that day, Konrád spotted Leó striding rapidly out of the yard by the police station on Hverfisgata, and called after him. When Leó saw who it was, he cut Konrád dead and kept walking until he reached the junction with Skúlagata. Konrád started running after him and caught up with him outside the Freemasons' Lodge. Aware that Leó was a Freemason, Konrád assumed he must be on his way to a meeting there.

'Leó!' he shouted. 'Don't be like that! I only want a quick word.'

Leó didn't answer or stop walking until Konrád grabbed him by the arm and hung on.

'There's something I need to ask you,' he said. 'Stop behaving like an idiot!'

Leó rounded on him. 'What do you want?' he snarled. 'Been listening to lies from any more old alkies?'

'A man was killed in a hit-and-run on Lindargata in 2009. I understand it was your case. The victim's name was Vilmar.'

'Haven't you retired?' Leó asked, tearing his arm out of Konrád's grasp.

'Yes, I –'

'Then I have nothing to say to you,' Leó said. 'Leave me alone.'

He made to climb the steps to the Freemasons' Lodge but Konrád blocked his path.

'Did you talk to an old woman called Vigga, who lived on Lindargata?'

Leó halted, radiating animosity.

'Do you remember talking to the old woman?' Konrád repeated.

Leó raised his arm to shove him away but Konrád refused to budge. He had been ready for an unpleasant scene and his old colleague never disappointed.

'I don't remember any old woman on Lindargata,' Leó said angrily. 'Leave me alone.'

'She was a witness,' Konrád said. 'How could you have missed her?'

'I don't know about any old bag from Lindargata witnessing anything. I have no idea what you're talking about.'

'She found the man lying in the street,' Konrád said. 'How could that have escaped your notice?'

'It's the first I've heard of it.'

'That's hardly a surprise. You obviously weren't bothered about getting that case "in the bag".'

'You can lie about me all you like. It wouldn't be the first time you've done that.'

'What about the driver? Why couldn't you find him?'

'What kind of questions are these? I don't have to justify myself to you –'

'How did you go about looking? What evidence were you going on? Who did you talk to?'

'What do you mean? You know how it works. Why are you wasting my time with all these stupid questions?'

'Who did you talk to?'

'Everyone who was relevant,' Leó snapped. 'Don't start getting on your high horse with me. You of all people can't afford to do that.'

'No, maybe not, but I wouldn't have thought the Lindargata case was that complicated.'

'We . . . I don't know why I'm telling you this, but we looked at repeat offenders who'd been picked up for drunk driving. We got descriptions of a few cars that had been spotted in the area that night, but there wasn't much to go on. Conditions were terrible, visibility was practically nil and there was hardly anyone about. We traced some vehicle owners but didn't learn anything from them. Their cars showed no signs of being involved in a collision and they were able to give a satisfactory account of their movements.'

'Did you consider the possibility that the man had been knocked down deliberately?'

'There was nothing to suggest that. Absolutely no evidence. Why should he have been?'

'Surely you'd know that better than me?' Konrád said. 'I wasn't the one who screwed up that particular investigation. And it wasn't me who forced the old man to tell lies about Hjaltalín in the Sigurvin case. What the hell were you thinking?'

'Shall I tell you? Do you really want to know?' Leó hissed. 'It was because you were fucking up the inquiry. The man had threatened Sigurvin. Not only that but he was the last person to see him alive: Sigurvin vanished after they argued in the car park. It wasn't hard to put two and two together. And we needed to get the case moving. It was going cold on your watch. We needed an arrest; some sort of progress to stop us looking like a bunch of useless pricks.'

'Meaning what? That two plus two equals throwing any poor sod in jail just to get a conviction?'

'Hjaltalín killed him. You fucked up the investigation. There was never anyone else in the picture. Face it. And Linda was mixed up in it with him. He wasn't with her that evening like she's claiming. She's lying. They both wanted Sigurvin out of the way. He wanted revenge; she made a packet out of getting rid of the guy. They kept their conspiracy secret all these years and couldn't risk being seen together again. It's like they didn't stop and think through the consequences – the fact that they lived in a little society like Iceland. Everything else went like a dream. If I was Marta, I'd lock her up.'

Konrád could feel himself trembling with anger.

'Hjaltalín got to you, we all know that,' Leó went on, twisting the knife. 'I don't know how he did it but he got to you and it messed with your judgement, so you let him off. They made a fool out of you, Konrád. A complete bloody fool!'

'You're full of shit,' Konrád snarled, beside himself with fury.

'Oh, shut your face,' Leó said. He barged past and pushed open the heavy door of the Freemasons' Lodge.

'Were you drinking when the hit-and-run happened? Is that why you couldn't be arsed to do a proper job?' Konrád called after him. 'I'd understand if that was the case.'

'Shut the fuck up!' Leó swore, his face crimson with rage.

'Have fun with your little Freemason friends,' Konrád sneered, as the door slammed behind Leó.

44

The last thing they ever did together was drive out to the Seltjar-narnes Peninsula at the westernmost point of Reykjavík, to watch a lunar eclipse. That whole year had been characterised by earth tremors and other unusual natural phenomena. A tourist-friendly eruption on the Fimmvörðuháls pass had turned out to be only the prelude to another, much more serious eruption under the Eyjafjallajökull glacier that had disrupted air traffic all over Europe. In Iceland, it had been accompanied by a massive ash fall and severe flooding. The cataclysmic year had ended with a lunar eclipse early in the morning of the winter solstice. Although Erna had been bedbound at home, she had insisted on seeing the eclipse and, as always, Konráð had bowed to her wishes.

She was terribly weak when he helped her out to the car. He had left the heater running first, to keep the piercing December cold at bay. A north wind had been blowing for the last few days and frost had settled like a crystalline blanket over the city's streets and squares. The frozen ground squeaked under his boots. The night sky was clear and, as they drove down the hill at Ártúnsbrekka, they got a good view of the full moon sailing high in the heavens to the west. The Earth's shadow had already begun its passage across it, and by the time they drove into the gloom at the end of the Seltjarnarnes Peninsula, the glowing disc had been veiled with a peculiar reddish darkness.

Konráð left the engine ticking over so they could keep the heater on, but switched off the lights. They weren't the only people out there. Several other cars had headed to the point to experience the eclipse away from the glare of the city lights. One man had set up a small telescope, angled towards the moon. Other figures, ignoring the cold, were standing on top of the shore ridge in front of them. The wind whistled around the car. The longer they sat there, their eyes adapting to the dark, the better they could make out the vast starry vault of the sky, with its sea of lights reaching them from far back in time.

'I want to get out,' Erna said.

'Erna . . .' Konráð objected.

'I have to get out.'

'It's too cold, Erna. I shouldn't have brought you here.'

'For a little while. Please. Just for a little while. It's no good trying to watch a lunar eclipse through the windscreen.'

Despite his reservations, he gave in to her wishes and got out of the car. He was wearing a thick down jacket and a woollen hat. Erna was similarly well wrapped up in a warm coat, a hat with ear flaps, a big scarf and thick gloves. Konráð walked round the front of the car, opened the passenger door, took Erna in his arms and lifted her out, taking her weight with his good arm. He carried her up to the top of the gravel bank, where he put her down, using his body to shelter her from the stripping cold of the wind. They could hear the waves breaking on the shore in the darkness. Erna gazed for a long time at the moon, now no more than a dim rose in the night sky. For the first time since she had told him she was ill, he saw that she was crying.

He took her in his arms again and carried her weak, exhausted body back to the car. It was warm and cosy inside as he laid her down with infinite care in the passenger seat.

'Thank you, Konrád, for everything,' she whispered, so quietly he could hardly make out the words.

They sat there in the car with the wind whistling outside, as more people arrived on the peninsula to watch the heavenly bodies sailing along their ancient orbits. Gradually the shadow lost its dark red tint and became a deeper black as it passed across the moon. The round shape of the Earth sank with infinite slowness, down over the glowing disc until only a tiny curved rim remained, then it vanished and the moon was whole again.

When they'd left home in the early hours, Erna had told him there hadn't been a lunar eclipse on the solstice since the seventeenth century, and it wouldn't happen again for a hundred years. She was glad they could share this moment, when time became both present and eternity at once.

Konrád reversed out of the parking space. Erna was sleeping peacefully; the morphine had taken effect. He drove slowly home, careful not to jolt her, but by the time he parked in front of their house in Árbær and prepared to take her inside, she had gone. Konrád sat there for a long time without moving, before gently freeing her from the seat belt and carrying her into the house, where he laid her in bed and told her what he had forgotten to tell her in the car on the way home: about how the moon was described somewhere in a poem. That it was the brooch of the night. The old friend of lovers.

It was the shortest day of the year and the longest in Konrád's life.

It lasted only four hours and twelve minutes.

And went on for eternity.

45

Her name was Pálína, she used to work as a taxi driver, and she'd been picked up for drunk driving on Frakkastígur the evening Villi was killed. Two years later she had lost her licence after knocking down a pedestrian and leaving him lying injured in the road. Shortly afterwards, she had been caught at home by the police and confessed to the whole thing. Her blood alcohol level had turned out to be way over the limit. As a result, she had gone into rehab and hadn't touched a drop since.

This was the story she told Konrád, sounding proud that it had taken only this one kick for her to conquer her addiction, pretty much on her own. She had never gone to AA meetings – well, to a couple at most – and had hardly any contact with her sponsor during that time. Admittedly, she still got the odd craving – which was only human – but it had never seriously occurred to her to start drinking again.

Despite her willingness to talk, she didn't go into what had caused her alcohol use to spiral out of control in the first place, but then it wasn't any of Konrád's business. No doubt time and habit had combined to undo her. But she did describe the drinking culture she had grown up with, back when beer was illegal and there had been nothing on offer but strong spirits. The streets of Reykjavík used to be heaving with people smashed out of their skulls at weekends.

'Of course, it wasn't healthy,' Pálína said, thinking back. 'Our Icelandic drinking culture.'

'It's not exactly healthy now,' Konrád replied.

'I always thought I had it under control – thought I was in charge – but the first thing you learn when you go into rehab is that drinking is completely out of your control. You're not in charge of anything. I mean, I drove a taxi! You know? Sometimes under the influence. I just thought I could get away with it. Christ, what idiots we can be!'

Pálína was the fourth person Konrád had spoken to since Marta had rung him with the information he had requested about Leó's investigation. She had compiled a list of the people who had been seen in the vicinity of the Shadow District the night Villi was killed. Konrád had promised to keep it absolutely hush-hush and thanked her from the bottom of his heart. He hadn't updated Marta on his enquiries recently, conscious that she had enough on her plate and unwilling to bother her with every minor detail he unearthed. All he had promised her was that he would let her know if he came across anything really significant.

The first man Konrád went to see had stolen his son's car on the evening in question and narrowly avoided an accident on Hverfisgata. The other vehicle had been driven by a couple returning from a party, who had been forced to swerve onto the pavement to avoid a collision. Despite the thickly falling snow, they had managed to get his registration and reported him for dangerous driving. The man, whose name was Ómar, had continued on his way without stopping, but had been picked up later that night at the central bus station. He had no memory of having driven along Lindargata.

He had demanded to know why Konrád was raking up the incident all these years later. But as soon as Konrád tried to explain, Ómar refused to listen, angrily retorting that it was a load of bloody nonsense and slamming the door in Konrád's face. Konrád was almost sure he'd caught a whiff of booze on his breath.

The second man had been equally unwilling to chat. He had treated Konrád with suspicion, repeatedly asking what he wanted. Konrád had explained that he was trying to track down a driver in connection with an accident on Lindargata seven years ago. He was asking on behalf of the sister of the man who had died in the accident – if it had been an accident. The driver of the car had never been found. He himself was following up a new lead and wanted to re-interview all those who had been spoken to in the course of the original inquiry.

'So you're not with the police, then?' the man had asked. His name was Tómas and he lived on Ingólfsstræti, a long street which crossed the bottom of Lindargata near the city centre. A neighbour had seen him get into his jeep in the middle of the night and drive off in the direction of the Shadow District, looking as if he was in a hurry. When Leó had spoken to Tómas, he had claimed he was visiting a woman in the east end of town. He'd provided the woman's name and she had confirmed his statement. In addition to this, there had been no suspicious marks on his jeep.

'No, it's more in the nature of a . . . private investigation,' Konrád said, 'but I was with the police for a long time, if that makes any difference.'

'So I don't have to talk to you.'

'No, not unless you want to.'

'Goodbye then,' the man said.

'You owned a jeep –'

'Goodbye,' the man repeated, and pushed the door almost to.

'Why, have you got something to hide?' Konrád asked, a little surprised by the man's reaction as he stood there in the stairwell of a rundown block of flats, talking to him through a crack in the door. But before he could say anything else, the man had shut the door in his face.

He had got a similar reception from the third man he talked to, though this one wasn't quite as rude. His name was Bernhard, he lived in a terraced house, and he was also in when Konrád rang the bell. When the man learnt that Konrád was asking about an accident on Lindargata, he explained that he had provided a statement at the time and knew nothing about the incident, then said a polite but firm goodbye. Konrád could understand. He would have reacted the same if a complete stranger had come to his door, asking questions about a serious incident. Bernhard had been seen driving east along Skúlagata. A witness, who had been trying to hitch a lift home in the blizzard, had come forward to say that a car had passed him, driving fast, and hadn't stopped. The witness hadn't been able to get a good look inside the vehicle and so couldn't be sure if the driver had been alone, but he had remembered part of the number plate because it contained three sevens. Bernhard had told the police that his wife had been in the car with him, and that they hadn't been mixed up in any accident.

The conversation with Pálína was quite different. She was positively welcoming, said she could perfectly understand why Konrád was asking about that evening, and readily answered his questions. She had never gone in for sports bars, never owned a jeep, it was out of the question that she had ever knocked anyone down on Lindargata, and she had never been a member of the Scouts or a rescue team. She was, on the other hand, extremely inquisitive and kept asking what it was Konrád was after. He deftly dodged her questions, rather taken aback by her nosiness, but soon got an explanation, which was as simple as it was understandable.

'You see, I'm a huge fan of crime fiction,' Pálína told him, 'and I rarely get the chance to meet a real detective.'

'Right, I see,' Konrád said, without enthusiasm.

'So, the thing is . . . it's quite a thrill for me to meet you, and . . . weren't you in charge of the case – the Sigurvin inquiry – the first time round?'

They were the only people in the cafeteria of the haulage company where Pálína was employed. She worked in the office; she'd given up driving, she explained. Konrád had accepted her offer of coffee but declined the custard creams. They didn't have much time to talk as things were busy, and one of the drivers, who should have set off by now for Höfn í Hornafirdi on the other side of the country, was waiting for Pálína in reception.

'That's right,' Konrád said.

'Is that why you're here?'

'No, this is about a different matter,' Konrád said, and for all he knew it could be true.

'A mysterious case,' Pálína said. 'The man you're looking for – was he out on the road at the same time as me?'

'That's one theory.'

'I remember very little about the hit-and-run on Lindargata,' Pálína said, frowning thoughtfully. 'It must have been all over the news. But of course I drank in those days. Worse than ever.'

'Did you notice anyone driving around town that evening that you happen to remember? Anyone behaving erratically? Or recklessly?'

'No, I don't remember anything like that. But then that period of my life is a bit of a blur.'

Konrád smiled.

'I'm afraid that's just the way it was,' Pálína said with a sigh, then started telling him the plot of a crime novel she had recently finished reading, about a mysterious murder in the Swedish countryside. She didn't seem to notice Konrád's complete lack of interest.

Konrád left the lights blazing in the kitchen, sitting room and bedroom when he went to bed. He had been feeling oddly spooked and unsettled all evening, sensing that he had missed something, though he couldn't put his finger on it. He mentally reviewed his visits that day, to the four people and the receptions they had given him. His thoughts lingered on the third man, the man in the terraced house who had turned him away. There was something familiar about his name but he couldn't work out what it was.

Bernhard, he was called.

Bernhard.

He was sure he'd heard or seen that name before. Recently, too. But he simply couldn't recall the context.

Eventually he gave up racking his brains and, as often happened before he fell asleep, he found himself aching with loss for

Erna. He remembered a bright summer's evening with her, many years ago, and could almost sense her presence in the room as drowsiness stole over him.

'Who is he?' He heard a low whisper in his ear. 'Who is this man?'

'I can't remember,' he replied. 'Can't remember.'

She was lying in bed beside him in a light-coloured summer dress that she had bought just after they met. He caught the faint scent of her perfume: of sunshine and flowers and the soft sand in Nauthólsvík Cove. He turned his head and gazed at her as she lay beside him, young and beautiful, as she always was in his dreams.

'I've come across that name somewhere,' he told her, 'I'm sure of it. But I've forgotten where . . . I never write anything down.'

Seeing that she was smiling, he reached out to her, longing to stroke her lips, longing to really have her beside him, to touch her one last time.

'I'm sorry,' he whispered. 'I'm sorry . . .'

Konráð opened his eyes to be met by dreary reality. He was lying alone in his cold bed, his arm stretched out across the duvet, and he knew that he had tried to catch hold of a dream.

46

The following day, Konrád looked after the twins. As it was a Saturday, this consisted of watching the English football together. Afterwards he took them out for burgers before dropping them off. Húgó tried to persuade him to stay for supper but he made his excuses, saying he wanted to go home. Shortly after that, his sister Beta came by, in rather low spirits.

'What's bothering you?' Konrád asked.

'Oh, nothing,' Beta said.

'Come on, what is it?'

'I've been dreaming about Dad.'

'Oh?'

'I don't like dreaming about him,' she said. 'It's never a good sign.'

'This time too?'

'Yes, the dream I had last night was a bad one. You were in it too. You and Dad together. Are you involved in something risky?'

'You needn't worry about me, Beta. I promise you.'

'Dad was standing behind the National Theatre – where they found that girl during the war.'

'Really?'

'And there was someone with him who didn't want to show himself. He was . . .'

'What?'

'There was something sinister about him,' Beta said. 'I got the impression he was covered in blood. And even though I couldn't get a proper glimpse of him, I knew it was you. Are you sure you're not in some kind of danger?'

'Absolutely. Don't worry about me, Beta. Honestly.'

'Are you planning to do something bad?'

'Something bad?'

'Yes.'

'Beta . . .'

'You were hiding in the shadows.'

Konrád shook his head. Beta was staring at him gravely.

'Are you sure?' she asked.

'Of course I'm sure. What am I supposed to do that's bad?'

'You don't know how much of Dad there is in you,' Beta said, standing up to go.

'Oh, I assure you I do, Beta,' Konrád said. 'I don't need you to tell me that.'

He woke up to find it was still pitch-dark, turned on the light and went for a pee. This happened once a night and had done for many years. He'd just crawled back into bed and was drifting off, when he unwisely started thinking about what Beta had said about the National Theatre. Although he'd tried not to let it show, the fact was that Beta's dream had got to him. It had taken a long time for him to relax after her visit and now his old insomnia was back.

Konrád tossed and turned, tense and restless, trying various tricks to find inner peace but without success. Even thinking about Erna, the method he used most often, didn't work this time. But it was while struggling with his sleeplessness that he finally remembered where he had come across the name Bernhard.

He got out of bed and found the printout Hólmsteinn had given him with the names of the boys who had been roughly contemporary with Sigurvin in the Scouts.

There it was.

Bernhard Skúli Gudmundsson.

After that, all hope of sleep was gone.

47

The first time he had been involved in a stakeout, CID had still been under the authority of the Reykjavík Prosecutor's Office. He and his colleague Ríkhardur had been sent to lie in wait for a man who had gone into hiding, suspected of smuggling large quantities of contraband spirits on one of the cargo ships. They had spotted him sneaking home, drunk, under cover of darkness, but had a hell of a job arresting him. Since that first time, Konrád had often taken part in similar operations, sitting outside premises in an unmarked police car, trying to catch people who had found themselves on the wrong side of the law. Not only was the waiting often long and mind-numbingly tedious, but there was something cringeworthy about it too, that made him feel as if he were taking part in a bad film.

And here he was again, on a self-appointed stakeout, in a foul mood and short on sleep. He had been sitting in his car for what felt like hours, watching the house without seeing any movement, and wondered now if he should risk edging a little closer. In an attempt to be inconspicuous, he had stopped some way down the street, where he was camouflaged among parked cars. Although he didn't know much about Bernhard yet, he had established that he was the only person registered at the address. According to the information in the online telephone directory, he was a car mechanic.

Konrád knew he didn't have much to go on. Even though the man was the same Bernhard as the boy who had been in the Scouts with Sigurvin, it wasn't necessarily significant that he had been driving down Skúlagata with his wife on the evening Villi died.

After failing to get back to sleep, Konrád had decided early that morning to drive over and take a look. There had been no car parked outside the house when he arrived, although it was a Sunday. Konrád guessed Bernhard might work shifts, but he didn't yet know where the man was employed. When he'd knocked on Bernhard's door on Friday, it had been late afternoon and he had probably just come home from work. Then again, it was unlikely he would be working the night shift at the weekend. No doubt he had been out having fun and slept it off somewhere else. Or he could have gone out of town for the weekend.

Time crawled by. Konrád had brought along a thermos of coffee and two sandwiches to eat while he waited. Eventually he heard the distant sound of church bells. It had never occurred to him to go to a service.

When the urge to stretch his legs became too strong to ignore, he got out of the car – though this was against all the rules. It was a relief to get his circulation going again and, since he was on his feet, he decided he might as well take a discreet look at Bernhard's house. The terrace lay at a right angle to the street, with an access path leading along it, but luckily Bernhard's house was at the near end, almost on the road. The back garden was enclosed by a high fence, which made it impossible to see in.

Konrád returned to his car and got behind the wheel again. He'd started running through the lyrics of old Icelandic pop songs to kill the time when sleep finally claimed him.

When he woke up, there was a vehicle in front of Bernhard's house. Not long afterwards, the door of the house opened and he saw Bernhard emerge and get into the car. Next minute, he was driving straight towards him. Konrád slid down low in his seat but Bernhard didn't appear to notice him. Once the other man had gone past, Konrád started his car, turned round, and set off after him, careful to hang well back.

Bernhard headed in an easterly direction, and before Konrád knew it they had reached the slope of Ártúnsbrekka, after which the car turned off into the industrial area that lay down by the coast. Bernhard threaded the streets between garages and car showrooms before finally pulling up in front of what looked like yet another garage. Konrád stopped a little way off and watched as Bernhard went inside. There was a small sign above the door but Konrád couldn't read it from where he was sitting. The cars parked in the yard outside appeared to be wrecks, good for nothing but spare parts.

Bernhard spent some minutes inside the garage before he came out carrying a part which Konrád couldn't identify from a distance. He jumped into his car and drove away again, but this time Konrád decided against following him.

He got out and walked, rather stiffly, over to the workshop. It looked like any other garage, apart from being dirtier and more of a mess than most. The reason for this became apparent when he got close enough to read the sign above the door, which announced that it was a scrapyard, not a garage. A notice stuck to the door said: *Used car parts for most models.* Konrád looked around. There was a stack of old tyres against the wooden fence separating the yard from the neighbouring premises. Beside it was a pile of rusty wheel-rims, with an upturned front seat on top. A couple of car doors were propped against the wall of the workshop. Konrád turned his attention back to the door, which was also rusty and contained two windows, their glass obscured by grime. He tried to peer inside but couldn't see a thing.

He surveyed his surroundings again and this time his gaze fell on a weathered tarpaulin that had once been green, which was spread over some large object in the corner by the workshop. Konrád went over and took hold of the tarpaulin, only to discover that it was firmly fastened. He took a quick glance around. He hadn't been aware of anyone else in the area on that quiet Sunday morning apart from him and Bernhard. Turning back to the tarpaulin, he started trying to loosen it. This proved far from easy as the knots seemed to have been tied a long time ago, with no intention of their ever coming undone. Only with considerable patience could he work them loose, after which he was able to free the cover and pull it carefully off the large object underneath.

An old Wagoneer jeep, or what was left of it, was revealed. The worn, colourless chassis was propped up on stands – minus wheels, both front wings, and one of the back wings. Almost everything had been removed from the interior except the steering wheel. Seats, dashboard and gearbox had all gone.

Konrád walked around the jeep. He didn't recognise the exact model but thought it could hardly be less than thirty years old. The front part was reasonably intact. The bonnet cover was still in place, though the bumper and grille were missing, leaving a large hole where the radiator had once been. The engine had gone too. Konrád knelt down and ran a finger over the metal behind where the bumper used to be, and reckoned he could see the impression where the cable from a winch had been attached.

He straightened up again. There was still no sound of traffic in the industrial estate but he thought he'd better get a move on, since for all he knew Bernhard might return any minute. He took hold of the tarpaulin and was about to drag it back over the wreck when his gaze fell on the bonnet. He bent down and ran his hand over the dented, rusty surface, peering at the little that was left of the faded paintwork.

Finally, not daring to stay a minute longer, he swung the cover over the wreck again and tried to secure it so there were no obvious signs that it had been tampered with. After wrestling with it for a while, he hurried back to his car.

On the way home he recalled the image of Bernhard standing in his doorway when he'd visited him on Friday. Konrád had rung the bell and waited a good while before the door had finally opened to reveal the houseowner. The man was quite tall, around the same age as Hjaltalín and Sigurvin, with thinning hair that was greying at the temples, big features, and thick lips under an impressive nose. He was short with strangers, if his behaviour towards Konrád was anything to go by. And he had claimed not to know anything about anything.

'Bernhard?' Konrád had said.

'Who are you?'

'I was hoping to speak to Bernhard. This is the right address, isn't it?'

'I'm Bernhard,' the man had said curtly.

'I'm here on a slightly strange errand,' Konrád had begun. 'I'm looking into a car accident that took place on Lindargata . . .'

'An accident?' the man said. 'I don't know anything about an accident.'

'No, I wasn't expecting you to. This was several years ago and they believe it was a jeep, so –'

'Why are you asking me about this?' the man interrupted.

'I'm working for the sister of the man who was knocked down,' Konrád said, 'and I understand the police interviewed you about the incident at the time. You were in the area when it happened.'

'Yes, they spoke to me,' the man replied, 'but I wasn't involved in any accident.'

Konrád had gone on to question him about his wife, who had supposedly been in the car with him, and to ask whether he could confirm the fact.

'Yes, she was with me,' the man said. 'Look, I told the police all this at the time.'

'Is she in, by any chance?'

'We're divorced.'

'Ah,' Konrád said. 'That's –'

'I'm afraid I can't help you,' the man said, preparing to close the door.

'Do you still own the jeep you were driving that night?' Konrád had asked quickly.

'No. Sorry, I haven't got time for this. I know nothing about the matter,' the man had said and closed the door.

Konrád thought about the skeleton of the Wagoneer jeep under the tarpaulin. Although he had no idea who it had belonged to or how it had got there, he could hardly think of a better place to dispose of an incriminating vehicle than in a scrapyard.

48

Sunday passed somehow. That evening, Konrád went round to his son's house for supper. Noticing how distracted he was, Húgó asked if it was the Sigurvin case that was weighing so heavily on him. Konrád changed the subject. He didn't stay long, making the excuse that he wanted an early night.

In fact, the night was long and restless. Konrád lay there, wide awake, trying to piece together what he knew about Sigurvin's fate, as he had so often before. He was sick to death of all the complications in the case that had dominated his life for so long. He kept trying to spot a new angle, new gaps, things that he had overlooked or overinterpreted or undervalued. He thought about the sequence of events from the point of view of each of the players in turn, trying to work out their role, what they had to gain and where their stories overlapped with those of others connected to the case.

But despite considering one scenario after another, he was still none the wiser when finally, mercifully, he dropped off and managed to sleep for a few hours.

The following day, Konrád drove the short distance from his house to the industrial estate on the other side of the big Vesturland road, and parked in front of Bernhard's scrapyard. The tarpaulin was still in place over the wreck of the jeep and Konrád reckoned he must have replaced it convincingly enough for the owner not to notice that it had been touched. The big doors to the workshop were closed but there was a smaller door beside them, which Konrád now opened. He found his way blocked by a reception desk that prevented visitors from coming any further inside. A couple of minutes passed. He stood by the desk, looking round the spare parts store, which was as filthy and cluttered as the yard outside. There were racks of engine parts and other odds and ends running the length of the workshop. From the ceiling hung exhaust pipes and silencers. The windows at the far end presumably faced west but they were so grimy that it was impossible to see out.

'Hello!' Konrád called.

There was no answer. He waited a short while, then went round the desk, saw a small kitchen and stuck his head inside, but it was empty. Off the kitchen was a tiny office in which he caught sight of a computer screen. The background was an image of a sunny tropical island.

He went back out and called again.

'Yes, just a minute,' said a voice, and Bernhard appeared almost immediately with an engine part in his hands and a pair of ear protectors round his neck. He recognised Konrád at once.

'What are you doing here?'

'I just wanted to talk to you about that accident I mentioned. I was going to –'

'No, I have nothing to say. I know nothing about it, as I've already told you. Will you please leave me alone.' Bernhard turned to go back into the parts store.

'Is that your old jeep outside? Under the tarpaulin?'

The mechanic turned back to him. 'Please could you leave, mate,' he said, his tone serious. 'I have nothing to say to you.'

'Am I right that you used to be in the Scouts with a boy called Sigurvin? Does that ring a bell?'

'Just get out.' Bernhard started to advance, as if he meant to throw Konrád out physically if he wouldn't leave of his own accord.

'I'm sure you've heard of him,' Konrád persisted, not budging an inch. 'He's connected to a famous criminal case. Sigurvin's frozen body was recently found on Langjökull. You must have heard the news.'

Bernhard hesitated. First it had been an accident on Lindargata, now the body in the ice. 'I haven't a clue what you're talking about,' he said.

'Do you remember Sigurvin from the Scouts?'

'Who did you say you were?'

'I'm working for the sister of the man who was knocked down on Lindargata. I believe the two cases are linked. So does she.'

'You aren't a cop, then?'

'I investigated Sigurvin's disappearance thirty years ago but I'm not a policeman any more, no. I've retired.'

Bernhard's expression didn't change.

Konrád smiled. 'It happens to all the best people.'

But Bernhard wasn't amused. 'I have nothing to say to you. I have no idea what you're wittering on about. None of this means anything to me.'

'A witness saw a man talking to Villi in a sports bar the evening he died. That was the victim's name, incidentally – Vilmar, known as Villi. Do you remember meeting him? Do you recognise the name?'

Bernhard shook his head.

'Did you follow him to Lindargata?'

Next minute, Bernhard was right in Konráð's face, shoving him towards the door.

'What the fuck has it got to do with you what I did or didn't do?' he swore, opening the door. 'Get out of here! You're mixing me up with somebody else. You should do your job better. I'll call the police if you don't stop harassing me. I don't want to see your face here again.'

Konráð was outside in the yard now. He had been more or less expecting this kind of reaction. Bernhard was standing in the doorway, blocking it. Konráð pointed over at the tarpaulin.

'Was it originally silver or grey?' he asked, but by then Bernhard had shut the door and vanished back inside. Konráð remained where he was.

'Did you seriously never get rid of the wreck?' he muttered under his breath, before heading back to his own car.

Konráð hadn't noticed anything unusual or distinctive about Bernhard during that brief encounter, apart from his lack of care for his surroundings and one oddly anachronistic detail of his appearance. It had struck Konráð more forcibly this time than it had on the first occasion he met the mechanic. Although the eighties were a distant memory, Bernhard had hung on to his mullet.

49

Bernhard had a clean record. Apparently he'd never had a run-in with the law. From what Konrád had been able to find out online or from ringing old contacts, the man was also divorced and childless: he had married late, at around forty, but the marriage hadn't lasted. He had bought the terraced house with his wife and he had held on to it after they split up. The scrapyard had come into his possession some time before he married but, judging from his public tax returns, it wasn't making much of a profit.

Konrád had been mulling over his options and decided he needed to dig up more information on the man before involving Marta or giving Bernhard another opportunity to show him the door. It didn't concern him that the man might get wind of the fact that questions were being asked about him in connection with Sigurvin or Vilmar. If he had a guilty conscience, with any luck he would lose his nerve and make a mistake, inadvertently giving himself away.

It occurred to Konrád to go and visit Bernhard's ex-wife, whose name was Jóhanna, and after a bit of detective work he discovered that she was now living in a council flat in Efra-Breidholt, a down-market suburb on the eastern edge of the city. He drove up there and parked in front of a large block of flats that was badly in need of maintenance. The blue paint had weathered to grey, streaks of rust ran down the walls from the windows and balcony railings, and the window frames looked battered.

The door to the staircase wasn't locked, so Konrád walked straight in and climbed up to the first floor where he pressed a bell. Hearing no sound of ringing from inside, he pressed the bell again. Then, since it was obviously broken, he tried knocking. He waited a good while, then knocked again and this time heard a rustling sound on the other side of the door. Someone coughed, then the door opened at last.

An obese, rather seedy-looking woman stood there staring at him. She was in her fifties, her hair stuck up in tufts, and she was regarding him with a look of perplexity, as if she had never expected another visit in her life.

'Good afternoon,' Konrád said.

'Who are you?' the woman asked bluntly.

'My name's Konrád. I'm trying to find out some information about your ex-husband, Bernhard.'

'Bernhard?'

'Yes.'

'Find out what . . . ?'

'Information.'

'What . . . what kind of information? What do you mean?'

Konrád got the impression he'd woken her up. 'You were married, weren't you? You and Bernhard?'

'Who did you say you were?' Jóhanna asked, her voice slurring a little.

'I'd like to ask you a couple of questions about your ex-husband, if that's all right,' Konráд said. He found himself feeling sorry for this shabby-looking woman and wished he could do something to help her, though he didn't know what. 'It's about an accident that happened several years ago on Lindargata,' he added. 'A pedestrian was knocked down.'

'Eh?' said the woman. 'What accident?'

'A young man died after being hit by a car. I'm working for his sister. Could I maybe talk to you for a minute?'

'Does Bernhard know you're here?'

'Bernhard? No.'

Jóhanna stared at him. 'Have you met him?'

'He won't talk to me,' Konráд said.

Jóhanna wavered. 'Come in,' she said at last, turning and going back inside the flat, leaving the door open for him to follow. Konráд slipped through and closed it behind him.

'Excuse the mess,' Jóhanna said.

She picked up a few things in a desultory way, as if that would achieve anything, but it was an empty gesture. It was one of the most chaotic and squalid flats Konráд had ever seen – despite all his years in the police, during which he'd been inside plenty of dumps. The place was littered with clothes and other possessions, cardboard boxes and newspapers, bits of furniture and kitchen utensils, dirty plates, saucepans coated with cooking residues, used glasses and empty wine bottles. A sour fug filled the air. As Konráд took in the chaos, he thought of Bernhard. If slovenliness had been one of the reasons for their divorce, it was hard to see who had been more to blame.

He could hardly bring himself to enter the cluttered room and, besides, he didn't want to disturb the poor woman any more than necessary, so he paused in the doorway.

'I never seem to have time to tidy up,' Jóhanna said, looking helplessly around the room.

'No,' Konrád said, groping for something to say. 'It tends to get left to last.'

'We're not friends, you know, Bernhard and me.' She sighed. 'I don't know how I put up with him all those years. I told him. Often. But he never listened. Never listened to a word I said. He was depressed. I reckon that must have been it. You couldn't get a word out of him for days on end, but if you did something he didn't like, he'd fly into such a violent sulk that he wouldn't talk to you for days – weeks, even. Who would put up with that kind of behaviour for long? No one. No one would put up with it.'

'Did he drink?'

'Yes, that too. Oh, yes. But then he went into rehab and I don't think he's touched a drop since.'

'Did he used to hang out in bars a lot?'

'No, not much, except to watch the football. He didn't want to fork out for the sports channels. He was crazy about football; he just didn't want to pay for it. So . . . yes, he used to go out to watch matches. It gave him an excuse to drink too. I thought maybe you were from social services. You aren't, are you?'

'No, I'm here about the accident I mentioned.'

'Oh, yes, the accident, of course.'

'I understand you were with him at the time.'

The woman was staring vacantly at the mounds of rubbish.

'Would you like me to talk to social services for you?' Konrád asked after a while. He had the feeling that Jóhanna wasn't quite with it. 'Do you need help?'

'What? Oh, no, I can manage fine. I just need to tidy up a bit.'

'Were you surprised when Bernhard went into rehab?'

'Not given the way he used to hit the bottle. But the decision did come a bit out of the blue.'

'His decision to dry out?'

'Yes, it was all very sudden.'

'Bernhard says he doesn't know anything about an accident,' Konrád said, 'and he didn't get in touch with the police at the time, when they were appealing for witnesses. But he was spotted in the area that night. He claims you were with him.'

'Yes.'

'You don't know anything about an accident?'

'No.'

'Has Bernhard lived alone since then? Since your divorce?'

'Yes.'

'Do you have any contact with him?'

'No. None. I've hardly seen him . . . since . . . After all, we've got nothing to say to each other. We didn't have any kids.'

'Did he ever talk to you about his time in the Scouts?'

'The Scouts? No. He sometimes went on call-outs but . . .'

'Call-outs?'

'When they rang.'

'Who?'

'Those search and rescue people . . .'

'Was he in a search and rescue team?'

'Yes, but then he quit.'

'What about Sigurvin? Did Bernhard ever mention a man by that name?'

'Sigurvin?'

'The name's been in the news. His body was found recently on Langjökull.'

Jóhanna couldn't have looked more astonished if Konrád had slapped her across the face.

'Him . . . ? Did Bernhard know him?'

'They were in the Scouts together as boys,' Konrád said. 'Briefly.'

'Really? I never knew that.'

'Bernhard never mentioned it to you?'

'No. How strange. I never had a clue.'

'Was Bernhard comfortably off when you were married?'

'Comfortably off?'

'Did he have enough money?'

'He was unbelievably stingy. That was one problem. But no, he didn't have much at all. I mean, he had that scrapyard but business was so-so. He used to repair cars too. All cash in hand, of course. He did quite well out of that – much better than from selling parts.'

Jóhanna had been gazing unseeingly at a pile of clothes on the floor, but now she raised her eyes to Konrád with a questioning look. 'Was he involved?'

'In what?'

'Sigurvin and all that?'

Konrád shook his head. 'I wouldn't know.'

'Why did you ask me if he was comfortably off? Where was Bernhard supposed to lay his hands on any kind of money?'

'It's just a routine question,' Konrád said to pacify her.

'Excuse the mess,' the woman said again after a pause. 'I need to tidy up in here. It's just . . . I never seem to find the time.'

'Maybe I could come and chat to you another day,' Konrád said. He didn't want to linger too long in the woman's flat. She needed time to process this unexpected visit and then maybe something would come back to her that might be of use to Konrád.

'Does Bernhard have many friends?' he asked, preparing to leave.

'No, he hardly had any friends worth the name. Just a handful of people who came to our wedding, but then we didn't have a ceremony. We just got married in front of a magistrate. And his family's very small. The only time he ever got together with anyone was when he went to a school reunion and met up with his old classmates. I had a few friends myself but he wasn't interested in getting to know them.'

Konrád began backing away in the direction of the door. Jóhanna noticed his eagerness to leave.

'You don't want to ask about the girlfriend?' she said.

'What girlfriend?'

'His, of course.'

'Did Bernhard have an affair?'

'I always suspected him of it,' Jóhanna said.

'Really?'

'I asked him about it. Loads of times. But he always denied it.'

'Why did you think he was cheating on you?'

'A woman knows,' Jóhanna said. 'It's just an instinct.'

'Did he drop any hints?'

'No, he never said anything. But there was always something weighing on him that I couldn't understand. He was always so down, always so mean to me.'

'You asked him about it?'

'Yes, I did. He just told me to shut up. So I abandoned the struggle and left him. He was useless. Bloody useless.'

'You have no idea who he was seeing?'

'There were always bitches ringing him. He claimed it was business, to do with the scrapyard. But I reckon it all started after that reunion.'

'Do you know who they were?'

'No, he didn't introduce them to me, of course. Maybe you don't believe me?'

'Sure I do,' Konrád said. 'These things happen.'

'These things? What do you mean?'

'People cheat on their partners,' Konrád said.

'Yes, it . . . she was . . . one time some cow rang his mobile and hung up the moment I answered, but I . . . but he had a number display, you know, so I typed the number into the computer. I asked him who the bitch was. He just claimed it was about selling spare parts.'

'Can you remember her name?'

'Her name?'

'The woman who rang Bernhard.'

'No. I used to . . . I remembered it once . . . It was . . . what was she called? Something out of the Bible. I do remember that. A Bible name.'

50

Dusk was falling as Konrád parked his car at a discreet distance from Bernhard's scrapyard. Few people seemed to have any business there. In the two hours he spent watching the place, he saw just three customers go in and only one emerge with the part he'd been looking for. People could save themselves a fortune if a scrapyard had the part they needed, as Konrád had discovered when some completely unnecessary sensor had stopped working in his four-wheel drive and the dealership was charging the earth for a replacement. Konrád wouldn't have bothered to buy another if it hadn't been for the warning light that kept flashing on his dashboard. He had rung round the scrapyards and eventually found the part he wanted for a fraction of the cost. So Bernhard was offering a much-needed service, though he didn't seem to be making much of a profit from it.

Once, Bernhard stepped into the doorway to smoke a cigarette and drink from a plastic cup. Konrád watched. The man's overalls looked as if they had never been near a washing machine. Towards closing time, the lights went out one by one in the workshop and Bernhard emerged, locking the door carefully behind him. He was carrying a thermos and a lunchbox. He walked over to his car, got in and drove off. Konrád set out after him, careful to stay well back.

Bernhard drove straight home to his terraced house without noticing that he was being followed, and Konrád again parked a little way off and waited in his car, not knowing exactly what for. He wondered if Bernhard had shut up shop unusually early, since it wasn't yet six. Perhaps he'd thought there were unlikely to be any further customers that day. Konrád turned on the radio and listened to an unbelievably boring cultural programme on the National Broadcasting Service, before giving up and searching the airwaves for some Icelandic music instead. He sat there for a long while, watching Bernhard's house, before deciding he'd had enough for one evening.

On the way home, he drove past Bernhard's old school, which Jóhanna had mentioned in connection with his class reunion, and saw that all the lights were on. The surrounding streets were full of parked cars and adults were streaming in through the main entrance. Konrád guessed it must be some sort of parent-teacher evening and decided to seize the chance to have a nose around.

All afternoon he had been pondering what Jóhanna had said about a woman with a biblical name who had once rung up to speak to Bernhard. She had been convinced that Bernhard was having an affair with the woman.

As Konrád entered the foyer, the meeting for parents was just beginning. Chairs had been lined up in front of a small stage where a man in a jacket, presumably the head teacher, was fiddling with a microphone, tapping it, checking it was switched on, then tapping it again. The parents were chatting among themselves. By far, the majority of them were women.

Konrád headed down one of the corridors that led off the foyer in every direction. The old school building had been extended more than once, and long corridors connected it to the new wings. Doors were open into classrooms where the pupils' work was displayed on the walls. The drawings revealed a wide divergence in talents. Húgó had shown some artistic promise as a boy and had once tried, without much success, to teach his father to draw. The only remotely decent pictures Konrád had been able to produce were of cars. Erna had kept all his efforts.

The walls of the corridors in the old building were lined with framed class photos going right back to the founding of the school. A photo had been taken of every form in its final year and there were so many of them that they had to be displayed in two or even three rows. Like a journey through time they showed the changing fashions and haircuts, from the short back and sides, through the Beatles moptop, to the modern lack of any defining trend. Some of the older photos showed teenage girls with beehive hair, their faces plastered in thick foundation.

It took Konrád a while to work out what order they were in, but once he had he made his way slowly but surely towards Bernhard's leaving year. Although there had been four forms in that year, which made it harder, he was able to pick out Bernhard in one of the photos. It was black and white, and had obviously been taken in one of the classrooms. The pupils were smiling at the photographer, perhaps mindful that the moment would be preserved for posterity, for as long as the school lasted, and that they would be able to revisit their youth in these corridors whenever they felt the urge.

Bernhard had changed little in the intervening years. His tall, lanky figure could be seen in the back row towards the centre. His shoulder-length hair was parted in the middle, he wore a stripy jumper, and he was smiling along with the other kids at some remark the photographer had made to put them at ease.

According to Jóhanna, her ex-husband had gone to a class reunion where he had met all these people again, many years later, when the morning of their life was over, to be replaced by the daily grind.

As Konrád stood alone in the corridor, studying the class photo, his phone started ringing. It was Marta.

'I haven't heard from you for days,' she said. 'What have you been up to?'

'Not much,' Konrád said. 'You?'

'Same story here. I can't stop thinking about those car keys.'

'Car keys?'

'The ones to Sigurvin's jeep. I keep wondering why he didn't have them on him. I reckon there can only be one explanation, assuming they didn't fall out of his pocket.'

'Which is?'

'Sigurvin's killer was intending to move his jeep. To drive it up to the glacier, presumably.'

'Yes, sounds plausible.'

'Isn't that the only possible explanation?' Marta asked.

'The killer probably intended to make it look as if Sigurvin had driven himself to Langjökull and died of exposure. Of course, he wasn't dressed for a glacier trip but maybe they thought that didn't matter.'

'At any rate, there's something unfinished about the whole business,' Marta said. 'About how he was disposed of – his jeep in one place, his body in another. As you said yourself when they found him, it's like a half-finished job.'

'It's possible the weather put a spanner in the works,' Konrád said. 'There was a severe storm on the glacier for several days following Sigurvin's disappearance. Perhaps they had to abandon their plan before they could complete it.'

Konrád stared at the class photo. Another face suddenly caught his eye, the pretty face of a girl sitting on the floor in the front row; the only one who wasn't smiling, but gazing solemnly at the camera instead. He couldn't be entirely sure but the resemblance was striking enough for his heart to miss a beat.

Marta was saying something on the phone but he didn't hear her. He was thinking back to what Jóhanna had said about the woman who had once rung Bernhard, pretending she wanted to buy a part for her car. The woman with the biblical name that Jóhanna couldn't remember through her alcoholic haze. The woman she was convinced had been having an affair with her husband.

'. . . like a half-finished job?' he heard Marta's voice repeating in his ear. 'That's it, isn't it?'

Konrád didn't take his eyes off the picture.

'Yes,' he said distractedly, 'unfinished, sordid and ugly.'

51

Unable to wait until the following morning, Konrád drove straight back up to Efra-Breidholt to see Jóhanna and try to confirm his suspicions before deciding what to do next. He'd said a curt good-bye to Marta and hurried out of the school. Although the main rush hour had passed and the traffic was lighter, he was so impatient that he dodged his way between the other cars and once even jumped a red light.

As he drove, he reviewed all he knew about the Sigurvin case, followed by all the things he didn't know, despite the long years of investigating and working and thinking and interviewing and meeting people from all levels of society who had links to Hjaltalín and the missing man. The discovery of the body in the ice had certainly thrown up new information that narrowed the search, but Konrád thought that, ironically, if it hadn't been for Villi, the witness he had never even met, he wouldn't have found the leads he was following now.

His mind went back and forth over all the different pieces of the puzzle, thinking about Bernhard and the Scouts and Sigurvin and the girl in the class photo, about search and rescue teams, and the secret stash of money in Sigurvin's kitchen. About the rundown scrapyard and Bernhard's failed marriage. Hjaltalín's peculiar obstinacy. And the business Sigurvin had got mixed up in that had led to his death. What could it have been, and how come it had ended in tragedy?

From there, his thoughts led him to reflect on the impact the case had had on his own life, shaping him perhaps more than he had realised or was willing to acknowledge. He thought about the effect the failed investigation had had on him as a police officer, about the reason why he had been sent on unpaid leave back in the day. It had been one of the few times he had completely lost it.

He shook his head, cursing, and blasted his horn at the car in front of him, which was taking forever to get going again now that the lights had turned green. He had always regretted what happened. His colleague Ríkhardur had asked if he'd lost his mind. To be fair, he probably had. He had gone out to his jeep in the yard behind the police station, grabbed a tyre iron and stormed back inside, bursting into the corridor to the cells with the intention of beating the living daylights out of the prisoner. Instead, he had been seized, thrown to the floor and held down by his colleagues until he had recovered his senses, after which he had been sent home.

Konrád hadn't been able to claim extenuating circumstances, even though the prisoner he was intending to beat with the tyre iron had attacked him first by headbutting him in the face and breaking his nose, causing a fountain of blood and excruciating pain. Even though the prisoner had insulted him and threatened his family. Even though he had mocked him and jeered at him over his investigation into Sigurvin's disappearance, and called him the most pathetic piece of shit in the whole fucking police force.

Even though the prisoner's name was Hjaltalín.

Konrád should have been man enough to shrug the whole thing off, but instead he had cracked.

Cracked and broken into a thousand pieces.

Hjaltalín had been picked up for drunk driving one night in the run-up to Christmas. He had been uncooperative and resisted arrest, so he had been thrown in the cells at the police station to sleep it off. A blood test had been taken that confirmed he was way over the limit. Konrád had learnt of his presence in the cells when he came to work the next morning. As it had been a long time since he had last met Hjaltalín, he made the mistake of going down to see him. He'd realised too late that the night hadn't been long enough to sober Hjaltalín up and that he was still drunk and raging at his incarceration. The moment he saw Konrád he started yelling insults at him and accusing him of having ruined his life.

'I'll kill you and your whole fucking family!' Hjaltalín had snarled at the height of their confrontation. 'You pathetic cripple!'

'Shut up!' Konrád had yelled back.

They were standing face to face in the narrow cell, years' worth of tension boiling up to the surface.

'I'll kill them if I feel like it, you arsehole! Your wife and the whole fucking lot of you.'

'If you –'

Konrád never got a chance to finish the sentence; the attack took him completely by surprise. All of a sudden Hjaltalín sprang at him and headbutted him in the face. The pain was so agonising that Konrád cried out, his eyes filling with tears, and he felt the hot blood gushing. Hjaltalín flung him against the wall, grabbed him by the throat and swore he would kill him, then threw him on the floor and started kicking him until a guard rushed in and got him in a chokehold.

Konrád saw red. What happened next was something of a blur. He had a vague memory of fetching the tyre iron from his jeep, running back in and going for Hjaltalín, who was out in the corridor with his hands cuffed behind his back. Konrád had swung the tyre iron, smashing it into the wall beside Hjaltalín so hard that a chunk broke off and the concrete crumbled all over the floor. Before he could swing it again, he was overpowered by his colleagues.

Hjaltalín hadn't pressed charges and Konrád had dropped the charges he had initially wanted to bring for violence against a police officer and making threats against his family. Most of his year's unpaid leave had been spent in Sweden with Erna. She had been talking for a while about wanting to go back to Stockholm, where she had done her specialist training, so this had seemed like the perfect opportunity. She got herself a job at the Karolinska Hospital and they had left for Sweden at the end of February, not returning to Iceland until the autumn. Just over a year later, Erna was dead and he had retired from the police for good.

Konrád parked by the block of flats in Efra-Breidholt, sighing heavily at the memory of his attack on Hjaltalín. The block looked even more depressing in the dark. He saw a light on in Jóhanna's flat and hoped that meant she was home. He took the stairs two at a time and knocked on her door, out of breath. There was no sound from inside. He knocked again, louder and for longer, then pressed his ear to the door. There was a noise on the other side. He waited impatiently. Just as he was about to knock for a third time, the door opened and Jóhanna appeared, in an even more dishevelled state than before.

'What's all this racket?' she asked, squinting as if she had just woken up.

'I wanted to ask you something else about Bernhard and –'

'Who are you? What do you mean by banging on my door like that?'

'My name's Konrád. I was here earlier today. Excuse the disturbance but –'

'You again? Why do you keep coming round here?'

'I wanted to see if I could help you remember the name of the woman you mentioned – the one who rang Bernhard once, pretending she wanted to buy a part for her car.'

Jóhanna stared at him blearily.

'You said you knew he'd been seeing other women,' Konrád prompted.

'Why don't you come in?' Jóhanna said. 'We can't talk about things like that in the corridor. Konrád, was it?'

She was cottoning on.

'That's right.'

For the second time that day he followed the woman who had once been married to Bernhard into her grotty flat, closing the door behind him. Jóhanna obviously hadn't moved a thing since he left. She dropped heavily into the same chair.

'The woman's name?' she said.

'Do you by any chance remember it?'

'I was trying to after you left.'

'You said you thought it was a name out of the Bible.'

'Yes, it was.'

'Has it come back to you?'

Jóhanna frowned. Konrád waited impatiently for an answer. It would be better if she could remember it of her own accord. He shifted from foot to foot in front of her. It wasn't going to work.

'Was it Salóme?' he asked at last.

Jóhanna perked up a little. 'Yes – Salóme,' she said. 'That was her name, wasn't it? He pretended not to know who she was. Claimed he was just selling her a spare part.'

'Are you sure?'

'Yes. Salóme. I have a feeling that was it.'

Jóhanna looked at Konrád a little sheepishly and he saw that she had something on her mind.

'Did you have a question for me?' he asked.

'You told me before that . . .' Her voice died away.

'Yes?'

'You told me . . . you said Bernhard used to know Sigurvin.'

'Yes, a little. When they were boys.'

'Do you think he could have done something to him?'

'I don't know,' Konrád said. 'It's possible.'

'Killed him?'

'I don't know.'

'And the young lad on Lindargata?'

'I'm trying to find out. You should know – you were in the car with him.'

'Yes,' Jóhanna said. 'Of course, but . . . it's just . . .'

'What?'

'I don't owe that man anything.'

'Who? Bernhard?'

'Do you think I owe him anything?'

'I wouldn't –'

'The lying bastard.'

'What do you mean?'

'He treated me like dirt. And I'm supposed to . . . I'm supposed to lie for him.'

'Lie about what?'

Jóhanna sat up straighter in her chair. 'Bernhard rang me one day and asked me to say I'd been in the car with him on a particular night. There, I've done it. I've never told anyone that before.'

Konrád wasn't sure if he'd understood her right. 'He asked you . . . ?'

'Yes. I wasn't in the car with him.'

'But you were supposed to say that you were?'

'Yes. He asked me to lie for him. The cops had talked to him about some accident. He said he'd been driving drunk and didn't want to lose his licence, so he asked me to say, if they asked, that I was with him and that he'd been sober. That he'd picked me up from work or a party, I can't remember which, and that nothing had happened and we hadn't noticed anything unusual. I didn't even know what he was talking about.'

'Was that the night the young man was knocked down on Lindargata?'

'I think it might have been. It was around about then. I got to thinking about it after you were here earlier. It was the only time he ever asked me to do anything like that.'

'And you told the police you were with him?'

'No. The police? I didn't tell them anything.'

'Why not?'

'They never asked me. I never had to tell them anything about it.'

'What do you mean?'

'I never talked to any policeman,' Jóhanna said.

'So no one ever asked you to confirm his alibi?' Konráð's mind flew to Leó, scuttling off to his Freemasons' meeting.

'No one ever talked to me.'

'So he was alone when he claimed he'd been with you?'

Jóhanna nodded. 'I don't know why I should have to keep on covering for him. I don't mind you knowing. It doesn't matter to me. I don't know if he was asking me to lie because of that lad or not.'

'Didn't you find it odd that he asked you to lie for him like that?'

'I didn't ask any questions. He just said he'd been driving over the limit. I didn't connect it with that lad. But then I didn't take much notice of the news in those days. Do you think Bernhard knocked him down? And killed Sigurvin too? I can't get over that, I just don't believe it. I don't believe he'd be capable of it. Bernhard's just not like that. He was . . . I'd never have believed he had it in him.'

Konráð didn't know how to answer that. 'Do you remember noticing any change in him at the time?' he asked instead.

'Change?'

'Did his temper get worse, for example? Was he more depressed? Did he drink more or seem more on edge?'

'No. Well, except that was when he took himself off to rehab. I do remember that. Just all of a sudden, like.'

Konráð had heard enough. He thanked Jóhanna for her help, reflecting as he did so on the women he had encountered in the course of this inquiry; the women who had lied for their men, been codependent, eager to help, unsuspecting.

'Yes, Salóme, that was it,' Jóhanna repeated as she shook his hand in parting. 'I knew it was something out of the Bible. Didn't she . . . er . . . how did it go again? I used to go to Sunday school, so I ought to know. Wasn't she given what's his name's – John the Baptist's – head on a silver platter? Wasn't that her? The little dancing girl. Her name was Salóme, wasn't it?'

Konrád opened the door and stepped out into the corridor. It could hardly be a coincidence. Salóme wasn't a common name in Iceland. She'd been Hjaltalín's girlfriend. And Bernhard's classmate.

'Yes, that's the one,' he said. 'The little dancing girl who brought us Hjaltalín's head on a silver platter,' he muttered under his breath, as he closed the door behind him.

52

Konrád drove back to Bernhard's house, only to discover that his car wasn't there. He kept an eye on the place for a while but, when nothing happened, he drove slowly away again, heading for the scrapyard. When he got there he saw a faint light inside and Bernhard's car parked out front. Konrád switched off his engine. Apart from the buses roaring at regular intervals along the road behind the yard, all was quiet.

As he sat there, Konrád tried to make sense of the new connections he had uncovered, which he hadn't been aware of before, and kept coming back to Salóme, Hjaltalín's ex-girlfriend. Where did she come in? What role had she really played?

These days Salóme owned and ran a womenswear shop with her sister. How had it come into her possession? True, the unlikeliest people had got rich when the Icelandic economic miracle was at its height, so it was perfectly possible that she had been among them; that she had been canny with her finances and acquired the shop thanks to her own resourcefulness and good management. When looking into her background the first time round, Konrád had discovered that she'd been brought up by a single mother, left school at sixteen and had done a variety of jobs, mostly in retail. That's how she had met Hjaltalín: she'd been working in one of his clothes shops. They had been seeing each other for a while when Sigurvin went missing but, by a twist of fate, she'd ended up as one of the key witnesses in the case against her boyfriend. Having admitted that the alibi she originally gave the police was a lie, she had never budged from her subsequent statement that Hjaltalín had gone out, intending to meet a 'friend', on the evening of Sigurvin's disappearance. Although Hjaltalín had insisted that she was lying, her testimony had been considered credible and in the end he'd admitted to having met Sigurvin in the car park.

Next, Konrád considered the fact that Salóme had been at the same school as Bernhard, perhaps all the way through. What was the nature of their relationship? Bernhard had also known Sigurvin from their time in the Scouts. Could he be linked to Sigurvin's disappearance? Was he the man who had knocked Villi down on Lindargata?

Konrád sat patiently in his car, his mind running through different scenarios, while nothing moved outside apart from the half-empty buses trundling by.

It was past midnight when the door of the garage finally opened and Bernhard appeared in the gap. He peered out into the darkness and lit a cigarette. Then his phone obviously rang because he fished it out of his trouser pocket and answered it. The conversation lasted some time. Konrád saw Bernhard shake his head. Then the phone call ended and Bernhard remained standing in the doorway, smoking. Finally, he flicked away the butt and peered out into the night again, before going back inside and closing the door. Shortly afterwards, Konrád saw the faint light at the back of the workshop go out and expected Bernhard to emerge from the building immediately afterwards.

He waited, puzzled that the man didn't reappear, then noticed a car entering the street. It crawled past, then turned round and came back again. Konrád couldn't make out the driver in the dim street lighting. The car stopped in the road in front of the scrapyard. The headlights went out. Time passed but nothing happened.

Eventually, the car door opened and the driver stepped out and started walking slowly towards the workshop.

It was Salóme.

She scanned her surroundings carefully, as if afraid someone was watching her, but failed to spot Konrád sitting in his car. Then she quickened her pace, almost breaking into a run. The door was apparently unlocked because she turned the handle and slipped inside, pulling it to behind her.

Half an hour passed. Konrád was dithering over what to do when the door opened again and Salóme came out. She closed it and headed straight towards her car. Konrád braced himself to dash out into the road and block her way, but changed his mind. Another bus roared along the street behind. Salóme got into her car, the headlights came on and a moment later she was gone.

Why on earth had she been visiting Bernhard in his workshop in the middle of the night? What were the two of them up to? Konrád sat there racking his brains in a vain attempt to work out what was going on, his eyes fixed all the while on the door of the workshop. The lights were still off and there was no sign of Bernhard.

After watching the entrance for a while, expecting Bernhard to come out any minute, Konrád considered his options. Finally, he eased himself out of his car and walked hesitantly over to the building. Both yard and workshop were silent and the entire area was shrouded in darkness. There was no outside light and the nearest streetlamp was broken.

Konrád reached the door and paused doubtfully before taking hold of the handle. It was unlocked. But the dark made him nervous. He was filled with dread at the thought of what it might conceal, unable to shake off the memory of all those stories about bad things that happened under cover of darkness.

Bracing himself, he opened the door and stepped inside.

'Bernhard?' he called into the workshop.

He thought he heard a faint noise.

'Bernhard!'

The man didn't answer.

'I know you're in there,' Konrád called.

Unable to feel a light switch on the wall, he inched his way warily to the reception desk, trying to remember the layout of the place from when he had visited earlier. He recalled the racks of spare parts, and the mounts running the length of the ceiling with exhaust pipes, bumpers and wings hanging from them.

'Bernhard!' Konrád tried a third time, but got no answer. There was that faint sound, though.

'I know you're in here,' Konrád called. 'I can hear you.'

Still no answer.

Konrád felt his way round the reception desk, then halted, his heart pounding, his breathing coming fast and shallow. He wasn't sure he dared to venture any further inside. What had Salóme been doing in there? Why had they been meeting after midnight?

'Bernhard!'

Nothing.

'I know you know Salóme,' he called into the gloom. 'I know she was here with you. Why won't you talk to me?'

After a moment, overcoming a sick feeling of dread, Konrád made himself go on, picking his way through the workshop, towards the faint light from the windows at the back.

'Why were you two meeting?' Konrád called, his voice sounding thin and breathless. 'Why did Sigurvin have to die?'

He had reached the windows. The rustling sound was clearer now. He could make out the shadowy shapes of racks of engine parts on either side of him. The reek of metal, oil and rubber filled his senses. He continued his wary exploration, constantly glancing back towards the door, fighting a rising panic at being alone and defenceless in the dark.

A loud rumble announced the approach of the last night bus, which sped past outside, its headlights briefly illuminating the innermost corner of the workshop through the filthy window-panes before receding into the distance. Konrád stared, stunned, at what it had revealed.

Then everything went dark again.

Konrád had no idea how long he had been standing there, rooted to the spot, when he noticed the rustling again. It had nothing to do with Bernhard but came from a torn plastic bag, which had blown against the window outside and was caught in a crack where it was flapping against the glass in the night breeze.

The rustling of the bag must have been the last thing Bernhard heard in this life. His body was hanging from a ceiling bracket by a thin cable. He had climbed onto a shelf in the wall rack, slipped the noose over his head and let himself drop, and now rested up against the engine parts that he had once removed from written-off cars and placed on the shelves.

Konrád shuddered. The wind's cold fingers played with the plastic bag in the window, the rustling passing through the garage like a requiem for the damned.

53

The first proper snow of autumn was falling, silently settling in the streets, when Konrád finally set out for Salóme's house. She lived in ostentatiously prosperous style in a large detached property in the upmarket suburb of Gardabær; alone, unmarried and childless. But all Konrád got to see of the house was the enormous kitchen into which she eventually invited him after some initial resistance at the front door. Konrád had insisted on having a word with her, in spite of the early hour, on a matter that couldn't wait. The bit about not being able to wait was quite true. Konrád had persuaded Marta to let him talk to Salóme before the police took action, pointing out that, in the circumstances, she owed it to him. Marta had conceded, after a brief argument, but warned him that she couldn't give him long.

He had phoned Marta from the scrapyard and the police had arrived a few minutes later. Some reporter must have got wind of a serious incident too, as the night had been lit up by a camera flash.

Konrád had filled Marta in on everything he knew about the links between Bernhard, Salóme, Sigurvin and Hjaltalín, going right back to school and the Scouts, and how he had picked up the trail thanks to Villi's sister; how it had been Villi's fate that had led him to Bernhard and now to Salóme.

'You've got ten minutes,' Marta had said. 'Not a second more.'

And now here he was, confronting Salóme, more than thirty years after notification had reached the police on that cold February day that Sigurvin was missing. Could she be the person he had been pursuing for half his working life? The owner of a clothing store? He didn't know how he was supposed to feel. Whether he should be blaming himself for all the difficulty he'd had solving the case, or experiencing a sense of triumph now he'd finally done it. The feeling of triumph didn't come. He felt neither relief nor pleasure. Instead, he was plunged into a mood of profound sadness and gloom.

Although it was past two in the morning, Salóme was still up. She explained that she'd been out. She seemed agitated, though, and couldn't hide her astonishment over Konrád's visit at such an hour. He said he had just come from Bernhard's scrapyard, and watched her try to conceal her shock.

'I saw you outside,' he said.

'The poor man . . . he . . . is he all right?' Salóme asked. 'Did you talk to him?'

'I understand you two were lovers,' Konrád replied, his eyes straying to the six gas rings on the hob, the double fridge and double oven, surrounded by all the marble and polished oak.

'Lovers?'

'His wife suspected him of cheating on her. She reckoned you were the guilty party. What were you and Bernhard up to?'

'I've known him since we were kids. He was . . . we never had an affair. That's some kind of misunderstanding.'

'What was his connection to Sigurvin?'

'I didn't know about that until tonight,' Salóme said, her tone anxious.

'Do you expect me to believe that?' Konrád asked. 'What were you and Hjaltalín and Bernhard up to, and why did Sigurvin have to die?'

'Hjaltalín? It had nothing to do with him. Or me. That's . . . that's a crazy thing to say. How could you believe that?'

'Then what were you doing at Bernhard's scrapyard in the middle of the night?'

'He rang me. He said he was at the workshop and wanted to see me. He begged me to come. The poor man was beside himself. He said it was all over – that you'd been to see him. I had absolutely no idea what he was talking about. All I knew was that he was scared and having some kind of breakdown and had turned to me for help.'

'Why? Why you?'

'We were neighbours when we were kids,' Salóme said. 'We lived in the same block. On the same staircase, in fact. He came from a broken home. His dad was . . . he was an alcoholic and the kids used to spend a bit of time round at our place – Bernhard and his sister, who's dead. We were at school together too but we lost contact when my mother moved out of the area, and after that I didn't see Bernhard for years, not until our old class got together for a reunion some time in the late nineties. Since then, he's been keen to stay in touch. He had a drink problem a while back but managed to sort himself out. Then he fell off the wagon again and became a complete mess . . .'

'Do you know why?'

'I didn't at the time. All I knew was that he was depressed and in a bad way. It wasn't until tonight that I found out why . . . why he was such a mess. Why he'd been so keen to stay in touch with me. Why . . . It was awful. He admitted everything. I urged him to talk to the police and as far as I know he was going to – first thing tomorrow morning. I offered to go with him, for moral support. He was in a dreadful state. Did he tell you . . . did he tell you about Sigurvin?'

'I didn't get a chance to talk to him,' Konrád said.

'Had he already gone?'

'Yes, you could say that. After you left him, he decided to end it all.'

Salóme stared at Konrád uncomprehendingly. 'What?'

'Bernhard's dead.'

'What ? How . . . ? You're not serious!'

'He hanged himself in the workshop.'

Salóme didn't seem able to take it in, and Konrád knew he could have broken it to her more tactfully. She put out a hand to the kitchen table for support, then sank into a chair, staring at Konrád, her face a mixture of bewilderment, questions and horror.

'I went in to talk to him,' Konrád said, 'but by then it was too late. I'm sorry to have to break the news.'

'He . . . he was going to talk to the police,' Salóme said, dazed. 'To come clean. To tell the whole truth. He promised me. He was actually relieved – relieved to be able to unburden himself at last. He'd been living with the guilt all these years and now he was finally going to tell the truth.'

'When you said he was keen to stay in touch with you,' Konrád said, 'was there any particular reason for that? Apart from the fact you used to know each other as kids?'

'It was to find out if anything was happening,' Salóme said. 'He admitted that. Naturally he knew I'd been with Hjaltalín and had got dragged into the affair, and he wanted to know what was going on – whether the police were still investigating the case. Whether you lot were still in touch with me about it. He used to ask me about it, you know: how Hjaltalín was doing, whether I had any contact with him, whether I was in touch with Sigurvin's sister. All that sort of thing. Now I know it was more than just natural curiosity . . . The poor guy, he was so down about it. Sometimes he used to wonder aloud about what could have happened and said what a waste it was – when people were snatched away like that. Of course, it must have been a cry for help all along.'

'So he admitted that he'd been involved in Sigurvin's death?'

Salóme nodded. 'He admitted it to me.'

'Was he alone?'

'No, there were two of them.'

'Who was the other person?'

'He wouldn't tell me.'

'And they hid his body on the glacier?'

Salóme nodded.

'What about Villi – a young man called Vilmar? Did he mention him?'

'No,' Salóme said. 'He hinted at something else but it was very vague. He talked about having to live with it and how it had driven him to do something desperate, but he didn't say what.' She shook her head. 'Maybe I should have seen it coming. He was very distressed when he rang me but I got the impression he was feeling a bit better after he'd told me about Sigurvin. He was determined to talk to the police. Those were his very words as he said goodbye to me. I thought he was feeling better about everything. But then . . . then he goes and does this.'

'I think I've found the wreck of the jeep that killed Villi,' Konrád said. 'It's parked in front of his workshop. Hidden in plain sight. It's nothing more than a skeleton now but it's the jeep all right, and I've been wondering why Bernhard didn't get rid of it.'

Salóme looked at him blankly. 'I don't know anything about that. He only talked about Sigurvin.'

'Why the glacier?' Konrád asked. 'Why go all the way up to Langjökull with the body? Couldn't he have found a simpler, more effective way of getting rid of it?'

It seemed Salóme had no answer to that.

The doorbell rang, then kept ringing as someone leant on it.

'They're here,' Konrád said. Marta and her team had arrived.

54

Konrád returned to Bernhard's scrapyard before dawn. He was feeling far too worked up to go home to bed. Although Bernhard's body had been removed and Forensics had finished their examination, there was still a police guard on the building: two men sitting in a squad car in the yard outside. The older officer turned out to be an acquaintance of Konrád's. They exchanged a few words and the officer let him in without comment after Konrád explained that he was working on the investigation with Marta.

'I thought you'd retired ages ago,' the man said.

'No rest for the wicked,' Konrád replied.

The lights were on in the workshop, providing Konrád with a better view of the place than when he had fumbled his way inside earlier, hesitant and fearful in the dark. He went round behind the reception desk and into the little kitchen with its grubby coffee machine, table and solitary chair, testimony to the fact that Bernhard had worked there alone. Konrád looked into the office, which proved to be even smaller, furnished with the same kind of basic table and chair. There were shelves of files, loose papers on the table, a phone and a card reader, and a monitor, mouse and keyboard that must once, long ago, have been white. Under the desk was the computer tower, a green light blinking on the front. Apart from that the office was drab, a wall calendar its only decoration. The same worn, filthy lino covered the floor of both kitchen and office.

Konrád sat down at the desk and started going through the mess of paperwork: printouts of invoices, clients' phone numbers, comments on spare parts, bank statements. The papers were covered in Bernhard's oily fingerprints. As far as Konrád could tell from a brief glance, the man's bookkeeping had been in disarray.

He looked around him, at the groaning shelves of files, the out-of-date calendar, the shabby lino and ubiquitous dirt. It all bore eloquent witness to the scrapyard's failure to earn money, but also to neglect and a sort of general apathy, as if there was no point in keeping things in order or reasonably clean or trying to create a good atmosphere. It was as if Bernhard had long ago lost interest in his business. Perhaps this had coincided with the point at which his life had taken a dramatic, unlooked-for turn for the worse, which had ended with him here, dangling from a cable.

There were two drawers in the desk, neither of them locked. They contained more junk. An old telephone directory. A folder of invoices. More bank statements. Nothing personal. Nothing from Bernhard's private life.

Konrád switched on the monitor and pressed a button on the keyboard. The computer under the table began to whirr, and soon the desktop wallpaper appeared on the screen. It was different from the one he had seen when he looked into the room the previous day. Konrád stared at it, wondering if Bernhard had really wasted precious time during the last few minutes of his life on selecting a new background.

The photo had obviously been taken many years ago and appeared grainy when stretched across the screen like this, but its subject was nevertheless clear. It was a colour snapshot of three boys of around the same age, posing with an ancient tractor. One sat in the driver's seat, another perched on the big rear wheel and the third was standing beside the tractor. The picture looked as if it had been taken in the countryside. The sky was a cloudless blue and the boys' faces were radiant with happiness. All three were dressed in Scout shirts, long green socks and shorts, and beaming at the camera.

Bernhard had added each boy's name.

He himself was sitting in the driving seat.

Sigurvin was standing beside the tractor.

Least familiar was the third boy, who was perched on the back tyre. But Konrád had met him once and liked him.

Konrád studied Bernhard's face in the picture. He was sure there had been nothing coincidental about his decision to change his wallpaper to this particular photo, just before taking his own life.

55

He'd had no sleep at all that night, and was acutely aware of the fact when he got back behind the wheel of his car and took the road out of town. After being awake for so many hours on the trot, he felt oddly detached from his surroundings. He hadn't even tried to go to bed. The rest of the night had been spent in a meeting with Marta at the police station, during which they had come to an agreement about the next move. The local police had been duly alerted.

While at the station, Konrád had apologised to Salóme for bursting into her house in the middle of the night, full of wild accusations. She was understanding, though he didn't feel he deserved it. The statement she had given Marta was consistent in every detail with the story she had told Konrád: she and Bernhard had been childhood friends; many years later, their paths had crossed again, and ever since then he had made an effort to stay in touch with her.

'I've been thinking about the time we met at the class reunion,' Salóme said.

'He was still with his wife at the time?'

'Yes, he told me he was married. But our relationship wasn't like that. We were never an item. Like I said, it felt as if he needed someone to talk to. He was having a really hard time. His behaviour was seriously paranoid. He didn't trust anybody and was convinced people were talking about him behind his back. Of course I had no idea what was bothering him. Bernhard was very cagey, and if you tried to ask any personal questions, he was liable to fly off the handle and walk out on you. He was a nervous wreck by the time he went into rehab. I went to see him once and he just broke down in tears but wouldn't tell me why. After he came out of the treatment centre he seemed better and I didn't hear from him as much. But he got in touch again when they found the body on the glacier. He wanted to discuss the case. He asked if the police had spoken to me again and if you'd got a lead; if you had your sights set on anyone.'

Salóme paused. 'Why were you spying on Bernhard?' she asked abruptly. 'Why did you think we'd been mixed up in something together?'

'Because I found out that you two knew each other and it seemed suspicious, in the circumstances.'

'That Villi you mentioned – who was he? Did Bernhard do something to him?'

'Possibly,' Konrád said. 'We don't know for sure.'

'Did you really think Bernhard and I had conspired to kill Sigurvin?'

'I got carried away,' Konrád said. 'This case has messed with my head, messed with my judgement, but I'm hoping it'll all be over soon. I really hope there's finally going to be an end to this bloody business.'

Konrád was in no hurry. He drove towards the sun as it rose over the Bláfjöll mountain range. The days were growing perceptibly shorter; winter was just around the corner. Soon the sun would only crawl above the horizon for four brief hours, in a feeble attempt to light up the night-filled vault of the sky.

56

The man wasn't home. As agreed, Konrád had informed the local police of his arrival, and a squad car had accompanied him to the address. The house was in a residential street on the west bank of the River Ölfusá, above the old bridge. When no one answered the door, Konrád followed a hunch and wandered down to the river, where he spotted a figure sitting with his back to them, his legs dangling over the steep, rocky bank, and thought he looked familiar. Turning, Konrád signalled to the uniformed officers that he was going down there alone. They nodded.

There were small birch trees growing close to the water's edge and a carpet of moss that extended to the rocky outcrop where the man was sitting. A short way off was the semicircular shape of a Second World War Nissen hut, roofed with grass, its grey-painted front facing onto the river. But most picturesque of all was the sheer rocky islet that rose out of the milky water a stone's throw from the bank, as if trying to withstand the destructive power of the torrent. It was capped with grass and at the very end perched a lone fir tree, looking as if it might topple into the flood at any minute.

The man on the bank heard Konrád approaching and turned his head.

'You've come then?' he said, as if he'd been expecting him for a long time.

'Hello, Lúkas,' Konrád replied, approaching him warily. 'This is a beautiful spot.'

'It's not bad having the river right on your doorstep like this,' Lúkas said. He was inadequately dressed for the chilly weather, his jaw was covered in several days' worth of stubble and he had entrenched dark circles under his eyes. Below his feet the Ölfusá surged and boiled.

'Do you mind if I join you?' Konrád asked.

'Be my guest,' Lúkas said. 'I can sit here for hours, watching the river.'

'I'm not surprised.'

'I discovered this spot after I moved to Selfoss, and I come here from time to time to enjoy the view and just savour the feeling of being here. Of course you have to be careful and know what you're doing. To be honest, I've always been shit-scared of the river. It has a strangely magnetic power that draws you to it. You have to respect that.'

'It's powerful, all right,' Konrád replied.

'I've been expecting you, to tell the truth.'

'For quite a long while, I would guess,' Konrád said.

'Yes, of course. For years – decades, in fact. I see you're not alone this time.' Lúkas glanced round at the police officers, who were hanging back at a discreet distance.

'No. I'm not alone.'

Konrád watched the grey waters of the glacial river churning against the rocks as they had for countless millennia, long before humans ever set foot in this place. The turbulence was accompanied by a deep-throated roar, as one would expect from the largest river in the country. Konrád could feel what Lúkas meant about its magnetic force.

'Why did Sigurvin have to – ?'

'Stupidity,' Lúkas cut in, as if reluctant to hear the rest of the sentence. 'Inexperience. Foolishness. But mostly stupidity. Goddamn, fucking stupidity.'

'Bernhard's dead,' Konrád said.

Lúkas stared out over the river to where its banks narrowed above the bridge. 'Dead?' he exclaimed belatedly, turning to look at Konrád. 'How . . . ?'

'He hanged himself. In his workshop.'

'Oh no . . . Poor Benni.' Lúkas groaned. 'He's . . . It's never going to end . . . There's no end to it . . .'

'He'd had enough,' Konrád said.

'So fucking stupid,' Lúkas swore again.

They were both silent.

'Did he say anything?' Lúkas asked after a while.

'He directed me here,' Konrád said.

Again they were silent.

'Do you . . . do you mind if we sit here by the river for a bit?' Lúkas asked.

'We've got a few minutes. Do you want to tell me about it? What happened? And why?'

Lúkas didn't reply.

'Lúkas?'

'Yes, sorry, where . . . where should I begin?'

'Maybe you could begin by telling me about Villi.'

'Villi?'

'The young man at the sports bar. Was it Bernhard who knocked him down?'

'Was he called Villi?'

'His name was Vilmar and he had a sister who wants to know how he came to die.'

'Bernhard bumped into him when he went out to watch the football. He immediately started getting jittery because he'd never got over what we'd done. He said the young man had recognised him. He rang me in the middle of the night, panicking that the guy was going to go to the police. I told him to calm down and take it easy. But Bernhard was in a state. He said he'd told the guy his name. He was drinking heavily in those days. It had got out of hand and he couldn't control it any more. He'd become a nervous wreck, constantly frightened and paranoid.'

'Because of Sigurvin?'

'Yes. The whole thing affected him very badly and he just got worse and worse over the years.'

'He must have remembered the boy he encountered by the hot-water tanks.'

'That was the thing. Bernhard was forever obsessing about that kid, saying he'd seen him on Öskjuhlíð and spoken to him. He couldn't stop thinking about the boy by the tanks. Kept going on about him. He was terrified of what he might do. Terrified of being found out.'

'Did he follow Villi from the bar?'

Instead of answering, Lúkas changed the subject. 'How do you mean, he directed you here?'

'He'd kept an old photo of the two of you with Sigurvin. And he talked to a childhood friend of his called Salóme and told her what he'd done.'

'Hjaltalín's girlfriend? I was aware he knew her. I'm actually . . . I think he was doing me a favour,' Lúkas said. 'Because, to be honest, I'm relieved it's over at last. You can't imagine how difficult it's been living with this. The constant hiding. The dread. The nightmares. It's . . . No one can imagine what it's like . . .' He didn't finish.

Konrád couldn't bring himself to feel sorry for him. 'Did Bernhard follow Villi in his jeep?' he asked, returning to his theme.

'Yes.'

'And deliberately run him down?'

'Yes.'

Away on the opposite bank, a young couple appeared pushing a pram. They paused while the mother bent over the pram to tend to the child, then continued on their way without paying the two men any attention.

'He kept his promise, then,' Konrád said.

'What?'

'Of killing the boy, as he'd threatened to when he was a kid. He kept his promise, all those years later.'

Lúkas made no reply to this.

'Did he stop drinking after that?' Konrád said. 'Go into rehab?'

'Yes.'

'Is that the wreck of the jeep under the tarpaulin in his scrapyard?'

'No,' Lúkas said. 'He broke his old jeep up for parts a long time ago. He got rid of it little by little, selling the parts until nothing was left but the skeleton, and I believe he even managed to sell that.'

Neither of them spoke for a moment or two.

'Why did Sigurvin have to die?' Konrád asked.

Lúkas drew a deep breath. 'We were amateurs,' he said. 'Bernhard and me. We hadn't a clue. Didn't know what we were getting into. You see, Bernhard had this brainwave of how to make some serious money by using the search and rescue team as cover for smuggling drugs into the country. Well, that was the plan, but the whole thing was a disaster.'

They locked gazes – two strangers who had been led by fate quite literally to the brink. Konrád could sense Lúkas's distress and believed him when he said that he had been suffering for a long time.

'You probably know where most of this water comes from,' Konrád said, following the river upstream with his eyes towards the highlands and ice caps of the interior. He was still preoccupied by the irony of it all. 'Which glacier the river comes from?'

'Of course,' Lúkas said. 'I know it comes from Langjökull.'

'It must have been a constant reminder.'

'It was.'

'Hearing the cries in its waters at night.'

57

Lúkas stared downstream to where the river took a sharp bend into the gorge on the other side of the bridge, continuing on its tireless journey to the sea.

'Are you planning to do something stupid like Bernhard?' Konrád asked.

Lúkas peered over the rocky ledge and shook his head. 'You needn't worry about that. I've always been afraid of the river, like I told you.'

'You said your plan was a disaster.'

'None of it would have happened if we hadn't bumped into Sigurvin at the cinema one day. I don't remember the name of the film, only that it was crap. We hadn't seen each other for years, not since we were in the Scouts, but we got chatting, and for some reason we started talking about booze because I used to work on the cargo ships. I said I could get hold of some vodka for him, if he liked. I had some gallon bottles smuggled in by a mate of mine and took a couple round to Sigurvin's place the following evening. He liked the price and after that I used to sell him the gallon bottles from time to time, whenever I had some to spare, and we used to chat a bit and got to know each other better and –'

'I don't remember any bottles like that turning up at his house,' Konrád interrupted. He was constantly on the lookout for any details he had missed during the original investigation. 'There was nothing to connect him to smuggling. Not a single piece of evidence.'

'No. He was careful. I think he used to empty out the gallon containers into normal-sized vodka bottles. He said something about it once.'

'And the drugs?'

'No one had a clue that we were mates with Sigurvin,' Lúkas said, seeming eager to tell the whole story at last. 'And he was the only person we knew who had any money. So I told him about Bernhard's idea of using the search and rescue team. Sigurvin thought it over, then said he was up for it. He was greedy. "You can never have too much dosh," he said. We told him he could get twenty times back what he'd paid for the drugs, which was perfectly true. His involvement would never come out, and even if it did he could simply deny everything. We'd make sure we didn't leave any tracks that could be traced to him. Bernhard and I offered to go to Amsterdam on rescue-team business. I'd done a bit of drug smuggling before on a very small scale, so I knew where to lay my hands on the goods. Everything went according to plan. We bought the drugs – cocaine mostly, which was starting to be popular in Iceland at the time – and packed it in with a consignment of equipment for the rescue team that was due to be transported home in a container. We hid the stuff in two second-hand German snowmobiles. The whole thing went like a dream, right up until Sigurvin lost his nerve. First he said he couldn't trust us; that we were cheating him and he'd never have any way of being sure that we weren't. We weren't cheating him but he didn't believe us when we denied it. In hindsight, I reckon he just wanted an excuse to withdraw from the whole thing. He'd got his profit and we'd given him some extra money as a sweetener because he made such a fuss, but then, stupidly, we decided we wanted him to return part of it. He flat-out refused.'

'We learnt recently that he'd kept a considerable sum in cash in his house,' Konrád said reflectively. 'Presumably, you two met him to talk things over?'

'Bernhard met him on Öskjuhlíd.'

'Had they met there before?' Konrád asked, remembering Ingvar's story about the big off-road vehicle by the tanks.

'Yes, once before. Bernhard had invested part of his profit in the scrapyard. He'd bought it off some bloke and was planning to sell it on quickly and open a garage instead. He had other big dreams too. We'd made a hell of a lot on that consignment. My brother had connections in the drugs world and helped us with the distribution. He was under the impression that me and Bernhard were responsible for smuggling it in on our own. I never told him about Sigurvin. By then, things had got so bad that we couldn't talk to him any more without it blowing up into a row. But Bernhard wanted to fix things, so he met Sigurvin on Öskjuhlíd and persuaded him, with a lot of difficulty, to come over to the scrapyard, where I was waiting. All we meant to do was smooth things out between us. But of course tempers got lost immediately and it turned into a shouting match. Sigurvin threatened to shop us. He talked about ringing the police with an anonymous tip-off. Said we'd never be able to prove he'd been involved. Which was true. We'd made sure there was no evidence pointing to him.'

'Which of you hit him on the head?'

Lúkas hesitated for a moment, then said: 'It would be easy to blame Bernhard now.'

'Sure,' Konrád said. 'If that would let you off the hook.'

'I often wondered if I should say it was Bernhard. If we were ever caught. Blame it on him and see if I got a more lenient sentence. It would be easy now he's dead to claim it was Bernhard, but I'm fed up with lying. *I* hit him. Twice.'

'What with?'

'Some junk I saw on the counter in the workshop.'

'What was it?'

'A tyre iron. Sigurvin was leaving and I lost it. I . . . I wasn't entirely sober and I'd done some of the coke too. I was so angry.'

'Did he die instantly?'

'Yes. It wasn't supposed to happen. I didn't mean to kill him, I meant to stop him. It's up to you whether you believe me. It was never supposed to go that far.'

'No. All the same, there were two blows,' Konrád pointed out. 'Heavy ones. So you were obviously pretty determined, whatever it was you intended to do.'

'Yes,' Lúkas said. 'I . . . I went too far. It was . . . I . . .'

'What happened to the tyre iron?'

'I . . . Bernhard got rid of it. I don't know how. I never asked him.'

'Have you been involved in any smuggling since then?'

'No.'

'And Hjaltalín? Did neither of you give a shit about what he was going through?'

'Of course we did, but what were we supposed to do? We weren't suspects; we were in hiding. So we didn't come forward. Time passed. And the investigators never came after us. You lot took the inquiry in a completely different direction, and Hjaltalín was never charged. The case was dead. Until Sigurvin turned up on the glacier.'

'Why did you take him up there?'

'It was Bernhard's idea. He wanted to hide the body and had been on the glacier the previous week. It was the only place he could think of. And even though we messed up, it worked. For thirty years, anyway. We knew we'd have to take him quite high up onto the ice if he wasn't to be found. That was about two days after he died. But we hit such crazy weather that in the end we had to save ourselves and we completely lost track of where we'd put him. It got dark, there was a complete whiteout and . . . we'd been meaning to throw him into a deep crevasse to explain his head injuries if he was ever found, but . . .'

'You took his car keys?'

'We wanted to make it look like Sigurvin had got lost and died of exposure on the ice. But by the time we finally remembered his jeep and decided to drive it up to the foot of the glacier, it was too late because you lot had already found it. That's how come Sigurvin vanished without a trace. If we'd managed to leave his jeep near the glacier, you'd have had an explanation for his disappearance. We knew the glacier would be searched if his car was there, but we doubted his body would ever be found. It was Bernhard's idea to make it look like Sigurvin had died of exposure. Like he'd fallen into a crevasse. Bernhard had often taken part in searching for people in all kinds of circumstances and said it couldn't fail.'

Lúkas shrugged, defeated. Below them the water flowed relentlessly past and Konrád felt as if he could sense the power of the glacier in its deep roar. The uniformed officers were slowly moving closer.

'Then people started talking about the greenhouse effect and saying the world's glaciers were melting. The amount of tourist traffic on the ice kept increasing too, and we knew it was only a matter of time before someone stumbled on Sigurvin. We went up there ourselves to see if we could find him before anyone else did but we failed. We knew he'd turn up one day. Knew it all along and it was a horrible feeling. Waiting for him to be found. Sometimes it was almost more than I could bear.'

'What did you do with the car keys?'

'Threw them away. I went to the rubbish dump at Gufunes and chucked them as far as I could onto the mounds.'

'Rescue team members searching for a man they had lost themselves,' Konrád said. 'Not to save a life but to dispose of a body. There's something sick about that, isn't there? Can't you see it?'

'In every single nightmare,' Lúkas said. 'It was the same for Bernhard . . .'

'That's no –'

'We'll never be forgiven,' Lúkas said, meeting Konrád's eye. 'It's been very hard but it'll only get worse from now on. I think Bernhard realised that.'

'Oh, my heart bleeds for you,' Konrád hissed, tired of fighting back rage.

'What was that?'

Konrád had listened to Lúkas and heard the regret and penitence, mingled with self-justification, but hadn't been able to summon up any sympathy for him. Hadn't felt anything except anger: anger on behalf of those who had died because of him. On behalf of those who had been made to grieve. Anger because the two men had never come forward and told the truth. Because they had crawled into their holes and disappeared. But, most of all, anger on behalf of Hjaltalín, who had protested his innocence all those years to deaf ears. The longer Lúkas's story had gone on, the angrier Konrád had grown. He looked down into the raging torrent and felt as if his emotions were in a similar turmoil. He hadn't experienced such a sense of revulsion since he'd walked out on his father that last time all those years ago, and before he knew it his disgust was whispering to him about how easy it would be to give Lúkas a little push.

'You didn't give a damn about Hjaltalín, did you?' Konrád said, rising to his feet to put an end to their meeting. 'About what you did to him? Sigurvin was dead and you couldn't hurt him any more, but Hjaltalín went through sheer hell because of you. Do you have any idea what that man had to endure? What you did to him? How you destroyed his life? Smashed it to pieces?'

'Yes, of course, yes, it's . . . it was always . . . Of course we were worried . . .'

Lúkas started to scramble to his feet. Konrád didn't see exactly what happened next, but Lúkas never finished his sentence. Instead, he gave a muffled cry. Either his foot had slipped or he'd lost his handhold. It all happened incredibly fast, but Konrád caught the flash of terror in the other man's eyes as he fell and began to slide over the edge. Konrád reached out to him and Lúkas snatched at his hand. Before Konrád could brace himself, he was almost pulled over the ledge with the falling man. Lúkas scrabbled frantically for a hold to save his life, but seemed to sense, even as he clutched at Konrád's hand, that it wasn't enough.

Konrád saw the realisation dawn. Saw it in the man's wide-open eyes as it came home to him that there was no hope; that his grip wouldn't hold. Then Lúkas emitted a blood-curdling scream.

He plummeted into the river, where the current whirled him away, curling him up, spinning him round and hurling him onwards, shooting him up to the surface, only to submerge him again an instant later. Lúkas couldn't see a thing in the murky depths, his limbs were paralysed by the cold, and when he tried to shout for help in his anguish and terror his lungs filled with water. He shot up to the surface again, coughing, to see a rock towering above him and the silhouette of a fir tree against the sky.

Again he was plunged head first into the depths, where he bashed into stones and, flinging out his arms, grasped at a jutting rock below the surface, only to lose his hold. He groped in the darkness like a madman, unable to tell which way up he was in the tumbling water, until the next minute he had emerged again and caught hold of a rock, momentarily slowing his headlong progress before his grip was torn away. The skin of his fingers ripped, but despite that he grabbed at a snag and this time managed to stop himself. The water flung him against a rough rock wall, he glimpsed a fir tree overhead, and only now did it dawn on him that he had been carried out to the islet in the middle of the river.

The water pounded him ceaselessly as he clung to the rock for dear life and slowly worked his way along it to a slightly calmer patch of water, out of the fiercest current. Then he hung on to the low cliff with his torn, numb fingers, his head just above the surface, the waves constantly breaking over him, glimpsing a faint chance of rescue. He didn't dare move for fear of losing his hold and being snatched away, but flattened himself against the rock wall, trying to present as little resistance as possible.

Konrád, observing the battle from the ledge, saw that it could only end one way. Lúkas's hands couldn't have any feeling left in that freezing water. He watched the man fighting for his life until, inevitably, Lúkas lost his grip on the rock and was borne away by the flood, disappearing under the surface, this time for good.

58

The search for Lúkas's body along the banks of the Ölfusá and down by the river mouth went on for days without success. In the end it was called off, on the assumption that he had been washed out to sea.

Konrád went to see Sigurvin's sister, Jórunn, who said she knew nothing about the two men who had killed her brother. She'd heard the whole sordid tale from Marta about how Sigurvin had been murdered in a fight over drugs. She'd had no idea her brother had been involved in anything like that and was grieved to think that he should have got mixed up in such a stupid business, with such fatal consequences. Konrád ended up sitting with her for a long time. Despite her sorrow over the tragic events, he could tell that it was a profound relief to have answers at last to the questions that had been plaguing her all these years. When he left, she hugged him and thanked him for never giving up.

After the initial media frenzy over the solving of this notorious historical case had died down, Herdís slipped round to see

Konrád, as quietly as she had that evening, weeks ago, when she first told him about her brother, Villi. They took a seat in the sitting room and he was about to fetch a bottle, saying they could both do with a drink, when she declined.

'I'm trying to cut down,' she added dully.

'Good for you,' Konrád said, and went without wine himself.

'I don't know. We'll see.'

Konrád admitted to her that he couldn't stop thinking about Hjaltalín; about the way an innocent man had been forced to suffer half his life, wrongly suspected of murder. Of course Hjaltalín hadn't helped matters by deciding not to tell the whole truth; by convincing himself that if he did, he would only be digging a deeper grave for himself and dragging down the woman he was trying to protect as well.

'And Villi?' Herdís asked.

'It was largely thanks to him that the case was solved,' Konrád said.

'It cost him his life.'

'I know.'

'That Bernhard, he . . .' Herdís couldn't find the words.

'He suffered torments over Villi,' Konrád said. 'That was another life down the drain. He wasn't responsible for Sigurvin's death, except indirectly. But he couldn't see any alternative to getting rid of Villi. The secret turned him into a nervous, paranoid wreck and in the end it killed him.'

'I find it hard to feel any sympathy for him,' Herdís said.

'I know it's not much comfort, but perhaps it might help a little to think that without Villi the case would almost certainly never have been solved. You have to see it like that.'

'That doesn't help me at all.'

'Maybe with time.'

Herdís shook her head. 'It's such a waste. The whole thing. Such a waste.'

'I probably shouldn't have gone and sat with him,' Konrád said, his thoughts distracted. 'I should have got him to leave that ledge straight away. But I wanted to approach him cautiously. I thought he might be intending to –' He broke off.

'I don't know,' he carried on after a moment. 'Lúkas said he knew the place well, knew the river and the rocks, and that he wasn't planning to do anything stupid. He was afraid of the river. It wasn't deliberate. The policemen who were there with me all say the same. That he was getting to his feet, when suddenly he fell over the edge. There's nothing to suggest he did it deliberately. Marta, my friend in the police, won't stop giving me a hard time about it. She's furious. She'd rather I'd drowned too.'

They sat there in silence for a while, each pursuing their own thoughts.

'We wrongly blamed Hjaltalín all along,' Konrád said at last, his bitterness breaking through. 'He should have lived to see how the case ended. He should have lived to see himself exonerated. But it's too late now. He was telling the truth all those years and no one believed him. Not a single person. I can't stop thinking about how the poor man must have felt. All that time. All those years with no one believing him when he protested his innocence. I've been thinking a lot about my part in that. About the way I treated him – even when he was dying. How the system failed him – how we all failed him.'

'But you didn't know any better, did you?' Herdís asked.

'No, maybe not,' Konrád said. 'But we should have done. That's the point. We should have made more of an effort. We should have known better.'

After Herdís had left, Konrád stayed in the sitting room, still brooding over Lúkas and Hjaltalín and thinking about how it might have been possible to run the investigation differently, now that he knew the whole story. The silence was abruptly shattered by the noisy ringing of the phone. He looked at the clock. Seeing that it was getting on for twelve, he guessed Marta had been drinking and needed a friend to talk to. But he was wrong. It was Eygló.

'Sorry to call so late,' she said. 'Am I disturbing you?'

'No, not at all.'

'I've been thinking about what we discussed when we met. About our fathers and whether they'd been in contact with each other. Are you intending to look into it?'

'I don't know,' Konrád said. 'I hardly know what I can do. Do you think there's any point?'

There was a pause during which neither of them spoke.

'Do you really think they'd started working together again?' Eygló asked. 'Is there any way you can find out?'

'Well, I know they met during the war when they were both members of the Society for Psychical Research,' Konrád said. 'Since we last talked, I've been wondering if anyone from the society is still alive and might know something about them. Might even be able to tell us whether they'd started meeting again. But I don't suppose their deaths were linked in any way. I can't see why they should have been.'

'Perhaps we should forget about it,' Eygló said. 'But I've . . . the thought's been bugging me . . . ever since you . . .'

'I can understand that.'

'Will you let me know if you're planning to look into it? If you learn anything new?'

'I will.'

'Promise?'

'Yes, of course.'

'Sorry to disturb you so late. I shouldn't have called. You're not in a good way.'

'No, it doesn't matter,' Konrád said.

'Why . . . what's upsetting you?'

'I'm fine. There's nothing upsetting me.'

'Are you sure?'

'Yes, I'm sure.'

'What happened on that ledge?' Eygló asked.

'It was an accident. He fell in the river.'

'There was something else.'

'No, nothing else.'

'Fine, have it your own way,' Eygló said curtly and hung up on him.

59

Konráð stroked his withered arm and thought about what Eygló had said, his mind returning yet again to the events on the riverbank. He had been trying to avoid letting it go there because the thoughts were unbearable, but they could be sparked off without warning, for the slightest reason. This time Eygló had been the trigger. She was right, however she had managed to divine his state of mind during their brief phone call. The regret had begun to steal over him as he watched the rescue team doing their utmost to find the man in the river, and slowly but surely the guilt had taken up residence in his soul.

Days had passed and the commotion ran its course. People accepted his explanation. Accepted the testimony of the police officers, and of the witnesses on the opposite riverbank who had seen Lúkas slip and Konráð do his best to save him, almost falling into the Ölfusá himself. The police authorities weren't going to take any action. The bystanders hadn't noticed anything beyond what would be considered natural in such an unusual, horrifying situation: Konrád had offered the man a helping hand.

No one except Konrád knew the truth – that he had held out his weak arm, knowing full well that it wouldn't afford the same help. That too would be forever obscured in darkness.

Sleep wouldn't come. He stroked his wasted arm and tossed and turned until the early hours, staring up at the ceiling, a succession of images flashing through his mind: Villi lying in the road, the attack on his father by the abattoir, his mother's fears, Polli howling with pain on Skólavörduholt hill, the psychic Engilbert and his daughter Eygló, Bernhard hanging from the rack in his workshop, and the aghast expression on Lúkas's face as he clutched at Konrád's withered arm.

The suffering in his eyes as he confronted death.

And, lastly, Hjaltalín in his prison cell. Those limpid eyes staring at him from the haggard face like twin oases in a desert. 'If you ever find him,' Hjaltalín had said in parting, 'make him pay. Will you do that for me? Will you make him pay for what he's done to me?'

Not until Konrád finally managed to fix his thoughts on Erna could he find any peace. And as sometimes happened when he felt low and was missing her most, the poignant notes of 'Spring in Vaglaskógur' stole into his mind and he slipped into a dreamless sleep, remembering the soft sand in Nauthólsvík Cove, children playing by the water's edge, and a flower-scented kiss.

60

As Villi came to, he sensed someone approaching, slowly and warily, through the storm. He heard the crunching of footsteps and what sounded like laboured breathing. He opened his eyes to slits but couldn't see anyone, only darkness and blinding snow. Yet he had the feeling that someone was there with him, that he wasn't alone, and the knowledge comforted him.

When he surfaced again, a moment or two later, he saw that someone was kneeling beside him, holding his hand, and he felt warmth on his cold fingers and a warm palm stroking his forehead.

Although he couldn't see who it was, he felt a strange sense of peace settling over him and relief that he wasn't alone any more, that someone was there to protect and take care of him.

Next time he awoke, he was able to recognise the figure as the old woman who lived on his street. She had taken pity on him and he could hear her saying something, some words of comfort that touched him, and he felt that everything would be all right now because she was there to take care of him. He tried to tell her about the man who had run him down; how in that split-second glimpse of him hunched over the wheel, he'd known it was the man he'd been talking to at the bar; the man from Öskjuhlíd.

'I'm . . . cold,' he whispered.

The woman laid his head in her lap. 'Hush-a-bye, baby,' she said.

His strength was running out. Somewhere far away he heard the woman crooning a refrain from an old nursery rhyme.

Then all went quiet.

'My poor baby,' the woman whispered. 'Oh, my poor little boy . . .'

Gassi

ARNALDUR INDRIDASON worked for many years as a journalist and critic before he began writing novels. His books have since sold over fifteen million copies worldwide. He won the CWA Gold Dagger for *Silence of the Grave* and is the only author to win the Glass Key for Best Nordic Crime Novel two years in a row, for *Jar City* and *Silence of the Grave*.

DISCOVER THE THRILLING FLOVENT AND THORSON SERIES

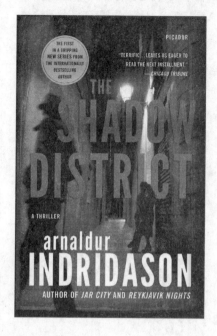

"Terrific . . . The deftly spun
Shadow District leaves us eager
to read the next installment
in the series."
—*Chicago Tribune*

"Gripping and deeply satisfying."
—*The Seattle Times*

"Haunting and elegant . . .
A writer of astonishing
gravitas and talent."
—John Lescroart

"Mesmerizing."
—*The Wall Street Journal*

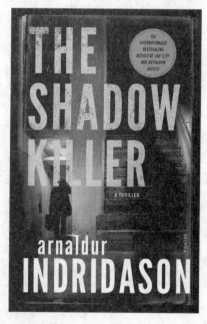

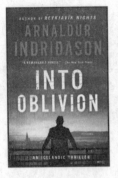
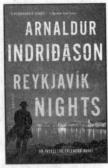

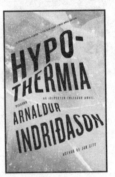
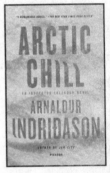
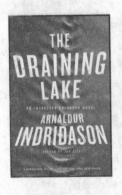
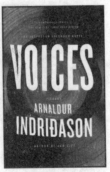
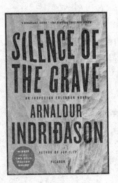
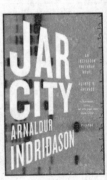